Since 2004, international bestselling author **Sherrilyn Kenyon** has placed over fifty novels on the *New York Times* bestseller list; in the past two years alone, she has claimed the No. 1 spot fifteen times. This extraordinary author continues to top every genre she writes within. Proclaimed the pre-eminent voice in paranormal fiction by critics, Kenyon has helped pioneer – and define – the current paranormal trend that has captivated the world and continues to blaze new trails that blur traditional genre lines. With more than twenty-three million copies of her books in print in over thirty countries, her current series include: the Dark-Hunters, League, Lords of Avalon, Chronicles of Nick and Belador Code.

Visit Sherrilyn Kenyon's websites:
www.darkhunter.com | www.sherrilynkenyon.co.uk

www.facebook.com/AuthorSherrilynKenyon |
www.twitter.com/KenyonSherrilyn

Praise for Sherrilyn Kenyon:

'A publishing phenomenon...[Sherrilyn Kenyon] is the reigning queen of the wildly successful paranormal scene'
Publishers Weekly

'Kenyon's writing is brisk, ironic and relentlessly imaginative. These are not your mother's vampire novels'
Boston Globe

'Whether writing as Sherrilyn Kenyon or Kinley MacGregor, this author delivers great romantic fantasy!'
New York Times bestselling author Elizabeth Lowell

Retribution

SHERRILYN KENYON

piatkus

PIATKUS

First published in the US in 2011 by St. Martin's Press, New York
First published in Great Britain in 2011 by Piatkus

A CIP catalogue record for this book
is available from the British Library.

ISBN 978-0-7499-5563-2 [HB]
ISBN 978-0-7499-5483-3 [TPB]

Printed and bound by CPI Mackays, Chatham ME5 8TD

Papers used by Piatkus are from well-managed forests and
other responsible sources.

MIX
Paper from
responsible sources
FSC
www.fsc.org
FSC® C104740

Piatkus
An imprint of
Little, Brown Book Group
100 Victoria Embankment
London EC4Y 0DY

An Hachette UK Company
www.hachette.co.uk

www.piatkus.co.uk

For my husband, for too many reasons to count.

For my boys, who make me laugh and fill my life with joy.

For my friends, who keep me sane.

And for my readers, who have been begging for Sundown's book.

Thank you all for being part of my life and for filling my heart with love.

Don't let yesterday use up too much of today.
—CHEROKEE PROVERB

RETRIBUTION

WILLIAM JESSUP
"SUNDOWN" BRADY
MAN. MYTH. MONSTER. 1873

WRITTEN BY
SOLACE WALTERS

They say the road to Hell is paved with good intentions. In the case of William Jessup Brady, it's been hand carved with a lever-action Henry rifle over his shoulder and a Smith & Wesson six-gun strapped to his hip.

At a time when the world is at its most violent, he's the meanest of all. Untamed. Uncivilized. A half-breed mongrel dog spawned from the bowels of the Devil's lowest pit, he is the worst of the scourge that haunts our towns and kills indiscriminately. No one is safe or immune from his wrath. No one is safe from his aim. A gun for hire, he doesn't shirk from any target. Man, woman, or child.

If you have the cash, he has the bullet. A bullet he will deliver to his victim right between the eyes.

There are those who would make a romantic hero of this villain. Some who think of him like Robin Hood, but Sundown Brady takes from everyone and gives only to himself.

He is truly soulless.

The bounty on this man is $50,000—a fortune, to be sure—and still people are terrified even to try to bring him in. In fact, authorities continue to find the scattered remains of the poor, virtuous marshal who made the mistake of shooting at him in Oklahoma when Brady was robbing a bank. Not one shot hit its mark. Is there any doubt Brady sold his soul to Lucifer for immortality and invulnerability?

Though Brady takes pity on no one, this reporter wants to know if there is anyone out there with the temerity to end Brady's wickedness. Surely one of you fine, upstanding, decent men would like the fame and money that would come from ridding the world of the most sinister being ever to walk it. I pray you courage, good man. Straight aim.

Most of all, I wish you luck.

E*verything changes today.*" Unable to believe he'd lived long enough to see this undeserved dream, Jess Brady stood outside the church in his best, itchiest clothes. This was the last turn he'd ever expected for his miserable life.

He'd been robbing banks and staring down experienced men in a gunfight without flinching or breaking a sweat since he was thirteen years old. Yet here, right now, he was as nervous as a one-eyed buck in a barn fire. Every part of him was on edge. Every part of him fully alive, and for the first time since his birth, he was actually looking forward to the future.

His hand shaking, he pulled his old, banged-up gold pocket watch out to check the time. In five minutes, he'd leave his brutal past behind him forever and be reborn a new man. No longer William Jessup Brady, cardsharp, gunslinger, and hired killer, he was about to become William Parker, farmer. . . .

Family man.

Inside those bright white church doors was the most beautiful woman in the world, and she was waiting for him to come inside and make her his.

Dreams do come true. His precious mother had told

him that when he was a boy, but his harsh life and drunken father, who'd been consumed by jealousy of and hatred for the entire world, had kicked that out of him by the time he was twelve years old and standing over her pauper's grave. Nothing good had happened to him since the day she took sick, and the years of her suffering had left a deep-seated bitterness inside him. No one so pure of heart should ever hurt so much.

Not a single thing had ever given him pleasure or made him think for even a second that the world was anything but utter misery for the fools unfortunate enough to be born into it. Not until Matilda Aponi had smiled at him. She alone had made him believe that the world was a beautiful place and that the people in it weren't all vicious animals out to punish everyone around them. Made him want to be a better man. The man his mother had told him he could be.

One free of hatred and bitterness.

He heard the sound of a horse approaching. That would be his best man, Bart Wilkerson. The only other person in his life he'd ever trusted and the one who'd taken him in when he was a thirteen-year-old runaway. Bart had taught him how to survive in a cold, hostile world that seemed to begrudge him every breath he took. He'd taken bullets for Bart on three separate occasions, and the two of them had been through more turmoil together than two demons scaling hell's thorny walls.

Like Jess, Bart was dressed in a long dark coat suit with his graying hair freshly combed. No one would ever be able to tell, looking at them right now, that they were two notorious outlaws. They looked respectable, but Jess wanted more than that. He wanted to *be* respectable.

Bart slid from his horse and tied her up beside Jess's buggy, which he'd bought just for this day. Hell, he'd even decorated it with lilies—Matilda's favorite flower.

"You ready, kid?" Bart asked solemnly.

"Yeah." Scared though he was, there was nothing else in this world he wanted.

Nothing.

He'd already given all his ill-gotten gains away so that Matilda wouldn't find out about his past. For her, he'd do anything.

Even be honest.

Jess started for the doors with Bart one step behind him. He'd just reached the steps when a gunshot rang out.

He sucked his breath in sharply.

Sudden pain invaded every part of his body as the impact of the shot knocked his hat from his head and sent it flying. It landed a few feet away and tumbled until it got caught in a nearby bush. Jess tried to take a step forward, but more shots followed the first. And all of them hit various parts of his body.

Those shots made him do something he'd never done before.

He fell to his knees in the dirt.

His fury igniting, he wanted to return that fire, but Bart knew he'd sold his guns to buy Matilda's ring—that had been his final act of ridding himself of the old Jess Brady. He was completely unarmed. The one thing he'd sworn he'd never be.

How could I be so stupid? How could he have put someone at his back when he knew better?

Maybe this was his penance for the sins he'd committed. Maybe this was all a bastard like him deserved.

Gunned down on what should have been the happiest day of his life.

Bart kicked him to the ground.

Panting from the weight of the pain and tasting blood, Jess stared up at him. The one man he'd risked his life for countless times. "Why?"

Bart shrugged nonchalantly as he reloaded his gun. "It's all about the money, Jess. You know that. And right now, you're worth a fortune."

Yeah ... how could he have forgotten their code? Having killed him, Bart would be the richest man in Gull Hollow. Not that he wasn't already.

Bart was the one Jess had given all his money to.

Jess coughed up blood as his vision dimmed. He was so cold now. Colder than he'd been even as a kid working in an early-spring field without shoes or a coat. His father had always told him he'd end up like this. *You're trash, boy. All you'll ever be, and you won't live long enough to be nothing else. Mark my words. You'll come to a bad end one day.*

And here he lay dying at age twenty-six. So evil, God wouldn't even let him reach the doors of Matilda's church.

But in the end, he was Sundown, and Sundown Brady didn't go quietly to his grave. *No damn man would kill him and live.* "I'll be back for you, Bart. Even if I have to sell my soul for it. So help me, God. I *will* kill you for this."

Bart laughed. "Give the devil my best regards."

"William!" Matilda's agonized scream hurt him more than the bullet wounds did.

He turned for one last look at her, but before he could take it, Bart coldly finished the job and denied him even the solace of seeing her face before he died.

J*ess came awake* with a curse. At least, he thought it was awake. Hard to tell, though, to be honest. It was darker here than the corner of his father's heart that had been reserved for any tender feelings the old bastard might have had for him. The silence was so loud, it rang in his ears.

He didn't even hear his own heartbeat.

'Cause I'm dead.

He remembered the pain of being shot, of trying to see Matilda in her wedding dress. . . .

So this is hell.

But to be honest, he'd expected flames and excruciating agony. Demons flying at him with pitchforks and smells akin to the stuff he'd mucked out of stables as a kid.

Instead, there was nothing inside the blackness.

"That's because you're on Olympus. At least your soul is."

He turned as a lonely light came up to show him the most beautiful woman he'd ever seen. Tall, lithe, and curvy, she had hair so red, it shimmered in the dim light. With glowing green eyes, she looked ethereal. More like an angel than like a demon, especially given the flowing white dress she wore that hugged her body. Something about its style reminded him of the white statues he'd seen in some of the fancier hotels he'd boarded in after they'd made a good haul over the years. "What's Olympus?"

She made a sound that reminded him of a filly about to buck off her rider for irritating her. "I grieve for the poor education of so-called modern man. How can you not know the name of the mountain where the Greek gods dwell?"

He rubbed his jaw and forced down his own irritation at her insult. Until he knew who she was, it probably wasn't wise to make her too mad. "Well, ma'am, no of-fense, but it probably has a lot to do with the fact I'm not Greek. I was born in Possum Town, Mississippi, and ain't been no further east than that."

She growled low in her throat, then spoke angrily in a

language he couldn't understand, which was probably for the best. No need in both of them being angry.

Clenching her fists, she settled down and pinned him with a killing glare. "I will try to speak so that you can understand me. I am the Greek goddess Artemis."

"I don't believe in gods and goddesses."

"Well, you should, because this one has a deal for you that I think will interest you."

Now, that made his ears perk up. "Deal how?"

She closed the distance between them so that she could whisper in his ear. "I heard what you said when you were dying at the feet of your best friend. Your soul screamed out for vengeance so loudly that it summoned me here to intercept you from your final destination."

He locked gazes with her. "You can send me back to kill Bart?"

"Yes, I can."

Rapid joy tore through him at the mere prospect. For that, she could insult him all day. "At what price?"

"You named it when you were dying."

"My soul."

She inclined her head to him before she patted him on the cheek. "That's the going rate for vengeance around here. But don't fret. There are other perks to being soulless. If you agree, I'll give you twenty-four hours to do whatever you wish to the one who betrayed you. No consequences for you whatsoever."

That he could sink his teeth into. His blackened soul had never been much use to him anyhow.

Artemis smiled. "You will have immortality and all the wealth you could ever imagine."

"I can imagine a lot."

"And still it won't fill even a corner of what you'll be given."

When something sounds too good . . .

He ran his thumb across his bottom lip as he eyed her suspiciously. "What's the mouseprint?"

She laughed evilly. "You are intelligent, after all. Good. It makes the job easier."

"Job?"

"Hmmm. You will serve in my army of Dark-Hunters."

He scowled. "Dark what?"

"Hunters," she repeated. "They are immortal warriors, foot-selected by me."

"Foot selected?" What was she talking about?

"Whatever the term is," she snapped irritably. "They are my soldiers who protect the humans against the Daimons who prey on them."

Technically, they were speaking the same language, but dang . . . Hard to follow a woman who used so many words he'd never heard before. "What's a Daimon?"

She set her hands on her hips as she paced in front of him. "In short, my brother Apollo's mess. Centuries ago, he created a race called Apollites." She paused to look at

Jess. "Arrogant of him, no? He thought man was weak and that he could do better." Then she returned to her pacing. "Anyway, he set them loose on mankind, and the Apollites turned on him and killed his favorite human concubine and *my* nephew. Not really wise. Why they thought Apollo wouldn't figure out who killed them is beyond me. So much for improvements, no?"

She rolled her eyes. "Apollites . . . ridiculous. At any rate, they are now cursed by him, and the only way they can live for more than twenty-seven years is to kill humans and steal their souls—we have an Atlantean whore goddess to thank for that little benediction to them." She flung her hand up in a gesture of supreme agitation. "Don't even get me started on how badly I'd like to kill her."

Artemis dropped her hand and faced him. "Anyway, that's where you come in, if you've been paying attention. You sell your soul to me, and you will spend eternity seeking and destroying the Daimons—the name given to the Apollites who feast on humanity. Are you out?"

"You mean in?"

"Whatever. Yes."

Jess considered it. Last time he'd made a bargain to go in with someone was Bart.

That hadn't worked out so well in the end.

"I don't know. I need to think about it."

Artemis splayed her hand out and waved it to her right. A shimmering light flickered there until images appeared.

Jess gasped at the sight. It was incredible. He saw every-thing as if looking through a glass window—so real, he felt that he could reach out and touch it.

The images showed Bart kicking him to the ground and then the final bullet that went straight into his skull.

This time, he saw not only Bart killing him from a dis-tance, but also what Bart did after he stepped over his body. Rage swelled up as Jess watched him kill Matilda's father and the preacher, then drag his bride into a back room.

"Enough!" he roared, unable to take any more. He'd always known Bart was part animal, but that only proved it. How dare he defile Matilda like that . . .

God damn him.

His fury raging, he glared at Artemis as he literally shook from the weight of his need to bathe in Bart's blood. "I'm in."

"There are a few more details you should know, such as—"

"I don't care," he snarled, cutting her off. "So long as it starts with me gutting that bastard, I'll do anything. And I do mean *anything*."

"All right, then." A bright gold medallion appeared in her palm. She grabbed his arm and pressed the medallion to it.

Searing pain tore through him as he gasped in agony. Still, she kept that medallion on his bicep, oblivious of the smell of burning flesh, which was so foul, it made his stomach pitch. When she finally pulled it away, he felt completely drained and weak. And there was a strange double bow and arrow mark on his arm, where she'd pressed the medallion.

Just as he was about to ask her how he could fight anyone like this, a new warmth crawled up from his toes to the top of his head. Suddenly he felt stronger than he'd ever been before. More alert. He could hear things that made no sense. Things like Artemis's heartbeat and the whisper of voices from far away. He held more knowledge than he'd ever been taught.

It was like being a god, and yet he knew for all his newfound power, it was nothing compared to what Artemis had.

Cupping the medallion in her hand, she stepped away from him. "You have twenty-four hours, horseguy, to kill your betrayer any way you see fit and to take your revenge. Make them count. Oh, and know that you can't let daylight touch you. If you do . . . Well, you don't want to die without your soul. It's highly unpleasant. Sometime in the next few days, a man named Acheron Parthenopaeus will find you and teach you everything you need to know about being a Dark-Hunter. If you're smart, you'll listen to him." She gave him an evil smirk as she stepped back and raised her arms. "Welcome to the madness."

1

138 *years later*
Las Vegas, Nevada

"How are you doing?"

Abigail Yager barely understood those words as the male doctor stood over her bed, injecting her with a substance that could very well be lethal. But if it worked, it would be worth the risk. "What?"

"Abby? Can you hear me?"

She blinked slowly and tried to focus on Hannah's question. Everything was blurry. Even so, she could see the way the light played in Hannah's blond hair. The concern on her sister's beautiful face. "Um . . . yeah."

Hannah cursed. "You're killing her. Stop!"

The doctor didn't listen.

Hannah started for him, but before she could reach the far side of the bed, her older brother, Kurt, intercepted her. "Stop it, Hannah."

"We don't know what that will do to her. She's human!"

Kurt shook his head. "She needs it. If it strengthens us, it should do the same with her. Besides, it's too late. At this point, it'll either help her or she's dead. Plain and simple."

Could there be any less care in his tone?

Hannah shoved Kurt away. "I'm ashamed of you. After all she's done for us, you still see her as nothing but a human." She returned to Abigail's side and took her hand. "Stay with me, Abby. Don't leave me alone with an insensitive prick as the only member of my family."

"I'm not a prick!"

Hannah ignored him. "I need my big sis. C'mon, girl. Don't let me down."

Abigail couldn't really follow the angry exchange they were now engaged in. Honestly, all she heard was her heart pounding in her ears. She saw images of her past playing through her mind as if they were on a DVD. The old two-story house where the three of them had grown up. Of her and Hannah sneaking up past their bedtime to whisper and giggle about their latest celebrity crushes.

So many happy memories of that time . . .

Her thoughts turned to Kurt and Hannah's mother and father, who took her in after Abby's own parents had been slaughtered. They, too, had died years ago from their curse, and there was nothing she wouldn't do for her adoptive siblings.

And you just might be paying the ultimate price.

"Wait . . ."

Was that the doctor's voice?

The thrumming grew louder as she felt something shatter deep within her body. Arching her back, she screamed as every molecule in her body seemed to catch fire.

"What's happening to her?"

"Get your sister out of here."

Abigail heard Hannah protesting as Kurt jerked her from the room and slammed the door behind them. Tears streamed from the corners of her eyes. She could no longer see anything, and yet she saw everything. There was no way to describe it. It was as if she had a mirror to the world.

"Breathe," the doctor whispered. "Just breathe. I'm not about to let you die."

That was easier said than done. Pain lacerated her body. It was as if she was burning from the inside out.

Unable to stand it, she screamed until she could stand no more. This was it. In spite of what he said, she was dying. She had to be. Surely no one could withstand this much pain and live. There was no way she'd survive.

In fact, she felt the darkness coming for her. It was swallowing her whole. Piece by piece. Shredding her completely.

She turned her head from side to side, trying to breathe. Something had its hands on her throat, choking her.

Was it the doctor?

She couldn't focus. Couldn't see.

"Stop!" Her cry echoed in her ears.

Then as quickly as it'd come, the pain left her—like a bird that shot skyward for no reason. It was gone.

Her throat was so dry now. She tilted her head to meet the doctor's gaze. Concern etched his brow as he lowered the mask on his face.

"How do you feel?" There was only the smallest bit of his fangs showing as he spoke. Something else flashed. A memory of him that was gone so fast, she couldn't grasp it.

Was it important?

"I need water," she rasped.

"Do you crave anything else?"

"Yes," she breathed.

"What?"

Abigail licked her lips as the memory of her birth parents' deaths seared her. Even all these years later, that memory was perfectly intact, as if it'd happened only yesterday.

Barely four years old and dressed in her red Sesame Street pajamas, she'd hidden under the bed while the man her parents had called friend mercilessly slaughtered them with a shotgun. Those horrendously violent sounds were forever carved in her heart. From where she'd been, she saw the man's black cowboy boots, which caused the floorboards to squeak while he searched her room. Terrified, she'd watched him track blood all over her pink princess rug. She'd held her favorite teddy bear to her mouth and bit him hard to keep from crying out and betraying her location. He'd paused before her dresser, and there in the mirror she'd seen his face so clearly. So perfectly.

And as she heard those heavy footsteps leave her home, she'd sworn one thing.

To find that man and kill him as brutally as he'd killed her parents. To make him beg for a mercy she had no intention of giving him.

Retribution would be hers. . . .

"Abigail?" The doctor forced her to look at him. "What else do you crave?"

"The throat of Sundown Brady."

2

"Someone's killing Dark-Hunters."

Jess Brady scowled as his Squire, Andy,
burst into the obscenely huge kitchen, huff-
ing and puffing, with his dark hair sticking
out all over his head as if the boy had been
wringing at it—a habit Andy had whenever
he was duly stressed.

Much less excited, especially since he'd been up only a few, Jess blew his breath across his steaming coffee. "Settle down, pup. I ain't had my caffeine yet." And he wasn't a morning person, even though his mornings were what most people called early evening.

Still the boy jumped about like a filly around a rattle-snake. Had *he* ever been that nervous about anything?

The answer hit him hard in the chest and did nothing to improve his irritability.

Jess quickly turned his thoughts away from that memory and focused on the boy he'd known since the day Andy was whelped.

Even though Andy was nearing thirty now, he was about as high-strung as anyone Jess had ever met. Times like this, he missed the old calmness of Andy's pa. Nothing had ever rattled that man.

Not even the time he'd landed in a nest of scorpions.

"Sundown . . . you don't understand. It's—"

He held his hand up to stop the boy midsentence. "I get it, kid. Case you haven't noticed, Dark-Hunters are on almost as many menus as humans are. Having something trying to kill us is about normal. Now, why you more flustered than a preacher in a whorehouse?"

"I'm trying to tell you." Andy gestured toward the door as if expecting the bogeyman to charge through it. "There's a human out there who is killing off Dark-Hunters, and someone needs to stop them."

Jess took a slow drink before he spoke. Ah yeah, that hit the spot. Little more, and he'd be as close to human as a deadman could come. "Well, that's just plain rude."

All that did was frustrate Andy more. "I really don't think you understand what I'm trying to tell you."

Jess scratched at the whiskers along his jaw. "And my mama drowned the dumb ones. I hear everything you're saying. There's a group of Buffys thinking we're the bad guys. Ain't my first rodeo, pup. It's been happening so long, they were called Helsings long before your daddy was a gleam in your granddaddy's eyes. Thank you, Hollywood and Stoker for that. Not like being undead didn't suck before. They just made it worse for us by cluing the rest of the world in that we exist. Now every goth with a thirst for immortality is cruising for us, begging us to bite them and turn them. Did I ever tell you about that time when—?"

"Sundown," Andy snapped. "I—"

"You need to check that tone, boy. Remember, I used to kill people for a living, and I ain't been up long enough to have much tolerance right about now. Knock it down a notch before I forget I'm supposed to actually like you."

Andy let out a long sigh. "Fine, but answer me this."

Dang, when had the kid turned into the Riddler? He should have curtailed all those *Batman* reruns when Andy was a boy.

"Did any of those others ever come after you guys in the past leading a Daimon entourage?"

Now, that got his attention. While it wasn't unusual for Daimons to use humans as servants or tools from time to time, it wasn't normal for them to follow one.

Jess set the coffee down on the stainless steel counter. "Come again?"

"Yeah . . . this one travels in a pack of Daimons, and has been slaying every Hunter they can find. She's taken out three here and four others in Arizona and Oklahoma."

Jess took a full minute to digest that. "How do you know about this?"

"I was contacted by Tawny, who got it from her mother." Now, to most, that'd sound bizarre. But like Andy, Tawny was a multigenerational Squire. A few thousand years back, the Squire network had been set up to provide a "normal" cover for the nocturnal Dark-Hunters during the daylight hours when they were sleeping. The Squires helped them to pass for humans, and most of all, the Squires shielded their existence from the rest of the world and took care of their day-to-day necessities so that they could focus on their job. Killing Daimons and freeing the human souls they'd stolen before those souls died and were forever lost.

But the best part about the Squires was that some of them were Oracles who could speak directly to the gods and get information from them that the Dark-Hunters could use to track and kill Daimons.

Tawny's mother happened to be one of those Oracles.

Deciphering what the gods said, however, was another matter.

Jess leaned against the kitchen counter and crossed his arms over his chest. "Tell me exactly what her mother said."

"She said that there's an ill wind coming and that you should guard your back. Lionel didn't fail to make it home before dawn. He was murdered and that his killer, a human leading a Daimon guard, was on the hunt for more of his kind."

Lionel was another Dark-Hunter who'd been assigned to Las Vegas. He died three nights ago, after he'd failed to make it to shelter before the sun rose—at least that was what they'd been told. Immortality had its price, and while the things that could kill them were few, those few were an ugly way to die.

Jess rubbed his thumb against his brow. "And the gods spoke that plainly?"

Andy hedged. "Well . . . not exactly. You know how they are."

Yeah, they always spoke in riddles that were tougher to unknot than a two-headed cobra. "So how—?"

"It's taken them days to decipher it, but she swears she's right and that you need to watch your back."

That, he'd been doing since the day the goddess Artemis resurrected him. Bart had tutored him well on guarding every angle of his body and staying alert no matter what or who. Jess wasn't about to ever be a victim again.

"Andy—"

"Don't *Andy* me. I believe her. She's one of the best Oracles we have."

He was right about that. But . . .

"We all make mistakes." And Jess had made more than his fair share.

A tic started in Andy's jaw. It was obvious he wanted to throttle Jess, but he knew better than to even try.

"Fine," he said, finally relenting on the matter. "Whatever. You're the one they're after, so it's none of my business. Plenty of other Dark-Hunters to work for. They're probably a lot less irritating, too." Then he changed the subject entirely. "I repaired your tracker and phone." He held Jess's iPhone out to him. "Try not to get it wet tonight."

"Not my fault the Daimon I was chasing decided to run through a water fountain." Damnedest part about living here in Vegas, there were huge fountains all over the place, and for some reason, Daimons seemed to think Dark-Hunters were allergic to water. Or maybe it was their way to piss them off before getting killed.

Andy ignored his comment. "Mom overnighted some of her oatmeal cookies for you. They're in the jar by the sink." He pointed to the container that looked like a Conestoga wagon, which was really out of place in the commercial-grade kitchen designed to feed a large army.

The thought of those cookies perked him up a lot. Cecilia made the best in the world. That was what he missed most about Andy's pa working for him. C used to have a fresh batch cooling on the stove every evening when he came upstairs for coffee.

Andy continued his report. "I picked up your laundry and hung it in the hall closet. I checked with the company, and your horses will be transported out here next week from your ranch, so you can quit pouting every time you pass the saddles."

Wow, he had no idea he'd done that. Huh . . . he'd have to keep an eye on his expressions. He hated to be that obvious to anyone.

Andy gestured toward the door. "The boots you ordered are in the box on the hall table, as are the throwing knives Kell sent to replace the ones you broke the other night. I couldn't get the black Stetson reblocked, so I have a new one on order. Your bike is fully gassed, and Sin has offered all of you free valet parking at his casino while you hunt. He'll have his staff leave the bike parked in front so that you can grab it and go when you're ready to head home, and if you get trapped in the city and can't make it back here before dawn, you can hole up in one of his rooms—they'll have a key at the concierge with your name on it. Is there anything else you need?"

That was the best part of Andy. Like his father, he was

as efficient as the devil's desk clerk. "Nope. Can't think of anything."

"All right. I'll have my cell phone if you need anything." The boy always said that.

Jess moved toward the cookies. "Have a good night."

Andy nodded before he went to the door. He paused as if he wanted to say something else—then he quickly took his exit to head to his apartment over the garage. For some reason, as the kid left, Jess had an image of Andy as a little boy chasing after his father. He could still see Andy's chubby cheeks, wide eyes, and freckled face. Hear him asking in that youthful tone if Jess would teach him how to ride, and then picking the boy up from the dirt the first time Andy was thrown by the Shetland pony Jess had bought for him. Little booger had gotten right back up, dusted himself off, and then climbed into the saddle like a trouper.

Now that little boy was a man strangers thought was older than Jess.

That was the hardest part of being immortal. Watching people he cared about be kids, grow old, and die while *he* never changed. And just like with Andy, he'd known the boy's father from the moment Ed was born. The Taylor family had been his Squires from the beginning of his Dark-Hunter life.

Even so, he'd kept a wall between him and them. Never letting them in too close. At least not until Andy.

He didn't know why, but that little shit had wormed his way past Jess's best defenses. In many ways, Andy was like his son.

There was only one other person in his long life that Jess had felt that way about.

He winced at another memory he wished he could purge.

Aching with remorse and grief, Jess pulled his watch out of his pocket to check the time. The moment he opened it, he paused to stare at Matilda's face in the worn-out sepia photograph that had been kept inside his watch since the day he was reborn. No matter how many years passed, he still ached over the loss of her.

That had been the only thing he truly hated about his rebirth. Knowing she was alive and not being able to see her. Dark-Hunters were forbidden from having families, and they were never to let anyone from their past know that they'd come back. It was part of what they swore to when Artemis created them.

Still he'd kept tabs on her while she lived and made sure that she never once wanted for anything. She'd gone on to marry and have six kids.

Without him.

To the day she died, she'd never known who her benefactor was. The Squires told her it was a trust fund set up by a distant uncle who'd died and left it to her. She never knew that money came from a pact he'd made with a goddess to even a score that no amount of violence could tally.

Sometimes dead wasn't dead enough.

His throat tightening, he closed his watch. There was no use thinking about what should have been. He'd done what he'd had to. Matilda had probably been better off without him, anyways. Sooner or later, his past would have caught up to them, and the result would have been the same.

At least that was the lie he told himself to make it all bearable. But inside, he knew the truth. No one could have loved her more than he had.

More than he did to this day.

"I miss you, Tilly." He always would. No one would ever again make him feel like she had.

Worthy.

Cursing, he curled his lip at his melancholy thoughts. "I'm turning into an old woman. Might as well start knitting and bitching about soap operas, gas prices, and rude drivers."

That wasn't what Sundown Brady did.

Nope. It was killing time, and he was in the mood to bathe in blood tonight.

3

Ren Waya coasted on the breeze as he heard the heartbeat of the earth thrumming in his ears. It sounded like a tribal drum, summoning the ancient spirits out of their slumber to make ready for war. And as he flew, Sister Wind carried a new scent to him. One he'd never smelled before, and given his extreme old age, that said a lot.

Something was here, and it didn't belong.

Unable to pinpoint it, he dipped down, then recognized a rider on the road far below. The motorcycle slowed from its feral speed as the rider came upon the Vegas traffic and lights. Ren let out a cry while he followed the sleek black motorcycle into town.

Swathed in a black duster, the rider was oblivious of being watched. Of course, the loud, thumping music inside the rider's helmet that was turned to a level that should be deafening might have something to do with that. Styx's "Renegade." The irony of that wasn't lost on Ren. If he could smile in his current form, he would.

The rider skimmed past traffic and turned into the brightly lit Ishtar Casino, which was styled after an ancient Sumerian temple. Ren lost sight of the rider as he drove under the parking pavilion. He banked to the right to miss the wall and circled back.

Jess *pulled his* helmet off before he gave his name to the valet.

The attendant snapped to attention. "Mr. Brady, sir, we were told to give you white-glove treatment. You may park your bike anywhere you want, and we'll make sure no one bothers it. If you have any problems or needs, have the concierge contact Damien Metaxas, and he'll take care of it for you."

A man could get used to this level of service—it was like being at Disney World. "Thanks," he said, then handed the valet a twenty.

Jess slid into a tight space at the front of the line of cars and limos, where his motorcycle should be out of the way, then parked his 2006 MV Agusta F4CC on the curb. At $120,000 a pop, his ride was a gold mine for any thief who had knowledge of motorcycles. Not that the money was that big a deal to him. Replacing it, however, was another matter, since they were as rare as a loyal friend, and he'd long grown attached to it.

Hate to gut a human for being greedy. But back in the day, he'd done worse for less.

He locked it down, put his helmet on the seat, then dropped the keys in his pocket. It was a little warm for his duster, but he preferred it, since it helped hide the weapons he needed for his trade. No need in scaring the civilians any more than was necessary.

Bad thing about Vegas, you couldn't spit without dropping germs on a Daimon. They practically owned this place. In fact, three of the valet drivers here were Apollites, including the one who'd spoken to him. And the casino manager, Damien Metaxas was, in fact, a full-blown Daimon that no Dark-Hunter was allowed to kill. They claimed Metaxas fed only on humans who deserved to die—rapists, murderers, pedophiles. But why would you take their word on it? Was anyone really checking?

Even when the casino owner, Sin, was a Dark-Hunter, he'd had them working for him.

"You're a sick SOB, Sin," Jess muttered as he pulled his sunglasses out and put them on.

Keep your enemies close, I guess. Still . . .

"You're late."

Jess grinned, making sure to keep his fangs from showing as he did so. He turned at the deep, accented voice that had come from behind him. "Didn't know Grandma was keeping tabs and setting curfew."

Two inches taller, Ren had his long, jet black hair pulled back into a single braid that trailed down his back. Even without that pissed-off expression, he was intimidating as all get out. At least to those who could be intimidated.

Jess definitely didn't fit into that category.

The only color on Ren's body was the bone and turquoise choker he wore as an homage to his Native American heritage—other than that, he was swathed all in black from head to toe. Jess asked him once what tribe he belonged to, but Ren had refused to answer. Since it didn't matter to Jess, he'd never asked again, even though they'd been friends for well over a hundred years.

Jess scratched at his whiskers, wishing he'd shaved a little closer. "I thought you were communing with Chocolate tonight."

Ren shook his head. "Choo Co La Tah."

"Isn't that what I said?"

Now, there was a pained expression for you. It was quite impressive. "For a man who was born speaking Cherokee, I don't understand why you can't pronounce things correctly."

"Ah, *potato, potahto.* Does it really matter in the grand scheme of things?"

"It does if you ever come into contact with him. Believe me, your mixed Cherokee blood won't buy you any tolerance where he's concerned."

Yeah, that was the thing about immortals. Many of them weren't exactly good natured. Many more were downright intolerant. And as for Choo Co La Tah, Jess was more than acquainted with him, but it was one of those things he *never* talked about. "Then I'll just make sure that I call him Exalted Being."

Ren laughed. "Wise choice."

Jess decided to change the topic to what had bothered him a few minutes ago. "So was that you flying above me as I rode in?"

"You saw me?"

Jess shrugged nonchalantly. "Don't you know, I sense everything around me." Even before Artemis had bestowed him with psychic powers, that was one ability he'd had from birth. No one had ever been able to sneak up on him.

Pulling a gun behind his back and shooting him was another story. Only someone as close to him as Bart had been could have killed him that way. Had Bart been a stranger, it would never have happened.

"And here I thought I was being stealthy."

Jess snorted. "With that girly caw you let out? Did a frog crawl down your throat and die, or what?"

Ren let out a short *heh* sound. "You better be glad I like you."

"I am indeed, for I have seen how you throw a knife, and it is truly awe inspiring. Now, if you don't mind . . ." Jess started away from him. If they stayed together too long, they'd deplete each other's strength. It was a fail-safe the gods used to keep Dark-Hunters from combining their powers and taking over mankind.

"Wait."

Jess paused.

"Choo Co La Tah wanted to warn me that something unnatural is coming from the west."

The direction of death for the Cherokee. He didn't know if Ren's people had the same beliefs as his mother's or not. "Yeah, okay. I'll watch for Daimons coming up the street."

"This is serious, Jess. We're nearing the Time Untime when everything resets. Of all men, you know what happens if things get misaligned."

Yes, he did. The Mayans weren't the only ancient Americans who had calendars. Many of the tribes had similar rotating cycles, including the Cherokee. "2012 ain't here yet."

"No, but the return of the Pale One has been sped up by whatever is coming. Be careful tonight."

Now, this was getting annoying, with everyone pecking at him like a bunch of hens. "Andy told me the same thing earlier."

"Two warnings. One night."

Time to listen. He understood. Too bad he hadn't had these warnings before he was gunned down as a human. That would have been a little more helpful than vague warnings to someone who was basically immortal and impervious now. But then, life was ever a study in a day late and a dollar short. "All right. I'll pay attention."

Ren inclined his head to him. "Good, 'cause you're the only reason I'm here, and I'd hate to think I uprooted myself needlessly." When Jess had been transferred out here a few weeks back, Ren asked to come, too. "Don't make me have to spirit-walk to cut your throat."

Jess snorted at the threat. "Got to say, dying would really wreck my best day. Been there, done that, and now that I think about it, Artemis forgot to give me the T-shirt."

Ren rolled his eyes. "You're psychotic."

"And we're down a Hunter, so we need to get patrolling before the Daimons start feeding."

Ren waved his hand in front of him and spoke a blessing in his native tongue.

Jess didn't understand it, but he appreciated the gesture. "Same to you, *di-na-da-nv-tli*." And with that, he started for the infamous strip, which was teeming with clueless tourists just waiting to become a walking Happy Meal for a Daimon.

Jess kept his pace leisurely as he used every sense he had to feel for any unnatural predator that was out and about. There was a strange vibe to the city, and it made him wonder about the depletion of the DH here.

The owner of the Ishtar Casino, Sin, he discounted from that list. Sin had fallen in love with one of Artemis's handmaidens and been redeemed from their service. So his was a happy exodus.

Lionel, Renee, and Pavel had all died over the last few months. Supposedly by bad luck. Lionel and Renee by not making it home before dawn. Pavel had been decapitated in a freak car wreck. At least, that was the official story.

After what Andy and Ren had said, Jess now wondered how accurate that was.

Two other Dark-Hunters had been moved in to replace those killed in action. Syra, who was better known as Yukon Jane, and Rogue, an Englishman whose proper speech belied his extremely psychotic ways. That boy definitely wasn't right.

Made him wonder who they'd move in to replace Lionel.

Guess I'll find out.

A pretty blonde walked past him on the street with a come-follow-me-cowboy look that grabbed his attention away from that line of thought. He let out a slow appreciative breath at the sass in her walk. He'd always been a sucker for a woman who knew how to handle herself and, more to the point, handle a man who was aching for her.

She smiled at him over her shoulder.

You got work to do, boy.

Yeah, but she was delectable.

Work, Jess. If Andy's right, there's a killer on the loose, and you need to find it and stop it.

He actually whimpered at the fact that he couldn't follow after the blonde. In Reno, doable. Here . . .

Too many Daimons.

Yet another reason they needed killing.

Sighing, he crossed Spring Mountain Road, heading north on Vegas Boulevard. He'd just passed the entrance to Neiman Marcus at the Fashion Show Mall and was nearing The Cloud when that familiar tingle went down his spine. One that was unmistakable.

There were Daimons nearby.

But where? People were all over the place. Hard to pinpoint a Daimon in a crowd this size. Not to mention the bright lights, even with his opaque sunglasses on, were hard on his light-sensitive Dark-Hunter eyes. Since Dark-Hunters were created long before the modern lightbulb, Artemis had given them incredible night vision that really hated anything bright. It was downright painful.

Closing his eyes, he focused his other senses. At first he was overwhelmed by everything he heard. But after a few seconds, it settled down so that he could pinpoint what he needed.

They were in the underground parking lot on his left.

Jess headed for it, making sure to keep himself away from any street cameras that the police might use for surveillance—that was one thing Rogue was the best at, since he'd come over from England, where their streets had more cameras than a fully stocked mega Best Buy store.

He ducked into the lot that was full of cars and vacant of people. At first he didn't hear anything more, and then . . .

To his right.

Pulling out his daggers, he kept them in his sleeves, just in case he happened upon someone who wouldn't understand why a tall, dark-haired man wearing really dark sunglasses and unseasonably warm clothing would be armed to his fangs. *Really, Officer, I was trying to protect humanity by killing these things that suck human souls out to live past their twenty-seventh birthday* just didn't cut it. Why no one would believe that, he couldn't imagine. Really, the audacity of modern courts and judges.

Jess came to an abrupt stop as he found something even more grisly than he'd expected.

There were four Daimons on the ground, literally feasting on what must be a demon of some kind. At first glance, it appeared human. But there was no missing the odd skin tone, slightly off from normal, and the smell of it.

That body wasn't human.

One of the Daimons looked up at him as if he'd sensed Jess's presence. "Dark-Hunter," he growled.

Now, normally, Daimons would do that and run away. That had been the standard operating procedure for the last 139 years.

These didn't run.

Well, not true. They ran *toward* him. Last time that had happened was his brief stint up in Fairbanks, Alaska, with Syra and a couple of others. And that hadn't gone so well for him. It was even worse for the other Dark-Hunters who had died there.

Jess caught the first one to reach him. He kicked the Daimon back and plunged his dagger straight into the Daimon's heart.

It didn't explode.

It just pissed the Daimon off.

Aw, now, wait a minute. . . .

"What the—?" His words ended as the Daimon picked him up and threw him against the far wall, where he slammed hard against the concrete. Pain exploded through his body. Been a while since he hurt this much. It brought back many an unhappy memory.

SHERRILYN KENYON

Still, he didn't take a lickin' and not give one back. No, sir. After flipping to his feet, he shrugged his coat off in one fluid movement and ran for his attacker.

Don't let them bite you."

Jess glanced over to where Sin had joined the fight. Almost a head taller, Sin wore his black hair cropped short. Dressed in black like Ren—something they all did, since it helped camouflage bloodstains they might collect in fights, and face it, it was a lot easier to look badass in black than in baby doll pink—Sin tossed him a new weapon, which was similar to a small scimitar.

He caught it just as the Daimon realized what was going on. The Daimon's eyes widened at the sight of the weapon. Now, that was what he was used to.

Respect.

Well, really fear, but he'd take it.

Sin flipped the Daimon nearest him flat onto his back and, in one swift stroke, beheaded him. He met Jess's gaze. "Now you know how to kill them."

Sure enough.

"Whatever you do, Jess, don't let even one of them escape."

Jess didn't. Of course, it took a little running, a near miss getting beheaded himself by a low-lying parking deck beam, couple of bruised ribs 'cause Daimons knew how to give a kick that counted, and more acrobatics than a man his age should be capable of, but he ran down the last one and made sure the Daimon took no more human lives.

42

Panting and sweating, he stood over the grisly body with a puzzled frown.

Sin grinned as he joined him. "That, I have to say, was highly impressive. You run like a jackrabbit. Too bad you were born before football. You, my friend, would have gone pro." He raked a hard stare over Jess's body. "They didn't bite you, did they?"

"Nothing but a willing female bites me, and definitely nothing without an explicit invitation." Jess indicated the body with a jerk of his chin. "Care to tell me why they're still here?" The one thing you could always count on with Daimons was the fact that they were self-cleaning. Kill one, and it exploded into dust. They didn't normally lie on the floor in a pool of blood, looking all grisly and nasty like that.

Sin kicked at the body. "Guess these haven't reached Reno yet."

"These?"

"Daimons who walk in daylight."

Ah, hell no . . .

This couldn't be good. "Come again?"

"We had a little bit of a problem here a couple of years ago. There was a hive of gallu demons who were preying on the tourists. I don't suppose you know what a gallu is."

"I'm a gunfighter, Jim, not a demonologist."

Sin moved past him so that he could burn the body on the ground. "Nice Bones impression. Roddenberry would be proud." He jerked his chin toward the burning body.

43

"Gallus are my pantheon's contribution to the nightmare list. Vicious and amoral, they don't care who they kill, and they are virtually indestructible."

"Nice."

"You have no idea. I had them contained here for a while. Unfortunately, they escaped."

That figured, and it was just like he feared. Suck City Limits was looming in the headlights. He should have known better than to take a detour from Normality. "So how many are running around now?"

"You miss the point, Dark-Hunter. They're not just here anymore, and they're spreading. Unlike a Daimon, one bite, and you become their slave. They can make more of themselves. That was bad enough. Then the Daimons realized they can feed on the gallu."

Jess shook his head. "Why do I have a feeling this is really about to piss me off?"

"Because it is. Once the Daimons feed on a gallu, they become immortal and absorb the demon's essence and powers into their bodies. As I said, Daimons can then walk in daylight, and the only way to kill them is to behead and burn them."

"And one bite, and I'm their slave?"

"Exactly."

Jess cursed. "And who thought this would be a good idea?"

Sin held his hand up. "Don't get me started. There are

idiots in all pantheons. Some days, I think the Sumerians had more than their fair share, and I only hope the idiocy is congenital and not something contracted later in life. Otherwise, I'm even more screwed." He accelerated the burning of the body. "But back to what needs to concern us most. So far the outbreaks have been containable."

That was one way of looking at it, he supposed.

Still . . .

"You know it might help if you'd actually told all of us about them before we run across them. Had you not shown up just now, I'd have been locked in a useless game of Whac-a-Mole, trying to kill them with a knife through the heart. I could have been gallu Daimon kibble. Really not cool, Sin."

"Hey, I just found out about these earlier today, and I was going to tell you about them."

"When? After they bit me and turned me into a Dark-Hunter gallu zombie?" Now, there was a horror movie in the making. He just didn't want to be the star of it.

Sin narrowed an angry gaze on him. "You left before I got down to you."

"I'm not that psychic, amigo. How was I supposed to know you wanted to talk to me?"

Sin scowled. "Didn't the valet tell you to wait?"

"Nope."

It was Sin's turn to curse.

Obviously the Apollite hadn't been as friendly as he

pretended. Jess tsked. "That's what you get for living with your enemies, Slim. Notice they don't flinch from stabbing you in the back."

"Neither do friends."

Jess grimaced at the touché. "Now, that's just cold, Sin. True," he admitted, "but cold."

"Yeah, well, I was trying to get your attention on the street. It's why I followed you down here. I wanted to warn you about them before you got into a fight with one."

That gave him pause. "You were following me?" And he didn't know it?

Impossible.

"Yeah."

Jess frowned at that. "Why didn't I sense you?"

"Maybe the blonde distracted you."

It didn't work that way. Never once had he failed to notice someone on his tail. Unless . . . "What are you?"

"Pardon?"

Jess raked a look over him, trying to find something to confirm his suspicion. "You can't be human, and I know you're not a Daimon or Apollite." Daimons, unless they partook of Clairol, were blond with lighter skin than Sin had. "You're no longer a Dark-Hunter, so . . ."

Sin gave a wicked half smile. "You're right. I'm none of those."

"What, then? Are you a god?"

Sin's smile went full blown. "Remember, Ray, whenever someone asks you if you're a god, the correct answer is always yes."

Jess snorted. "I saw that movie, and I think you misquoted it."

"The sentiment's the same."

Which meant Sin wouldn't answer. Fine. Jess wouldn't press the issue. He more than understood wanting to keep some things to oneself.

"Did you tell Ren about them?" Jess asked.

"Yeah. I caught him when I came down, then I went for you."

Thank God for that. He glanced at the scorched stain on the pavement that was the only thing left of the Daimons. He met Sin's gaze. "I appreciate the assist. And I have another question. Since I can't throw flames out of my hands like you did a minute ago, how do I dispose of these new Daimons we're fighting after I kill them?"

"We haven't worked out the kinks quite yet. But if you drop one, call me and I'll send out a cleanup team."

Jess shook his head. "Damn, you really can get anything in Vegas."

Sin laughed. "You have no idea."

No, but Jess was beginning to.

"Since you have so many of the enemy working in your casino . . . Have you heard of a human working with Daimons to kill Dark-Hunters?"

Sin's eyes widened. "What?"

That expression answered the question. "My Squire got word about it from the Oracles. I was just wondering if they might have misinterpreted whatever they got from the Powers That Be. I keep thinking if there was such a beast, Acheron would have called all of us with a warning." As their unofficial leader, Acheron tended to watch out for them, and he had powers that defied belief and understanding.

"Ash's powers don't necessarily work that way."

"What do you mean?"

"Think of it like having a fire hose turned on full blast," Sin said. "The water flows so fast, it's hard to control. He blocks his abilities unless he needs something, so that he doesn't get overwhelmed by it."

Jess wasn't so sure he believed Sin. Acheron was a walking contradiction who never spoke to anyone about himself. He couldn't imagine Acheron having a heart-to-heart chat with Sin, never mind explaining to the ancient Sumerian how his powers worked. "How do you know this?"

"Married to Artemis's handmaiden, remember? She knows a lot about Ash."

Now, that he believed. Be hard for Acheron to keep secrets from the goddess they all served. Sin was right. If anyone knew some of those secrets, it was probably his wife.

"So," Sin continued with his explanation, "if Ash isn't

focused on here, he won't know what's going on. You want me to call him about it?"

"Nah. I'll do it later." Jess never liked getting second-hand information. Too much room for people to forget something or get it misconstrued. He'd much rather have it straight from the horse's mouth.

Sin nodded. "Well, I won't keep you. I know you have a lot to do, and I have a casino to run and a wife and toddler to see to."

Yeah, but Jess envied him that last bit. A lot. However, he wouldn't begrudge Sin his good fortune. It was nice to know that life worked out for some people, and since Sin had been a Dark-Hunter, Jess knew the man must have suffered greatly in his first life. It did his heart good to see someone happy, even if it wasn't him. "Give the missus my best."

"Will do."

Jess went back for his coat while Sin took his leave. He glanced around at the remains Sin had burned and let out a tired breath.

New rules. New playing field. The gods must have gotten bored with them all. In the back of his mind, he could picture these new Daimons spreading like in a bad SF movie. Hell, he could even see the map with a superimposed image of a red horde spreading out like an epidemic.

And somewhere out there was a human playing vigilante on them.

Yeah, it was a good time to be in Vegas. He was so happy Acheron had reassigned him, and that was said with all due sarcasm.

He shrugged his coat on and returned to the street to continue his lonely patrol. As he walked among the crowd, he tried to imagine what it would be like to be one of them—an innocent person going about completely ignorant of the preternatural around him. A part of him had forgotten what it was like to be human.

Another part wondered if he'd ever really been human at all. His enemies and victims would definitely deny it. And he'd been nothing more than an animal.

Until Matilda.

"Gah, I'm maudlin again." Must be his lack of horses. Riding always made him feel better, and he'd been away from them for way too long.

Soon though, they'd be here and he'd be back to normal. At least as normal as an immortal could be.

Hours went by as he searched and found no target. It amazed him that the nightlife in Vegas didn't let up. The crowds did thin, but still . . .

Totally different world from what he was used to in Reno.

His phone buzzed in his pocket, letting him know it was time to head back so that he'd be home a few minutes before dawn. When it came to that, he never liked pushing his luck. No one wanted to spontaneously combust into flames, especially not in traffic. The thought of going Johnny Blaze just didn't appeal to him in the least.

He headed back for Sin's casino to collect his ride.

Jess hadn't gone far when a flash across the street caught his eye.

It was two Daimons pulling a woman into a storm drain. Jess sucked his breath in. Underneath the city was approximately a five hundred mile maze of drainage systems. It wouldn't take much for the Daimons to lose him down there.

He bolted across the street, hoping to catch them before they killed their prey or lost him.

The minute he was inside the drain, he all but let out a sigh of relief from the soothing darkness.

After removing his sunglasses, he slid them into his pocket and made his way through the smelly tunnel, which had about an inch of standing water in it. He curled his lip at the rotten garbage and other things he didn't want to think about. There were a number of homeless people who called these tunnels home. Some of them were every bit as dangerous to the average human as the Daimons he was after.

"Please let me go! Please! Please don't hurt me!"

He followed the sound of the woman's petrified cries. It didn't take long to find them.

Only it wasn't what he'd expected.

It was a trap, and he'd just barreled right into it.

4

Abigail had spent her entire life bracing for the moment when she'd see Sundown Brady again. Over the years, when she wasn't training to kill him, she'd played every imaginable scenario through her mind. Them meeting by accident. Her breaking into his house in the middle of the day to murder him in his sleep. A smoky, crowded bar where she walked up to him and then stabbed him in the heart and watched him fall to her feet as he died in utter agony. Even an abandoned movie theater where she trapped him inside and burned it to the ground. All to the tune of him begging her for mercy.

Yet none of those imaginings had prepared her for this.

For one thing, he was a lot larger than she remembered. Not just tall, which he was, but wide and extremely well muscled in a way very few men were. It was the kind of build that said he could snap her in two if he got close enough. His dark hair fell just past his ears and was a bit shaggy, as if he'd missed a haircut appointment. Two days' growth of whiskers shadowed a face that was so perfectly formed, he didn't look real. His eyes were black, and the intelligence there said nothing, absolutely nothing, escaped his notice.

Even with her new powers, she swallowed at the thought of fighting him. He wouldn't go down easy.

He'd probably take her with him.

But all she had to think of was her parents and the merciless way they'd died by his hands, and the fiery rage in her ignited to a level that wouldn't be intimidated or denied. It demanded his blood.

Sundown Brady was going to die tonight, and she was the harbinger who'd deliver it.

Jess froze as he saw the woman close up. Her black

hair was pulled back from her exotic features into a tight ponytail. Dressed in a pair of jeans and a dark purple shirt, she was armed from head to toe. But that wasn't what stopped him dead in his tracks.

For one instant, he could swear he was looking into Bart's face.

Time seemed to freeze as he took it all in. Her deep blue eyes that were shaped like a cat's. The dimple in her chin. The way she looked at him as if she could kill him.

It was like he was lying on the ground wounded again, looking up at Bart right before he pulled the trigger one last time.

"You bastard!" she snarled in a voice that was hauntingly familiar. One that brought back excruciating memories.

Before he could recover, she lunged at him.

Jess jumped back and twisted, sending her into the wall. He looked at the two Daimons, who were staying out of the fight for some reason. But he didn't have time to contemplate that as she came back at him, slashing at his body with a black KA-BAR.

He blocked her slash with his forearm across hers, then grabbed her hand. Dang, she was strong. Supernatural strong. Not to mention, she kept kicking at him. She fought like a well-trained wildcat.

"Let go of me!" she snarled, head-butting him.

That rattled his senses, but he refused to let go of her.

She was too quick and too close for that. If he released her, she'd get a shot in someplace that was going to hurt.

She looked past his shoulder to where the other two were sidelined. "Get him!"

Great. He slung her toward the Daimons. She collided with them, but it didn't slow them down.

His phone buzzed again, warning him he was running out of time. *I'm going to be a crispy critter if I don't do something quick.* While he could probably hole up here, he didn't want to chance it. Police and workers did occasionally venture down into the drains. All he needed was for one of them to find him loaded up with weapons.

Or worse, a flash flood could swoop down on him. Lionel had warned him on his first night here about seeking daytime shelter in the drains. Every year, there were a number of homeless who died from the flooding. While he couldn't drown, he could be swept into daylight, which would really suck for him.

He had to get out of here. Fast.

The really bad thing was he couldn't kill her. Dark-Hunters weren't supposed to kill humans, even when they were attacked by them. Stupid rule, granted. But it was one Acheron would have their ass over if they violated it.

And then there was the terrible suspicion he had about her identity. He wasn't sure if he wanted to be right or wrong. "Abigail?"

Anger darkened her blue eyes. "You do remember me."

How could he forget? "I thought you were dead."

She shrieked in rage before she attacked him with a fury that seemed to come from somewhere deep inside her. It was the same force that he'd had when he went for Bart.

Now that he knew who she was, there was no way he could hurt her. He choked on conflicting emotions. Relief, sorrow, and the deep need not to let her end his life. "I take it you're the one who's been killing Dark-Hunters?"

She lifted her chin proudly as she swung at him. "With relish. But you're the one I really want."

Why? All he'd ever done was protect her and her family.

He caught her arm and yanked her closer. "Ah, sugar, for that, all you had to do was get naked."

She curled her lip before she attacked even more viciously.

He staggered under a couple of well-placed blows. She was very well trained.

But then, so was he.

Jess twisted the knife from her hand and managed to finally catch her in a sleeper hold. She was harder to grip than a hungry greased pig. Luckily, he was used to pinning such ornery things. But if he'd been human, she'd have freed herself and been back on him.

He turned to the Daimons. "One step closer, and I snap her neck."

They exchanged a doubting frown.

"I mean it," he said as they looked like they were about

to pounce. He increased the pressure on her carotid and jugular. Within seconds, she was out. Still, he waited a few seconds more, in case she was faking. At this point, he wouldn't put anything past her.

Once he was sure she was unconscious, he slid her to a dry spot on the floor. "All right, punks. Bring it."

The moment he took a step forward, they ran deeper into the tunnel.

Well, at least they weren't the infected Daimons who could convert him.

Jess started to go after them, but rethought it. It was too close to dawn, and right now he had the prize of all time.

The woman who'd been hunting them.

A woman he'd once known . . .

"I can't believe you survived." But how? He had so many questions, they made him dizzy.

Best thing to do would be to interrogate her and find out what was going on and why she had such a hard-on for them. Hoping he didn't live to regret this decision, he picked her up and carried her back to the street. Now that she wasn't trying to kick his jewels into his throat, he realized just how tiny she was. Very well muscled, but short.

Like Matilda.

He squelched that comparison quick. She was nothing like his mild-mannered, soft-spoken bride-to-be. No one was. It was why he'd fallen in love with her and why all these decades later, he still ached from the loss of her friendship.

The woman in his arms was like everyone else he'd ever met. Treacherous. Lethal. Only out for herself. Whatever he did, he couldn't let himself forget that. She wanted him dead, and if he didn't stop her, she'd kill him and then move on to the rest of his colleagues.

No good deed goes unpunished....

He'd protected her and her mother, and how did she pay him back? By trying to kill him.

How utterly typical.

Jess made it out as the sky was just starting to lighten. *I better hurry and be quick about it....* It was getting a little too close at this point.

He hadn't gone far from the drain when he saw a police car driving by on the street.

Crap.

What were the odds that they'd not see him and keep going? Probably about as good as them believing he was carrying his wife back to their room after a heavy night of drinking.

Yeah . . .

He hadn't been *that* lucky in a long time. "I hope lockup doesn't have a window," he muttered under his breath.

The patrol car pulled up to the curb and stopped. "Hey, you there! Come over here."

Yeah, it was nice to know his bad luck was the only stable thing in his life.

Jess tightened his grip on Abigail as he debated his

options. None of them were good, especially since he was packing an arsenal under his coat. One they were sure to object to if they discovered it.

Making sure to act nonchalant, he moseyed over to the car. "Yes, sir?"

The officer glanced down at Abigail. "Is there a problem?"

Uh, yeah. You people are bugging the shit out of me when I need to be rocketing home. Jess forced himself not to betray his annoyance. "Little too much to drink. I was taking her back to the casino where we're staying."

The man narrowed his gaze suspiciously. "You need a doctor?"

No, he needed a break. "Nah, Officer. Thank you very much for the offer, though. She'll be all right. Well, the hangover will be pretty ferocious, I'm sure, but after a few hours, she'll be good as new."

"I don't know, George," the other officer said from the passenger seat. "I think we should call it in, just in case. Last thing we need is for him to be kidnapping her or something and we let him go. Think of the PR nightmare that'd be if he turns out to be a serial rapist or killer."

Jess had to bite back a curse at the paranoid asshole. Yeah, he *was* kidnapping her, but still . . .

She was the serial killer, not him.

"Hey, Jess."

He turned his head to see another police officer

approaching from the sidewalk. At least this one he knew. "Kevin, how you doing?"

Kevin stepped between Jess and the car. "Is there a problem here?" he asked the other officers.

Was that drilled into them at the academy, or what?

"No," the officer in the car said quickly. "We saw him carrying the woman and just wanted to make sure nothing was wrong."

Thank God neither he nor Abigail had been bloodied or bruised during their fight and their clothes weren't torn. That would have been even harder to explain. As it was, her clothes were no more rumpled than if she had simply passed out from drink.

"Ah," Kevin said, dragging the word out. He indicated Jess with a jerk of his chin. "Don't worry. Jimmy and I'll take it from here."

Jimmy, Kevin's partner, came up behind Jess to wave at the officers in the car.

Both of them appeared relieved that they could pass this along to someone else. "All right. Thanks for sparing us the paperwork. See you guys later." The car pulled off.

Turning around, Kevin arched his brow at Jess and the woman he was holding. "Should I even ask?"

Jess shifted Abigail's weight. "Not if you want to keep your job, and I don't mean the one that doesn't afford you your million-dollar house." His phone started buzzing again with another warning about sunrise. Not that he needed it. The sky was turning a scary shade of light.

Kevin glanced up as if he were reading Jess's mind. "You're cutting it a little close to dawn, aren't you?"

"Closer than I meant to."

Jimmy gestured to their car, which was parked a few feet away. "C'mon, we can get you back in time."

"Thanks." Jess finally breathed easily. This would also keep him from having to wrangle her onto his bike and hold her there, especially since she'd be coming to any time now. He had to admit, having Squires who were cops came in handy. That was one thing Sin had set up well in this city. In Reno, they'd been light handed with a Squire network. But this place was hooked up to the extreme.

Jimmy held the door open for them. Jess got into the backseat and rested his package by his side and tried not to notice how amazingly pretty she was. It seriously messed with his head to see mixed in her features the person he'd once loved most and the only one he'd ever truly hated.

Life ain't fair.

And it was never simple.

Kevin and Jimmy got in and turned the siren on. They called in their break and sped him toward his house at warp speed.

"I appreciate y'all doing this."

"No problem," Kevin said with a grin. "It's nice to run through the streets when we're not really on a call. Makes me feel like Speed Racer."

Jess frowned as they passed the interstate ramp. "Wouldn't the freeway be faster?"

Jimmy laughed. "For you, civ. We don't have to stop for lights."

That made sense. It normally took Jess a little over twenty minutes to get from downtown to his eleven-acre compound on Tomiyasu Lane (depending on where he was when he started), but he did shoot out farther by taking the interstate. If they didn't stop for lights, they should be able to make it to his place in about the same time, maybe less.

With some luck, he might actually avoid combusting into flames in the backseat. *That* would be hard for the Squires to explain to their watch commander. Though it might be entertaining to see them try if *he* weren't the stain.

Kevin glanced at Jess in the rearview mirror. "So you want to tell us about the woman now?"

"Not really."

Jimmy scratched at the back of his neck. "Are we going to have to file a missing persons report on her later?"

"I doubt it. She's running with a group of Daimons. They're usually not the kind to call you guys." And he knew for a fact that she had no family.

Unless she'd married.

His breath caught as he realized he didn't know anything about her now. Hell, she could be married to a Daimon or Apollite. The very thought made him ill. But humans did occasionally fall in with them for one reason or another.

She could be someone's mother. . . .

Surely she wouldn't have been on the street hunting Dark-Hunters if she had dependents.

Would she?

Jimmy turned around in the seat with wide eyes to stare through the partition at him. "Is she the one the Oracles have been talking about? The human killing you guys off?"

I should have kept my mouth shut. Now all the social network sites used and run by the Squires would be lighting up like a Christmas tree. "I think so, but I'd appreciate it if you'd keep this between us until I have a chance to ask her some questions."

"Absolutely." Jimmy slapped Kevin on his arm. "Told you it was real. Hah! You owe me twenty bucks."

"Yeah, yeah, whatever," Kevin groused.

They didn't say anything else as they sped down South Las Vegas Boulevard. Jess felt that familiar tingle at the back of his neck. The sun was dawning. The sky turning brighter with every heartbeat. And they were still a couple of miles from his home. Worse? He had to knock her out again as she started coming to.

Jess rubbed his thumb and index finger together—a nervous twitch he'd developed as a gunfighter. It was the same feeling he had right now. One mistake. One delay.

He was history.

Only this time, he wasn't relying on his instincts and skills to survive. He was relying on theirs. . . .

The first rays were cresting just as they pulled up to the black wrought iron gates that protected his driveway. Jess slinked down in the seat as he used his iPhone app to open them. He also signaled for the garage doors.

Come on . . . let's go. . . .

His skin was already burning something fierce. It wouldn't be long before he'd be dead.

Kevin shot them through the gates before they'd finished opening and across his long driveway. Too long, he realized as Kevin hauled ass down it and they still weren't under cover. Why the hell had he bought a house with a two-mile driveway? Okay, slight exaggeration, but damn. It seemed like forever before they were inside the garage.

Jess breathed a long sigh of relief, and he leaned back in his seat. "That's about as close to bacon as I want to come for a while."

Without commenting on that, Jimmy came around to open his door and let him out. "You need any help with her?"

He shook his head. "Nah, I got it. Thanks, though."

Jess had just pulled her from the car and was heading to the back door when Kevin blocked his path. The Squire pulled out a pair of cuffs. "You need these?"

That actually made him laugh. "Think I can handle a little filly without them." Then again, given the whipping she'd put on him earlier, he might want to rethink that.

Pride goeth before a fall. . . .

Kevin returned them to the pouch on his belt. "All right. We'll see you later."

Jess inclined his head to them before he carried her into the house.

He hesitated inside the door. Now what to do with her? He hadn't thought this far ahead, and while he should have done it in the car, he'd been a little preoccupied with thoughts bursting into flames.

His best bet would be to take her into the basement with him. There was plenty of room down there to keep her locked up and away from anyone who might think about releasing her before he wanted her set loose.

Or worse, her hurting Andy while she was trying to escape.

That definitely wouldn't do.

All right. Back to the original plan. He'd hold her downstairs in his domain.

He carried her to the hidden elevator and into what Andy called his six-thousand-square-foot dungeon. It hadn't been all that easy to find a house in Vegas with a basement, especially one this size as well as a home that also had a stable for his horses. When Andy first told him about this place, Jess had thought he was joking.

Andy wasn't. The house was actually sixty-five thousand square feet. Seventy-two thousand under the roofline.

It was amazing what a man would do for his horses.

Hell, he'd lived in smaller towns. But all things said

and done, the house was perfect for him, since it allowed him to stay downstairs undisturbed. Down here, he wasn't locked in by the daylight. He could live an almost normal subterranean life.

The house had a total of eighteen bedroom suites, with three of them being in the basement. He took her to the one closest to his room and laid her down on the bed. He started to walk away, but something about her held him by her side. She looked so fragile like this. However, the painful throbbing in his jaw where she'd slugged him said she was anything but.

What had made a little thing like her hunt them so viciously?

The Daimons must have lied to her. They did that a lot. Countless humans had been used as their tools over the centuries. The Daimons promised them eternal life, and in the end, they murdered the humans when they were done with them.

But her anger had run deeper than that. She'd fought like she had a personal grudge.

He sighed as he thought about the last time he'd seen her parents. That had been one screwed-up night. To this day, he could still see the blood splatters that had covered the room. The blood that had covered him . . .

There had been no sign of Abby in the house, and he'd definitely looked for her. He'd always hoped she was at a friend's.

The most disturbing thought was that she'd been there.

That she'd seen them die. That thought made him sick to his stomach. No child should witness the horrors of that night. Just like he wished Artemis had spared him the sight of what happened after he'd been killed.

Some memories weren't worth keeping.

And when the police had been unable to locate her, they'd all assumed her dead.

Yet here she was . . .

Grown up and kicking ass.

Frowning, he ran his hand down the side of her cheek. She had the softest skin he'd ever felt. Smooth. Inviting. Warm. He'd always loved the way a woman's flesh felt under his fingers. There was nothing more succulent.

Her features were exotic and intriguing. So different from Laura's, and at the same time, he could see enough of Laura there that it tugged at his heart. Laura had been both a haven and a hell for him. Around her, he'd felt connected to the past, and that connection had stung as deep as it'd comforted. He'd tried to let her go, but he couldn't sever the tie.

Now he wished he had.

Maybe then Abigail would have had a normal life. A woman her age ought to be out with her friends, having fun and enjoying her youth. Not coming after Dark-Hunters. Definitely not killing them.

A smile tugged at the edges of his lips at her ponytail. He didn't know why, but that reminded him of her as a kid. She'd had a lot of spunk even then. And it was weird to be so attracted to her now, having been there when she was born. He tried not to think about that whenever he was with a woman. On a level he didn't want to acknowledge, it bothered him. He was old enough to be their great-great-great granddaddy.

But he wasn't altruistic enough to be celibate either. There was only so much a man could do. Especially since they didn't know how old he was. To them, he was another mid-twenty-year-old guy they met in a bar and took home.

However, Abigail knew.

And she hated him for it.

He turned her face toward him. Her eyes opened just a slit, and when he saw them . . .

He pulled back.

What the hell? His heart pounding, he gently lifted one lid. Sure enough, her eyes were red with yellow threads running through them.

She wasn't human after all.

At least not fully.

Oh yeah, this was bad. *Real* bad. Was she the enemy from the west that Ren had been talking about? Prophecy and Oracle warnings never made much sense to him. Trying to unravel them was enough to give even the stoutest mind a nine-day migraine.

And he was too tired right now to think it through. He needed some sleep before he dealt with this. Or at least a break . . .

He covered her with a blanket, then made sure that

she had no way out of this room until he was ready for her leave.

At the door, he lowered the lights so that she'd be able to see the room when she came to, but not so bright that they'd disturb her.

He glanced back at her, and his breath caught in his throat. With this light and with her head tilted, she looked so much like her mother that it temporarily stunned him and took him back in time.

He saw Matilda lying on the bank of the stream where she'd taken him for a picnic not long after their engagement. The sun had been so warm that she'd fallen asleep while he read one of her favorite dime novels out loud to her. Her serene beauty had enchanted him and he'd spent hours watching her, praying for that afternoon not to end.

I love you, William.

He could still hear her voice. See her beautiful smile. Clearing his throat of the sudden lump, he shook his head to clear it, too.

Abigail wasn't Matilda.

But as she lay there without the hatred shooting out of her eyes at him, she was every bit as beautiful, and it stirred emotions inside him that he'd sworn he buried.

Not wanting to think about that, he went to his room and pulled off his coat and weapons. While he undressed for bed, his thoughts sped around his head as he tried to figure out what had happened to her.

Where she'd been all this time.

I should have checked her for an ID. Yeah, no duh. That would have given him her address and let him know if she was still a Yager or if she'd married.

Feeling like a complete dolt, he went back to see if he could locate one.

He pushed open the door and froze.

The bed was completely empty, and she was nowhere in sight.

5

Abigail came awake with a jerk. The last thing she remembered was being strangled by her worst enemy. Pain hit her hard as she came to terms with what had happened.

I failed. . . .

After all these years, she'd finally found the man who'd ruined her life and killed her parents. And he'd overpowered her with an ease that sickened her. She'd risked everything and even allowed her body to be used as an experiment. Still, it hadn't been enough.

I hate you, Sundown Brady. You rotten bastard!

For a moment, she feared she might have died. But as she focused on the opulent room she was in, she realized she was alive.

And it was *o-p-u-l-e-n-t*.

The bed she lay on was an ornately carved California king with a dark blue silk duvet that was so light, it felt like moving air. The furniture was the kind of high-end quality that looked like an antique, but wasn't. There didn't appear to be any windows, yet the ten-foot ceiling seemed too high to be a basement. And the French tray above her had a beautiful mural painted inside it of a lush forest scene with gilded deer.

I've died and gone to a palace. . . .

That was what it seemed like. The room she was in was bigger than her entire house.

Biting her lip in trepidation, she slid off the bed and wandered around. Her first stop was the door that someone had locked. Not that she was surprised. Far from it. She'd have only been shocked had it opened.

Abigail closed her eyes and tried to use her newfound powers to feel what was around her.

Nothing showed. Which meant nothing. She was still too new to her powers to fully command them.

"You were right, Hannah," she whispered. "I should have honed them better before I took off after Brady." But from the moment Jonah told her he had the updated dossier that told them where Sundown was patrolling, she'd been impatient.

Now she was paying for that stupidity.

Where am I? She had no clue to anything. While the room was lush, it didn't have much in it other than the bed and a dresser and armoire along with two chairs and a coffee table. There was no phone, computer, or clock.

Had Sundown kidnapped her? It was the most likely scenario since she doubted she'd been abducted by a prince, and that made her heart rate speed up. Why would he do that and not kill her?

Unless he wanted to torture her . . .

Yeah, that would be more his speed. Dark-Hunters were said to be vicious killers who lived to hear their prey beg for mercy while they died. Though to be honest, this didn't look like a torture chamber. It looked like a palace. The kind of place Jonah would love . . .

And then she felt sick as her thoughts turned to Perry and Jonah, who'd been with her when she attacked Sundown. No doubt they were both dead. Tears choked her at the thought of their loss. They'd been good friends to her for many years. Better than she deserved some days. She could barely remember a time when they hadn't been part of her life.

Now they were dead because of Sundown, too. Damn him!

She cursed as she ran through their last few minutes together. Jonah was the one who'd first identified Sundown on the street. She'd wanted to go after him immediately, but Perry had come up with the idea to get him down to the drain so that they could ambush him and keep their actions out of sight of any passersby or police.

Why hadn't it worked? Her powers should have been enough to defeat him. It was like something else had shielded him from her attacks.

Frustration welled up inside her until she sensed someone approaching her room. She quickly returned to the door and glanced about for something she could use as a weapon. There really wasn't anything unless she yanked a picture off the wall, and those were so large and unwieldy, they wouldn't do her any good. Not to mention, they were actual paintings and didn't have a glass front for her to shatter and use. He didn't even have a lamp in here to bash him over the head with. The light came from overhead cans that were on a dimmer switch. She'd turn the light off completely, but that wouldn't help. His eyesight would be much better in the dark than hers.

It didn't matter. She'd beat him down by hand if she had to. He would not defeat her this time.

She pressed herself back against the wall as the door slowly opened.

. . .

Jess *paused as* he saw the empty bed. Having survived numerous ambushes in his human life, he knew she'd be nearby, waiting to jump him.

And not in a way a man wanted an attractive woman to jump him.

Since she wasn't in his line of sight, she must be behind the door. That thought had barely finished before she kicked it into him with everything she had, which was a lot for a little thing. The door hit him hard and slammed against his arm and face. Oh yeah, that was going to leave a mark.

Stunned, he staggered back.

That was a mistake. She came around the door with a feral growl and launched herself at him. Damn, it was like trying to fight off a mountain lion. Come to think of it, he'd rather fight a mountain lion.

Those, he could shoot.

"Stop!" he snarled, trying to get her off him as she pounded him with her fists.

"Not until you're dead!"

He hissed as she bit his hand. "Trust me, you don't want me to die."

She elbowed him hard in the stomach. "Why not?"

Jess tried to get a grip on her, but she twisted out of his hold and kicked him hard in the leg. He put some distance between them in the hallway. "You're locked in my soundproof basement, where no one will ever be able to hear you scream—and they won't dare come down here to check on me, since they're not allowed." Definitely not true—he always had a hard time keeping Andy out of his hair, but she didn't need to know that. "They'll just think I'm coming and going on my own. You got about a day's worth of food in the pantry down here. After that, hope you don't mind eating rotting Dark-Hunter carcass, 'cause, babe, that's all you're going to have."

Abigail paused at his words. She would call him a liar, but something in his eyes told her he was being honest. Besides, it made sense from what she knew about Dark-Hunters and their habits. She'd been told by her Apollite brethren that their Squires lived in fear of them and that the Squires interacted with the Dark-Hunters they served only when they had to. Some of them had even welcomed death at Apollite hands to be free of their Dark-Hunter masters. "I could break down the door."

He scoffed at her bravado. "This was designed as a fall-out shelter with ten-foot-thick steel walls. Unless you're packing some heavy artillery in your foundation garments, sweetie, it ain't gonna happen. Ain't no cell service down here or anything else. It's like a tomb, which it will be if you kill me. But that's up to you."

She wanted to tear his throat out. Unfortunately, even though she ached to kill him, her self-preservation kicked in. Last thing she wanted was to die . . . at least before he did. "Why did you bring me here?"

"Why are you killing Dark-Hunters?" he countered.

Stepping back, she raked a repugnant sneer over him. At least as much of one as she could, given his wardrobe change. Dressed in a pair of red flannel Psycho Bunny pajama bottoms that added a sense of humor and whimsy to his I'll-rip-your-throat-out tough guy aura, and a gray T-shirt, he looked . . .

Normal. The only thing lethal about him now was his giant size and those dark eyes that promised her death.

She swallowed before she answered. "Why do you think?"

"Other than the fact that you're as loco as a three-tailed cat in a rocking chair factory, I'm as clueless as a newborn colt."

Abigail's stomach churned at his words. "Oh I forgot. You think it's all right to kill innocent Apollites and humans and prey on them. Well, I have news for you, buster. We're not taking it anymore. Your days of killing us are over, and we're hunting *you* now."

Frowning, he snapped his head back with a baffled expression. "Come again?"

"Are you deaf?"

"No, ma'am. But I know you didn't just accuse *me* of killing the very things I protect."

His denial shot a fresh bomb of rage through her. Grinding her teeth, she lunged at him.

Jess caught her against his chest. She stomped his instep. Cursing, he bent over and stumbled back. Big mistake. She slammed her hands across his ears. Pain splintered his skull. She would have kneed him in the face had he not put a little more distance between them.

Sick of being beat on, he cursed himself for declining the handcuffs.

His only course of action was to wrap himself around her and brace her flat against the wall so that she couldn't continue to hurt him. "Stop fighting," he snarled in her ear.

"No! You took everything from me, and I'm going to kill you for it."

That only confused him more. "What are you talking about?"

"You murdered my parents. You bastard!"

For a few heartbeats, he couldn't breathe as he flashed back to his life as a human. Change out the word *parents* with *father* and make her a man, and he remembered the day when someone else had leveled that accusation. After it was said, the man drew his gun and shot him.

The bullet had gone into his shoulder. Acting on pure instinct honed by countless gunfights, Jess had pulled his own Colt out and returned the favor. Only his bullet went straight through the man's head. It wasn't until Jess checked him that he realized that man was a sixteen-year-old boy who'd stared up at him in agony while the light drained out of his eyes. The father he'd mentioned had been a card-sharp who'd tried to gun Jess down outside a saloon a few weeks before that. Stupid fool had pulled a derringer on him. Jess had disarmed him, and when the gambler went to stab him, he'd shot him at point-blank range.

Justified.

But the kid's death . . .

That was one of dozens of such memories he wished to God he could purge out of his mind.

"I haven't killed a human being in over a hundred and forty years, and I damned sure didn't kill your parents."

She shrieked at him, then thrashed about with enough force to free herself from his hold. "You don't even re-member? You worthless, rotten—"

He caught her hand before she slapped him. "Honey, I haven't shot a human since I was one. Only piece of loco around here would be you."

She shoved him back and tried to kick him. "I saw you with my own eyes. You gunned them down in cold blood."

That set fire to his temper. He might have been a lot of things, but that . . . that . . . "Oh, like hell. I have *never* in my life killed *anyone* in cold blood."

She curled her lip. "Right . . . You're a hired killer. It's all you've ever known. You've never cared who and what you put down so long as you got paid for it."

"*Was*"—he stressed the word—"and those I killed, I did so in a fair duel. They had as much a chance of living as I did." While he was the first to admit he'd been a cold-blooded criminal, unlike Bart, he'd had lines he wouldn't cross. Things no amount of money could make him do. "I swear to God that I did *not* kill your parents."

Abigail hesitated. He meant what he was saying. She could see it in his eyes and hear it in his indignant tone. "How could you forget that night? I heard you fighting with my father. You left and then came back and broke into our house."

He held his hands up to emphasize his point. "I have never broken into a house. A bank, most definitely. A train a time or two to rob payrolls, but *never* someone's home."

"You're lying."

He shook his head. "I don't lie. I've got no need to."

"Bullshit. I was there. I *saw* you."

"And I'm telling you right now that I wasn't. On the soul of my mother, I didn't kill them. And while I fought with your dad, I never once struck him or even insulted him." Then to her utmost shock, he went to a cabinet a little farther down the hallway and opened a drawer that had a safe with a hand scanner. He put his palm on top and opened the safe. Inside was a handgun and KA-BAR. He pulled the knife out.

Her heart pounded as she realized he was going to stab her. She braced herself for the fight.

It didn't come.

Instead, he flipped the KA-BAR around so that the blade faced his body and the hilt was toward her. "If you really, truly think I killed your parents, have your vengeance." He placed the knife in her hand.

Completely caught off guard, she stared at him with the weight of the knife heavy in her palm. *You've waited your whole life for this. Cut his throat.* So what if she died afterward? She'd have her vengeance.

She wanted his life with a passion that was undeniable. It was a primal need that screamed out for his blood. But something in her gut told her to wait.

And in that instant, she had another memory. Sundown sitting at her kitchen table, coloring with her. "Dang, Laura, you have a real artist here. I've never seen a better rendition of Scooby-Doo."

Abigail had beamed with happiness while her mother brought them both a cup of hot chocolate. When her mother turned her back, Jess had added his marshmallows to Abigail's cup because they were her favorite. He'd winked at her and then held his finger to his lips and cut his eyes to her mother's back to tell her to be quiet about it so that neither of them would get in trouble for it. She couldn't count the times he'd done something sweet like that for her.

Sundown had been their friend.

No, her rationale countered. He'd killed them. She'd seen his face in the mirror of her room. He didn't know how to be anyone's friend. He was treacherous to his core, and if he was offering her a knife . . .

"What kind of trick is this?"

He didn't back down or blink. He stood right in front of her, looking at her through his thick lashes. His presence was terrifying and overwhelming as a tic beat a fierce rhythm in his jaw. "No trick. Believe me, I understand that soul-deep need to kill the person who took what you loved away from you. I know for a fact that I'm innocent, but I won't fault you for your belief, wrong though it is." He dropped his arms to his sides. "You want to kill me, go for it. I won't stop you. But know that when you do, you'll be spilling innocent blood yourself. May God have mercy on your soul."

Growling in anger, she moved to slice his jugular, expecting him to catch her hand and use the knife on her.

He didn't.

"I *will* kill you," she said between clenched teeth. She *could* behead him. She had no doubts.

He continued to stare down at her. "Do it."

Determined, she pressed the blade so close to his throat that it drew a bead of blood onto the dark carbon steel. Still, he didn't budge. He merely stood patiently for her to end his life.

"What are you waiting for?" His words sounded like a taunt.

She ground her teeth in fury at herself. "I'm not you. I can't kill someone who's defenseless."

"Nice to know the other Dark-Hunters you murdered had a fighting chance."

She pulled the blade away from his throat. "Oh, spare me, you blood-sucking bastard. I know exactly how you prey on people and then blame the Apollites for it."

He scowled at her. "Wait, wait, wait. I'm confused. First I'm a murderer, and now I'm guilty of preying on all humanity. Woman, who have you been talking to? They done got your head screwed on backwards and then some. We're not the bad guys in all this. The Daimons are the ones killing humans, not us."

What in the world was he talking about now? "Daimons? What's a Daimon?"

He choked. "You work with Apollites and you've never heard the term?"

"No. Are they some kind of demon?"

Sundown folded his arms over his chest as he gave her a disbelieving grimace. "Daimons are the Apollites who live past their twenty-seventh birthdays."

Was he on something? Surely, he knew the history of her adoptive people even better than she did. "Apollites can't do that. It's impossible."

"Uh, yeah, they can. I know, 'cause they're what we hunt. Every night. Without fail."

She rolled her eyes at his lunacy. "You are such a liar."

"Why would I lie?"

"Because you're one of the ones who kills humans and then blames it on the Apollites," she repeated, stressing the words so that even he could understand them. "You use them as your scapegoats, and this must be the lie you tell to justify it."

"And that makes sense in what alternate universe? Really? Why would we blame something neither humanity nor Apollites know exists to cover up these supposed crimes we commit? Hell, it'd make more sense to blame little green men. Who told you this malarkey?"

Before she could answer, something bright flashed to her left.

Lifting her hand to shield her eyes, she cringed in pain. It was absolutely blinding.

When the light faded, there was another man in the hallway with them. One with an evil sneer, who looked like he'd been bred for no other purpose than to kill. Tall with jet black hair and icy blue eyes, he was gorgeous. Dressed in a blue shirt and jeans, he had a small goatee. He glanced at her, then locked gazes with Sundown, who seemed to know him. "Do I have to kill her for seeing me pop in?"

Sundown shook his head. "She already knows about us."

The unknown man tsked at him. "Risky, boy. Acheron finds out you've been spilling your guts to civs, he'll have your ass."

Sundown ran his thumb down the line of his jaw. He held an expression that said he was oddly amused. "It's not what you think, Z. Turn on those god powers and use them. I am not responsible for her knowledge of nothing."

Z scoffed. "Impressively screwed-up syntax there, Cowboy. Glad I could follow it . . . Sort of. As for the powers, don't really have time to scan her and I really don't give a shit. Rather kill her and save myself the expended energy for something I might actually enjoy . . . like picking my nose."

Ew. Someone was socially awkward. She wasn't sure at this point if she liked Z or not. He was rather off-putting.

"So why are you here?" Sundown asked.

"Got a huge problem."

Jess didn't like the sound of that at all. He slid his gaze to Abigail. "I already got one of those. Don't need another right now, little buddy."

Zarek laughed evilly at his term of endearment. Only Jess could call the Roman ex-slave that and live. The one thing about Zarek, it didn't take much to motivate him to murder. He hated all people and wanted nothing to do with the world at large. That being said, the two of them went way back, and but for Jess, Zarek would be dead now and not married to a Greek goddess.

It was a debt neither of them spoke about. Ever. However, Zarek wasn't the kind of man to forget it either. They had an unspoken bond of friendship that ran as deep as a blood tie.

Zarek sobered. "Well, that's just too bad, Hoss. 'Cause I'm here to drop this one right in your lap. Someone killed your buddy tonight."

His heart sank at the news. "Ren?"

"Other friend."

Jess scowled. Like Z, he tended to shy away from most folks. His past didn't exactly lend itself to trust. "I only have you and him. So I'm pulling a little blank here on who you might be referring to."

Zarek slapped him across the back. "Think, bud. Fierce immortal who likes to gamble in Sin's casino, wear tacky shirts and watch anime."

Jess sucked his breath in sharply as he understood. "Old Bear?"

"Give that boy a biscuit." Zarek's tone dripped with sarcasm. "He finally got it."

Jess couldn't believe what Z was saying. It wasn't possible. Old Bear was one of the four Guardians and powerful beyond belief. "How?"

"Some fool beheaded him around one A.M."

The woman frowned at them. "Are you talking about the Native American Dark-Hunter stationed here?"

A bad feeling went through Jess as he met her gaze. Surely she wouldn't have been so stupid as to . . .

"Say you didn't."

"Kill him?" she asked. "Fine. I didn't . . . but I did."

Oh yeah, this was bad. The kind of bad they made horror movies out of. In fact, he'd rather be naked in a zombie flick with no ammo or shelter, coated in brain matter and wearing a sign that said COME GET ME, than face what they were going to have to face now. "Honey, let me give you a quick lesson. Just 'cause someone's a few centuries old and fanged, doesn't make them a Dark-Hunter."

Zarek concurred. "And some of those fanged immortals we actually need. Old Bear happened to be one of them."

She rolled her eyes dismissively. "Pah-lease."

Jess ignored her. There was no need in arguing with her right now. They had much bigger problems than her pigheadedness. "How bad is it?" he asked Zarek.

"Well, he was the Guardian for the West Lands, where his people had banished some of the worst of their supernatural predators. Now that he's dead, the balance has shifted and those he guarded can be set free."

Jess hated to even ask the next question. But unfortunately, he had to. "And they are?"

When he answered, Z's tone was as dry as the desert. "Nothing too major. A couple of plagues. Some scary weather anomalies. . . . oh, and my personal fave—" He paused for effect, which told Jess how bad it was going to be. "—the Grizzly Spirit."

Oh yeah, that was quite a stellar lineup from hell. Literally. "You're kidding me, right?"

Zarek shook his head. "I don't have a sense of humor, you know that. The Dark Guardians will be moving after Choo Co La Tah now, since he's the North Guardian. If they can take him down, they can free the ones he guards, too."

And set loose an apocalyptic war that would make the Daimon leader, Stryker, look like a wuss. Yeah, that was just what they needed.

The woman set her arms on her hips in pique. "What are you people talking about?"

"Nothing important." Zarek raked a nasty glare over her. "Just the end of the world as we know it, and for the record, I don't feel fine. Neither will you when it all comes slamming down on your head."

Jess dragged Zarek's attention back to the more important matter. Saving the world from those who would put a major hurt on it. "Where's Choo Co La Tah now?"

"Ren was with him at the time Old Bear died. Now he's guarding him. When the sun goes down, Ren'll need help moving Choo Co La Tah to the Valley of Fire."

Now, that made no sense. "Why?"

Zarek shrugged. "You'll have to ask Ren yourself. I didn't inquire and no one elaborated. All I know is it's something to do with a prophecy from their pantheon, and for that reason, I can't go with you. Apparently the area you have to go into is protected from any god or demigod born outside their pantheon. I'm only here as a messenger. Ash would have come for this, but his wife's in labor."

"Why'd he call you?"

Zarek gave him a droll stare. "My charming personality."

Jess snorted in derision.

"Fine, asshole. I'm sure it had to do with the fact that he figured you wouldn't shoot me."

That was a good bet, and Ash had no doubt refrained from calling Andy because the boy was too high-strung to deal with news like this. Andy would still be in his room, freaking out over the end of the world and trying to get laid before it occurred. "Why didn't he call me himself?" For some reason, Ash's calls came through even down here. That man had the best cell service ever.

"He tried. You didn't answer your phone. And since he's a little busy with his wife threatening to castrate him over her labor pains, he sent me in."

Now, *that*, Jess would have paid money to hear. He couldn't imagine anyone threatening Ash.

He slid his gaze back to Abigail, who'd been nothing but trouble since the moment he followed her into the drain. The call must have come in when they'd been fighting.

Zarek walked over to her. "And thank you, Miss Priss, for making this easy on us." He snapped his fingers and a rope appeared on her hands, binding them together.

She shrieked in outrage until Zarek manifested a gag over her lips to stifle her insults.

"What are you doing?" Jess asked.

"Making it easy on *you*."

Completely baffled, he frowned at Zarek's actions. "Making what easy on me?"

"Transporting her."

At this point, Z was starting to wear on his nerves. "Would you stop acting like a third-rate Oracle and spit everything out so that it makes sense." 'Cause right now, he had no idea why Zarek had her bound up like a Christmas goose, and he was too tired to keep chasing answers.

"Glad to. In order to set everything back to normal and stop the hell to come, Choo Co La Tah has to go to the Valley and offer up a sacrifice of the one who killed Old Bear." He passed a wry grin to the woman. "That'd be you, sweet cheeks."

6

Jess gaped while Abigail backed away at Zarek's dire words, but she couldn't go far. Zarek threw up his hand to hold her in the hallway next to them. Even before he'd married a goddess, Zarek had held some impressive telekinetic powers. Nowadays, they were downright sick.

He gave Zarek a disbelieving stare as he digested his orders to kill her. "You're telling me that Acheron, my boss, the really tall Atlantean pain in most of our asses, actually authorized the killing of a human?"

Zarek shrugged. "I can see your confusion. It is highly out of character for him. But since she's been killing off Hunters . . . I guess he figures it's tit for tat. Or maybe he's just having a really bad day."

"You're seriously not joking?"

Zarek let out an irritated growl. "Really? How many more times are you going to ask me that? I could be on a beach right now with my wife, son, and daughter, baking in the sun while they frolic and play. Am I? No. I'm here, and I want nothing more than to yank you around with bullshit 'cause this gets me off more than my wife running in a bikini."

Jess counted to ten before he let Z rile him. That was the thing about Zarek. The man had a short fuse, and Jess's wasn't all that far behind his. Not that he blamed Z for it. As bad as Jess's childhood had been, it was a picnic in paradise compared to what Z had suffered.

Still, those orders were so contrary to what they normally were that he couldn't wrap his head around it. Acheron profaned hurting humans in any way. Why would he be okay with it now?

That alone told him just how scary this whole thing was. Playtime was over.

Jess removed the gag from Abigail's lips. No need in making this worse on her. He expected her to shriek and curse. At the very least, head-butt him again and fight.

Instead, she was remarkably calm, given the fact she'd just heard Zarek call for her death. "You are not sacrificing me . . . to anything," she said between clenched teeth.

Zarek scoffed. "You started this, babe. The choice is simple. Either you die alone, nobly like a good sport, or the entire world dies with you, which I don't think they'd appreciate much. So put on your big-girl pants and own up to what you and your stupidity caused. It's *Joe Versus the Volcano* time."

He folded his arms over his chest. "But in the end, I don't give a shit what you do. With the exception of the cowboy there and my family, I hate people with a passion that makes your feelings for Jess look like a schoolgirl crush. Lovely thing about my current situation, I'm truly immortal. You annihilate humanity and the world . . . I'm still good. So whatever you decide, it won't affect me personally. I would say you're the one who'll have to live with the guilt. But either way, you're dead. Whatever. I delivered my message. My job here is done, and I need to get back to the one that I'm still not sure how I let them talk me into doing—which is even weirder and scarier than the Dark-Hunter gig." He turned his attention to Sundown. "Jess, call me if she wusses, and I'll make sure you survive the holocaust." He vanished.

"Thanks, Z," Jess called after him. "Always nice chatting with you."

Now what should he do? Really . . . it was the kind of thing that even *his* vast and varied experiences had never prepared him for. Yes, he'd dealt with Daimon outbreaks galore. A run-amok Daimon slayer up in Alaska who'd walked in daylight. But Daimons who were demons and could convert anyone they bit, and all-out death prophecy were a whole new territory for him.

Jess wasn't sure where to go with that.

Abigail's eyes were filled with a mixture of panic and suspicion. She did not appear happy. Not that he blamed her. He'd hate to be told he had to sacrifice himself to save the world. It would seriously muck up even a great day. And honestly, he wasn't sure he'd be any more inclined to do it than she was.

"He was lying." Her voice had a tiny tremble in it.

Wouldn't it be great if life were that easy? You got bad news, you called it a lie and everything was fixed. . . .

One could only hope.

Jess sighed in sympathy. "Unfortunately, Zarek doesn't lie. And as you saw, he doesn't pull punches either. He's as frank and tactless as the summer day is long." He cut the rope on her hands and let it fall to the floor. "You still going to fight me?"

She rubbed at her wrists. "Given what he said, I was thinking about running."

Well, at least she was honest. That, he could appreciate. He slid his knife into the back of his pants, waiting to see when she'd bolt.

Abigail stood there, unsure of what to think or do. Sundown watched her with a nonchalance she knew was misleading. His reflexes were as honed as any she'd ever encountered or fought. The fact that her demon-enhanced powers weren't enough to subdue him said it all. None of the others she'd killed, including Old Bear, had stood toe to toe with her for very long.

Never mind knocking her out and kidnapping her.

In fact, Old Bear had barely put up a fight. Why, if he was so important, hadn't he fought harder?

Why hadn't she double-checked his identity? How could Jonah have made such a bad mistake?

And before she could decide on an action, the ground beneath them shook. The force of it was so great that it knocked both of them off their feet.

Abigail hit the floor with enough impact to steal her breath and bruise her elbow. Gah, that hurt. She definitely could have done without that on top of all the other delights this day had held.

Pushing herself up, she met Sundown's gaze from across the hall. "Was that an earthquake?" While rare in Vegas, they did happen. But usually they were minor. This one had felt much, much larger.

"I don't know." He got up and went into a room across the hall.

You should run for it while he's distracted.

The only problem was, she didn't know where to run to. Since there were no obvious windows or stairs, she'd have to search for an exit. That would probably be obvious to Sundown, who'd then stop her.

And that thought died as he turned on the TV and she heard the news.

It wasn't an earthquake.

The ground outside the city was bubbling and opening up, and scorpions were flooding out of the crevices like some bad horror movie as they overran everything. Thousands and thousands of them.

How could there be so many? She'd never seen more than a handful in her entire life. Honestly, it looked like the earth was vomiting arthropods.

She shivered in revulsion.

Sundown let out an audible breath. "Now, there's something you never think about seeing, huh? Zarek definitely wasn't exaggerating about the plagues he mentioned. Why couldn't it be locusts like other people have? No. Leave it to Old Bear to do something different."

She shook her head in denial. "I didn't do this." It wasn't possible. There had to be another explanation as to why this was happening. One that didn't point the finger at her.

Maybe the scorpions were bored?

Or the Scorpion King was ticked off that no one had built a casino for him? At this point, she was willing to grasp any straw that didn't tell her to kill herself to save the world.

"Hon, you're the one who said you killed Old Bear. I tried to deny it, but you corrected me. And if you did cut his head off, you *did* do this. Accept it." He flipped the channel to another view of the scorpions swarming over a road downtown toward people who were screaming and running to get away from them. "Welcome to the apocalypse. Ain't she pretty?"

Abigail felt sick as more tremors shook the ground under them. She braced herself against the wall to keep from being thrown off her feet again. "He looked like a Dark-Hunter," she insisted. "He didn't correct me when I called him one."

Sundown arched a brow at her. "He had fangs. So what? Plenty of things not a Dark-Hunter have fangs, including Hollywood actors and kids playing vampire. You should have checked his membership card before you attacked. Good grief, what if you'd run across a Masquerade group? Would you have slaughtered a bunch of innocent kids?"

"Of course not. I'm telling you, Jonah did do recon on him. He did recon on all our targets. The man I killed tonight was a Dark-Hunter. Jonah would never have authorized hunting and terminating someone else."

Sundown gestured to the TV with the remote in his hand. "Obviously somebody had bogus information. Or he just plain lied."

She started to respond when all of a sudden, the floor near her buckled. She'd no more righted herself than dozens of scorpions swarmed out, scattering across the floor as they'd done in the desert. And worse, these were the deadliest ones. Bark scorpions. Whereas a sting from a single one *might* not kill her, to be stung by this many would without fail. The neurotoxins in their stinger were known to be fatal.

And she was allergic to them.

Shrieking, she tried to get away, but the floor shifted even more, pitching her toward them. Frozen in terror, she couldn't move as she watched them wide-eyed.

I'm going to die. . . .

She had no doubt. They were going to overrun her and sting her all at once.

Everything seemed to slow down as they advanced on her with a swiftness that was indescribable. Those little bodies twisted as they moved their legs faster and faster, their tails arched and thrusting for a strike. . . . She couldn't breathe as the sound of their scuttling feet and snapping pinchers echoed in her ears.

Her entire body cringed in expectation of the pain. They were on her.

Just as they swarmed her feet, she was yanked off the floor and shaken until the scorpions fell away. Once they were clear, she was thrown over a well-muscled shoulder and carried from the room as if she were a rag doll.

Sundown slammed the door shut behind him and set her back on her feet. Unable to speak, she flicked the one remaining scorpion on her boot to the ground and then stomped it until it stopped moving.

Every millimeter of skin on her body crawled in revulsion. It was like they were on her again.

But her relief was very short lived. The scorpions were now tearing through the door.

She gaped in disbelief of their power and persistence. What were they going to do? "How are they doing that?"

"I ain't gonna ask them right now. Don't really rate on my importance scale." Sundown sprinted to a locked cabinet. He entered a code on the electronic lock, then opened the doors. It was a gun case with enough weaponry inside to arm a small nation.

Sundown grabbed a pump-action shotgun and a bunch of shells, which he put into his pockets. She ran toward him as the scorpions began flooding into the bedroom from the space they'd made under the door.

He slammed the cabinet doors shut and then pulled her behind him before she could arm herself. With a feral gleam in his eyes that was more frightening than the scorpions, he opened fire on them.

They blew back in every direction like a clawing cloud.

But it didn't stop them. They kept coming, and in greater numbers.

Desperate, Abigail looked at the cabinet. "You have a flamethrower in there?"

"Yeah. Bad news, though—it'd burn down the house if we used it, and that wouldn't do us any good."

There was that. However, she'd rather be burned alive than stung by that number of scorpions. "What are we going to do now?"

"Find a steam roller?"

If only . . .

"You're not funny." Growling, Abigail tried to think of a real solution. The first thing she'd learned as a kid when they found a scorpion in her bed was that scorpions didn't react to insecticide, and even if they did, Sundown would have had to have gallons of it to stop them. The only way she knew to kill them was to squash them.

Yeah . . . her feet weren't big enough to even make a dent in that horde. She'd be overrun and dead in a matter of seconds.

"What we need here, folks, is a really big chicken."

She scowled at his bizarre comment and the fact that his drawl had actually gotten deeper as he spoke. "What are you? Hungry? Now?"

He laughed at her irritation. "Nah. They love to hunt and kill scorpions. Damn shame I don't have a flock or two million of them right about now. Who knew? I just hope those damn things aren't chowing down on my Squire."

Sundown pulled her through a doorway and into another bedroom. He held the gun in one hand as he slammed the door shut and locked it.

They could hear the scorpions on the other side, scurrying about. The sound made her cringe. It wouldn't take them long to breach this door, too.

"We're dead, aren't we?"

Jess wanted to deny it, but right now, he couldn't think of anything else to escape. They were out of rooms to run to, and the scorpions were chewing his door down. Not that it mattered in his case. He couldn't die from their stings.

But the woman could.

And even without death, those sons of bitches would hurt. Not exactly something he was craving.

He glanced around the room, then grinned as an idea hit him. "Get on the bed."

She stiffened indignantly. "Excuse me?"

Jess grinned at the direction her thoughts had gone. Normally he wouldn't mind, but right now, sex was the last thing either of them should think about. "We need height. Get on the bed." He didn't wait for her. He launched himself at it. He loaded more shells into his gun, then fired up at the ceiling.

"What are you doing?"

He didn't respond as he reversed the gun and used the stock to widen the hole by slamming it against the plaster and knocking it down. *Don't let the damn thing go off by accident.* If it did in this position, it'd take out a piece of his anatomy that he sure would miss.

Abigail let out a squeak before she sidled up against him. She actually wedged herself between him and the wall. Any other time, he'd appreciate having those curves pressed so close against his body.

But right now . . .

"They're swarming in."

He glanced over his shoulder to confirm her words. "All right. I think there's enough room that I can lift you up into the floor above."

Sundown was trying to save her? Abigail was stunned by his offer. Especially since she'd been trying to kill him just a short time ago. Before she could respond, he dropped the gun, then braced his hands on her hips and lifted her up with an ease that was startling. She reached for the hole he'd made and pulled herself up through it.

It wasn't easy, but she finally wiggled all the way through the tight opening.

Laughing in triumph, she started for the front door, which was only a few feet away. She'd barely gone a step when she heard Sundown firing at the scorpions again.

He was still trapped.

Leave him. He didn't deserve anything better than to be stung until his head exploded. Every part of her wanted to hear him screaming in pain.

He saved your life just now.

So what? That didn't undo her parents' deaths.

But what if he wasn't lying? What if someone else had

really killed them? If he died, she might not ever find out the truth.

The thought made her pause. If Sundown hadn't killed them, who did?

And why?

There's more to all of this. She could feel it with every heightened instinct she possessed.

I've never been an unreasonable person. She prided herself on that fact. When others panicked and freaked, she was always calm and rational. Methodical.

More gunshots sounded.

Unable to leave him to the scorpions until she knew more, she reversed course toward the hole in the floor. She knelt down so that she could see him below. Sure enough, the area around the bed was crawling with the arthropods. "Give me your hand."

Sundown looked up at her with a shocked expression that would have been comical if they weren't in such a bad situation.

She leaned down and held her hand out to him.

"Get back," he snapped.

"I can help you."

He grinned at her, flashing his fangs. "I'm a little wider than you are, sweetheart. I won't fit through that."

She started tearing at the floor to widen it.

Jess arched a brow as he realized what she was doing. Damned if she wasn't trying to help him. Who'd have thought? Amazed, he turned the gun around and started pounding at the ceiling on the other side with the stock again.

Within a few minutes, they had the hole bigger.

And the scorpions were already on the bed.

Jess kicked at them before he handed her the shotgun. "Back up and I'll jump."

She took the gun and vanished.

Cursing as a couple of the scorpions stung his leg, he launched himself at the ceiling. He caught it barely and hung above the bed that was now completely swimming in those nasty little buggers. He kicked his legs until he was sure they were free of scorpions. His arms bulged as he pulled himself up, through the hole and onto the wooden floor. He made it, but his skin was stinging from the scrapes of wedging himself through. Not to mention his leg that was on fire from the scorpions.

Abigail was crouched by a wall, aiming the gun at him.

Jess ignored her as he moved to the bookshelf against the wall and slammed it down to cover the hole. Hopefully, that would delay them a bit longer.

Abigail cocked the gun.

Now, that amused him. "You can't kill me with a bullet, darling. You'll just piss me off."

"Maybe, but shooting you might be fun." She lowered the barrel to his groin. "And while I might not be able to kill you, I sure could ruin your social life."

He laughed at her conviction. "There's only one problem with that."

"Yeah?"

He indicated the shotgun with a jerk of his chin. "The gun's not loaded. I used the last of the ammo downstairs."

She opened the gun and cursed as she realized he wasn't lying. "Figures."

Yes, it did. He wouldn't have handed it to her otherwise. He hadn't been *that* stupid in a very long time. Still, he admired her gumption.

Jess took the gun back and made a mental note of where the sun was shining in his house and where it wasn't. *Man, I hope Andy remembered to lock the house down.* If not, she'd stand a good chance of escaping, and there would be nothing he could do until dark.

Unless he wanted to shoot her. He did still have a couple of shells in his pocket . . .

Another quake shook the house.

She gasped in alarm. "You think that's more of them?"

"Our luck? Probably."

"How do we stop them?"

He had no idea. Not this many of them. If he were Talon, he might could drop the temperature here to freeze them to death. But unlike the Celt's, his Dark-Hunter powers didn't include weather control.

No sooner had that thought gone through his mind, than the house went completely dark. As dark as a midnight sky from the days when he'd been human and out on the range. He hadn't seen anything like this in decades. Not since modern lights had dimmed the night skies.

"What's going on?"

He ignored her question as he peeked around the wall, toward a window. Thunder rolled like an angry growl. A moment later, snow started falling.

Jess gaped at the last thing he'd expected to see. Now, that was more startling than the scorpion invasion.

"It's snowing." In April. In Las Vegas . . .

Yeah, the world was definitely coming to an end.

Abigail didn't believe his words until she stepped past him to look outside. Sure enough, large clumps of snow fell from the sky. The contrast of the white against the black was absolutely beautiful.

And yet . . .

"I really did start the apocalypse," she breathed. There was no other explanation. Things like this didn't happen except in movies and end-of-the-world prophecies. "What have I done?"

Sundown rested the gun on his shoulder in a manner that smacked of his past. He looked like a rogue cowboy, locked and loaded and ready for the next round. All he needed was a hat, and he'd be the perfect cliché. But what really bothered her about it was how sexy that pose made him even in Psycho Bunny pajama bottoms.

I have lost my mind.

Surely the stress of the last few minutes had driven her insane. It had to. There was no other way she could see him as anything but a monster.

She swallowed. Her adoptive father had always told her that evil was beautiful and seductive. Otherwise, no one would ever fall for it. That was why Artemis had made the Dark-Hunters so sexy. It was how they lured their victims in before they slaughtered them.

Whatever she did, she couldn't let herself forget that.

Sundown shrugged. "Well, it appears to me that you have opened a big old can of worms. And according to what Z said, you're the only one who can close it."

She pressed her fingers against her temple to help relieve the ache that was starting right behind her left eye. "All I was trying to do was protect my people and family from *you*."

"I was never your threat."

Abigail started to argue, but she'd barely parted her lips before the floor beneath her feet literally opened up and sucked her down.

Oh, dear Lord, she was going to die!

7

Jess dropped his gun and launched himself at Abigail as she slid through the floor. At first, he was sure she'd fallen to her death right before his eyes. That thought hit him a lot harder than it should have. The pain was indescribable.

But somehow, against all odds, he felt

warmth in his palm and a weight on his arm that made his spirits soar with relief.

He'd caught her. . . .

Looking over the side of the hole, he saw her panicked face staring up at him, and that was the most beautiful thing he'd seen in over a century.

She was alive.

Abigail's heart thumped wildly as she swung in a precarious arc. The only thing that kept her from crashing onto the marble floor ten feet below was one hand.

And it belonged to her enemy.

"I gotcha." Sundown's grip tightened on her hand in a silent promise that he wouldn't let go.

She locked both her hands around his and hoped he wasn't holding a grudge against her for anything. "Please don't drop me."

He actually winked at her. "Not on your life." He pulled her up slowly, taking care not to scrape her against the jagged edges of the floor where pieces of wood waited to impale her.

In that moment, she could kiss him for his fast reflexes that had saved her life, and for the care he was taking to pull her up and not hurt her.

But her relief didn't last long. As soon as her head popped through the hole, something grabbed her leg from below and yanked her hard enough to take her back through it.

Sundown's eyes widened.

I'm going to die. She was sure of it as the pressure on her legs increased with a determination that said it wouldn't relent until she was a stain on the floor below.

Yet somehow Sundown maintained his firm grip on her hands. He pulled her up again.

Again, something jerked her down. She kicked her legs and struck nothing. Yet there was no denying that some invisible force had her by her ankles.

If only she could look down to see what it was. "What's going on?"

"I don't know. I don't see anything. I just wish whatever it is that it'd let go." His face turned bright red as he held on to her with a determination that said he really did care whether she lived or died.

Abigail blinked back tears from the pain of being the rope in a tug-of-war that would mean her life if Sundown lost.

He growled as the muscles in his arms bulged from the strain. She stared into his eyes, which were dark with conviction, and used those as her lifeline.

"Thank you," she whispered to him.

Inclining his head to her, Jess felt his grip slipping. Whatever had her was increasing its pressure to the point he knew it was only a matter of time before she fell from his hands.

He'd failed to keep his promise to her mother. The

last thing he wanted was to see her die, too. *I can't let go....*

What choice did he have?

The answer came from somewhere deep inside him. A forgotten prayer his mother had taught him from the cradle to use whenever things were too hard and he wanted to give up.

Aike aniya trumuli gerou sunari.... Those words whispered through his mind. *I am White Buffalo and I will not be stopped.* Yeah, okay, so it sounded better in her language than in English. Still, it echoed and he felt an inner strength rising with every syllable as he continued silently chanting it. *Our people never met an enemy they couldn't defeat. Their blood flows inside of you,* penyo. *You are my pride and my gift to the Elders who watch over us. Listen to them when you're weak and they will help you. Always.* He heard his mother's voice as clearly as if she sat beside him.

He saw the fear in Abigail's eyes as she realized her hands were slipping.

"Aike aniya trumuli gerou sunari!"

Abigail gasped at his angry words and the bright flash of red that shone through his pupils an instant before he jerked her up through the floor so fast, she barely realized she'd moved. He gathered her in his arms and hugged her close, as if he was as thankful she was alive as she was.

Even though she hated him, she was too grateful to

shove him away. Instead, she reveled in the sensation of his hard body pressing against hers. She clung to him while she shook from relief and tried to squelch the fear that the invisible force would grab her again and take her back into the hole. Her blood rushed thick through her veins as she buried her face in his neck and inhaled the warm scent of his skin.

He'd saved her. She was alive.

In that moment, with all the endorphins coursing through her, she felt as if she could fly.

Jess couldn't move with her cradled against him as she breathed raggedly in his ear, sending chills down his arm. Every inch of her body was pressed against his. And deep inside, he felt something in him stir. Something he hadn't felt in a long time. Before he could rethink his intentions, he nuzzled her neck. A low moan escaped her lips. He started to pull away, but she cupped his head, stopping him.

Then she did the most unexpected thing of all.

She kissed him.

For a full minute, he couldn't breathe as he tasted her. Her lips were incredibly soft as she swept her tongue against his, teasing and warming him. He couldn't remember the last time a woman had kissed him with this much passion.

Abigail knew she shouldn't be doing this. In the back of her mind was the voice that tried to remind her that she hated him. And yet he'd saved her life. More than that, he felt like heaven. Never had she experienced anything like this.

Like she belonged.

There was no explaining it. It was something deep within that welcomed him even while her mind called her all kinds of stupid.

But before she could examine that thought further, the floor started rumbling again.

They pushed themselves to their feet and then away from the hole as some unseen beast from below began a fierce howl. It sounded like a pack of hungry coyotes. . . .

Backing them up, Sundown put himself between her and the hole. He retrieved his gun from the floor.

An instant later, six men and one woman shot up from the opening. With dark hair and eyes, they curled their lips in a purely canine fashion as they stalked toward the two of them.

Jess braced himself for the attack he knew was coming. He'd never much cared for shape-shifters, and these were going to be brutal. "C'mon, punks," he goaded. "You want to fight or sniff each other's crotches?"

The leader ran at him. With a bright flash of yellow, he turned from a man into a coyote. Jess reversed his shotgun so that he was holding it by the barrel. Using the stock like a bat, he knocked the coyote into the wall, where it hit with a heavy thud.

The others changed form and came at him full force.

"Run!" he said over his shoulder to Abigail.

She didn't listen. Rather, she ripped the tacky antlers off the wall that Andy had put there as a sick joke—that boy had never been right in the head—and held them to defend against their attackers.

It was a bold move, and he seriously hoped those antlers broke during the fight so he'd never have to look at them again.

Even though Jess had a feeling he was wasting his time, he went ahead and loaded his gun with the shells in his pocket, then opened fire on the coyotes. The first one he shot yelped, skidded sideways, rebounded off the wall, then kept coming.

Yeah, all it did was piss the coyote off and give him some target practice. But what the hell? He kept shooting until he was empty again while he and Abigail backed down the hallway.

Until she stopped moving.

He slammed up against her.

"You're about to be in daylight."

He glanced over his shoulder to see the truth of that. Had she not stood her ground, he'd have been in some serious pain right about now. "Much obliged." With no choice and with their retreat cut off, he took a step forward to fight.

The coyotes launched themselves at the two of them.

Jess moved to hit one, but they never made contact.

The coyotes slammed into an invisible wall that magically appeared around him and Abigail. Yelping, the coyotes tried to attack again and again—they couldn't.

Yee-haw on that. He just hoped whoever was shielding them was a friend.

Abigail moved to stand beside him. She reached out to touch it, and apparently there was nothing there. She waved her hand around but it contacted nothing. Meanwhile, the coyotes couldn't touch them.

Interesting . . .

She frowned in confusion. "What is this?"

"Don't know. But given everything else that's happened so far, I'm not real sure it's a good thing." For all he knew, that magic wall might be protecting the coyotes from something ugly about to happen to the two of them.

As if on cue, an evil growl, low and deep, echoed around them.

The coyotes hesitated at the sound.

Abigail swallowed in fear. When the scariest of scary were wary, it was time to take note. She whipped out her mental notepad to wait on whatever evil was about to pounce.

She didn't have to wait long before a huge wolf launched out of the walls to attack the coyotes.

That was unexpected on several levels. She turned toward Sundown. "Is that on our side?"

He squinted as if trying to look into the heart of this

latest addition. "Looks like, but . . . hell, who knows at this point?"

Within seconds, the coyotes vanished into a mist. The wolf circled as if he was about to give chase. Until he turned into a man in the middle of the hallway.

Tall, blond, and extremely handsome, he still looked feral in his human form. There was a light in his eyes that said he wanted to taste blood.

She hoped it wasn't theirs.

Abigail held her breath as he moved forward with a deadly glower.

Here we go again. . . .

The wolf flipped the gun out of Sundown's hands. He cracked open the barrel to check its loaded status and shook his head. "Shells, cowboy? Really?"

Sundown shrugged. "Sometimes you just have to try even when it's wasted energy."

The wolf laughed, then handed it back. "I admire the tenacity, useless though it is."

Abigail relaxed as she realized the wolf was at the very least a frenemy.

Sundown leaned the gun against the wall. "What are you doing here?"

"Zarek sent me in, just in case."

Sundown scratched at the whiskers on his jaw. " 'Cause shit rolls downhill."

"Yeah, and what upsets Z gets my ass kicked. Have I

ever told you how much it chafes me that Astrid gave that psycho bastard god powers? I swear I go to bed every night with the one desire to rip out his throat, and I don't even live with them anymore. Sad, isn't it?"

Sundown bristled as if the wolf had struck a nerve. "Now, that's *my* boy you're talking about, and I don't want to get crossed up with you, Sasha. But you keep that tone and attitude about him, and we will."

Sasha held his hands up in surrender. "Sorry. I forget you and Ash are weird enough to actually like him. No accounting for taste." He turned that penetrating stare toward her. "And you must be the cause of this disaster."

Abigail was offended. What? Was there some cosmic social media feed somewhere with her photo on it, announcing her as the cause of the apocalypse? "I didn't do anything."

Sundown grinned. "She's in denial."

"Cool. We can feed her to the coyotes then, and I can go back to Sanctuary and continue scoping out this amazing brunette who keeps coming in with her friends."

She wasn't amused by that.

At all.

Sundown ignored her ire. "Speaking of friends . . . why did our new coyote buddies run from you?"

Sasha swaggered like a strutting peacock. "I'm *that* badass."

Sundown snorted. "Seriously."

"O ye of little faith. You doubt my rep? My skills?"

"And your brains."

Sasha tsked. "Fine. I'll be honest. . . . Absolutely no idea. They had me outnumbered. I should have been easy for them to rip into. Not that I wanted to be their early morning snack, but—"

"The wolf has always been a most natural enemy to the coyote. Wolves are one of the few predators known to hunt them when the season is right. And because of this, the coyote are wary of them by nature. Especially one from an unknown pantheon whose powers they can only guess at. No doubt, they thought retreat was the best course of action. As Sun Tzu would say, 'If ignorant both of your enemy and yourself, you are certain to be in peril.'"

Abigail turned at the voice of what sounded like an ancient Englishman standing behind them.

He wasn't English. Or anything like what she'd expected from his proper, thickly accented speech.

Barely taller than her, he wore a tan suede jacket with fringed sleeves and heavy Native American beadwork and carved bone all over it. His silver hair was parted into two braids that framed his withered face. However age hadn't dulled the sharpness of his hazel gold eyes, which stared at her with an accusation that cut her all the way to her soul.

She had a sudden desire to take a step back, but she refused to be a coward. So she stood her ground and put on the bravest face she could manage.

Sundown inclined his head respectfully to the man. "Choo Co La Tah, what are you doing here?"

Choo Co La Tah turned that frightening gaze from her to Sundown. "The Unfolding has started, and so I knew I couldn't wait, no matter Ren's protestations. As the Dineh would say, Coyote is always out there waiting, and Coyote is always hungry. I knew they would be after the woman as soon as they caught her scent. If they kill her before we reach the Valley, there will be no one to stop them. Hence my appearance here and now. The two of you must be protected, no matter what happens." He opened his jacket to show a crow that had been resting under his right arm. He pulled it out and, with a grace and dexterity that contradicted his apparent age, set it on the floor.

Letting out a caw, the bird flapped its wings, then manifested into a man. This one appeared to be in his early twenties with jet hair and eyes. Dressed all in black, he was stunningly sexy and even scarier than the coyotes had been.

He was also fanged.

And now all the men were staring at her, making her extremely uncomfortable and self-conscious. She felt like a mouse surrounded by hungry cats who were taking odds on who would be the first to pounce.

"Do you comprehend the gravity of your situation, my dear?" Choo Co La Tah asked her.

She did. But that didn't stop one cold, hard fact. "I don't want to die."

There was no sympathy in the old man's gaze. "As the

Duwamish would say, there is no death, only a change of worlds."

"I like *this* world."

"Then you should have thought of that before you took the life of Old Bear. I can assure you, even at his advanced age, he didn't want to change realms either. And he's only one of many you have killed who never once harmed you."

Her anger snapped at that. How dare he patronize her—something that was made even more pronounced by his accent and proper tone.

She hadn't stalked innocent people like some deranged serial killer. She was an avenger who was tallying a sickening score started by the true villains in all of this. "The Dark-Hunters have hunted my people for centuries."

"Your people, madam, are human . . . most of them qualify for that term, anyway. They are the ones the Dark-Hunters strive to protect."

"Yeah, right. They . . ." Her words broke off as images flashed in her mind. She heard countless humans begging for mercy as they were attacked.

Not by Dark-Hunters.

By Apollites who'd killed them so that they could take their human souls and feed on them and live past their twenty-seventh birthday—just as Sundown had told her. The horror of it slapped her hard as their screams resonated through her skull.

It couldn't be.

She shook her head in denial. "You planted those images in my head. They're not real."

Choo Co La Tah sighed. "My people have a saying. *Kirha tahanahna ditari sukenah.* To deny the presence of the sun doesn't escape its blister. I admire your loyalty. But sometimes you have to face the truth, even when it hurts."

No, she didn't. Because if he was right, if those images were the truth, then she was wrong on a level so profound that it made her sick. It would mean she'd done horrendous things to people who didn't deserve it.

People who'd been protecting the innocent from predators.

And if that was the case, she wasn't sure if she could live with herself.

I'm not a predator. I'm a protector.

Choo Co La Tah's eyes were filled with compassion. "I feel your pain, child. But you should have studied Confucius."

She frowned at his words. "How so?"

"Had you taken the time to learn his wisdom instead of war, you would have known that before you start down the road to revenge, dig two graves."

She bristled at that. "You don't understand."

"There you are quite wrong. Shamefully, all of us have wanted revenge on someone at some point for something. I've lived since before man and buffalo roamed this small planet. I have survived the beginning, bloom, and death of countless enemies, civilizations, and people. And the one truth I have learned most during all of these centuries is the old Japanese proverb. If you sit by the river long enough, you will see the body of your enemy float by."

That made her temper boil over. He made it sound so simple. But he was wrong, and she knew it. "Even if he's immortal?"

"Especially then. To quote the Tsalagi, you should never allow your yesterday to use up too much of today. The past is gone and tomorrow is at best a maybe. Live for this moment because it may be all you'll ever have."

She curled her lip in disgust. His pithy phrases were easy to spout, but living with her amount of pain was another story. And seeing your parents slaughtered was something no one got over. Ever. "What are you? A fortune cookie writer?"

The Native American Dark-Hunter started forward, but Choo Co La Tah stopped him before he could reach her. There was laughter in his tone as he spoke. "Respect must be earned, Ren. Not demanded. A questioning mind is the most cherished resource man has and the rarest. I admire her tenacity and her misplaced loyalty."

Those words embarrassed her, and somehow they made her feel like she was being childish.

"And I don't." Deep and resonant, Ren's voice rolled like thunder.

Choo Co La Tah placed a gentle hand on her shoulder.

"All feelings are valid, and I do not discount yours, Abigail. Our true journey will begin in a handful of hours after the sun sets. In the meantime, all of you need to rest and conserve your strength. Sasha and I will guard you while you slumber." He glanced to Sundown. "And I will notify Andy and make sure he, too, is safe."

Sasha arched a brow. "Why is the wolf always the one who's drafted?"

Choo Co La Tah smiled. "The wolf is the one who is most rested."

Sasha scoffed. "What? You want to toss logic into my emotional outburst? Where's the fairness of that?"

If she wasn't so upset, Abigail might have found Sasha amusing, but right now nothing was funny to her. Not when the agony of her past weighed on her and her conscience ripped at her with razor-sharp talons. *I'm not what they say.*

She wasn't. At least she hoped she wasn't.

But what if?

Sundown cleared his throat to get Choo Co La Tah's attention. "I agree we need to rest. But there is a small matter of scorpions in the basement, and that's the only safe place for me and Ren during daylight. No offense, I don't really want to nap with them crawling all over me."

Choo Co La Tah stepped away from her. "Ah yes, the scorpion infestation. Don't despair. I've taken care of your pest problem. All of them are gone now."

"You sent the snow?" Abigail asked.

He inclined his head. "The plagues that will come are designed to weaken me. The Coyote is forcing me to expend energy to protect mankind from his tools. For now, my strength holds. But I'm old and I must recharge my powers much more often than I did when I was young. If we don't make it to the Valley before I lose strength . . ."

It wouldn't be pretty for any of them.

And it will be all by my fault.

Jess saw the terrified look in Abigail's eyes before she hid it. That uncharacteristic frailty from her tugged at his heart. She wasn't the kind of woman to let her vulnerability show. The fact that she did . . .

She was in absolute agony, and he'd always been a sucker for a woman in pain.

"C'mon," he said to her gently. "I'll take you back downstairs."

For once, she didn't argue, and that told him exactly how torn up she really was. Ren followed after them while Choo Co La Tah and Sasha stayed topside to keep an eye out for any other enemies who might want to join them.

No one spoke until they were in the elevator. Ren folded his arms over his chest as he blocked the door and faced them. He glanced from Abigail to Jess. "You have no idea how much it bothers me to know that I was the man she meant to kill tonight and now I have to protect her."

Jess snorted. "Yeah, well, she tried to kill me, too, and I got over it."

"I'm not as good a man as you are, Sundown. I find it hard to give an enemy my back under any circumstance."

"Oh, I didn't say I was giving her my back. I'm not lacking all my noodle sense. But I'm not holding a grudge neither. Sometimes you just got to let the rattlesnake lay in the sun."

Ren muttered an obscenity about that under his breath.

Abigail cleared her throat. "Men? You do know I'm standing in this little box with you and can hear every word?"

They exchanged an arch look.

"We know," Ren said. "I merely don't care."

She rolled her eyes as the elevator stopped and Jess moved Ren aside so that he could open it.

Abigail hesitated before stepping out.

"Something wrong?" Jess held the door open for her with one arm.

She stuck her head out a little ways and squinted at the ground. "Making sure there's no scorpions on the floor."

He laughed at her uncharacteristic timidity. "Miraculously, they're all gone." The only proof of their ordeal was the hole in the ceiling that the coyotes had used to jump through earlier. "Looks safe."

Ren made a hostile noise before he pushed past them and took the rear bedroom suite.

Jess tsked at him. "You know, bud, that there's just plain rude."

Ren held his hand up over his shoulder to flip him off as he continued on without comment or pausing.

Abigail swallowed at his open hostility. Not that she blamed him, since he had been her target. Still . . .

"Don't take it too hard," Sundown said sheepishly. "Ren's . . . well . . . he's Ren. He don't mean nothing."

If it were only that simple, but she did appreciate his trying to make her feel better. "He hates me."

"He's wary of you. Big difference. Like he said, he was your target. Not exactly something a man gets over real fast."

"You seem to have adapted."

He flashed the most devilish and charming grin she'd ever seen before, and it did peculiar things to her stomach. "I'm not as bright as he is."

Oh yeah, he could be devastating when he wanted to. "I somehow doubt that."

"Is that a compliment?"

"Well, hell has indeed frozen over, in case you missed the snow on your front lawn."

He laughed as he led her toward the room he'd taken her to earlier. Now that they weren't in fear of their lives, she could appreciate the beauty of his home. The hallway was painted a peaceful ochre with white wainscoting. The wall sconces were baroque and seemed at odds with the down-home simplicity of Sundown Brady.

"Did you decorate this place?"

He cast a frown at her over his shoulder that said he

thought she was a few gallons shy of a load. "Yeah, no . . . decorating ain't exactly something I strive to do in my spare time. It came with the house."

"Why did you want to live here? No offense, but it doesn't really seem to be your style."

He paused at her room. "I think I might ought to be offended by that. What exactly are you saying about my style?"

She paused, too, then shrugged. "I don't know. You just seem to be the kind of guy to have a man cave, not something this . . ."

"Refined?"

She shook her head affirmatively.

"Well, that just shows what you know. For your information, I do like some fancy things."

"Like what? Lacy underwear?"

"On my women, yeah." He flashed that grin at her that she was learning to hate. Not for any reason other than the fact that it softened his features and made him terribly irresistible.

"And—?" she asked when he didn't continue.

He scratched at the back of his neck. "Well, opera for one and foreign films for another, especially French ones."

She scoffed. "No, you don't."

"I can show you my Opera Guild membership card if you want to see it. Been a season ticket holder for decades."

Out of all the things about him that took her by surprise, those actually floored her. She just couldn't imagine a man so large and tough wedging himself into an opera seat.

"Heck, I even play violin."

"You mean fiddle."

"Play that, too. But Mozart and Grieg are my favorite pieces that I like to unwind with after a hard night's work."

In the back of her mind was a vague memory of him playing Wagner on her toy piano and then showing her what the keys were. "You taught me 'Chopsticks.'"

"I did."

The thought of a man so huge and ripped handling such a delicate instrument was incongruous and yet . . .

Why can't I remember more?

Sundown opened the door for her.

Abigail went to the bed, then paused. Instead of leaving, Sundown pulled a blanket and pillow out of the closet and made a pallet on the floor.

"What are you doing?" she asked, dreading the obvious answer.

"We tore my room up, remember? I don't want to sleep with a big hole over my head. Plaster or something might fall down and scare me enough, I could scream like a woman and humiliate myself. I definitely don't want to do that with Sasha in the house. He'd laugh at me forever, and I'd have to skin him."

She started to protest, but honestly she was glad to have him in here. Just in case. After everything that had happened, her nerves were shot.

You should be running from him or at least trying to kill him.

Perhaps. But if the coyotes were really after her, the last thing she wanted to do was lead them home so that they could kill her adoptive family, too. Hannah and Kurt were all she had left. And while the Apollites were good, she wasn't sure they'd be enough to fight them. Not to mention Choo Co La Tah was right, she was exhausted to a level she'd never known before. She needed rest. At least for a couple of hours.

Then she might be up for an escape attempt.

Kicking off her shoes and pulling the band from her hair to release her ponytail, she climbed into bed. Before she could think better of it, she glanced to where Sundown lay on the floor. One thing she didn't miss was the fact that he had one foot against the door so that if anyone opened it, it would wake him immediately. And the shotgun was on the floor only millimeters from his fingertips.

Weird . . . she couldn't remember him picking it up again. Where had it come from?

Man, she must be tired to have missed that.

Pushing it out of her mind, she changed the topic. "You need another pillow?"

He covered his eyes with his arm. Something that caused his shirt to ride up and give her a glimpse of his rock-hard abs. Oh yeah, she could do laundry on that. "Nah, thanks. I'm good."

In more ways than one. He was definitely scrumptious, lying on the floor like that.

I have lost my mind. And then some. *You can't possibly find him attractive. He killed your family.*

Or had he? Could he have been telling her the truth earlier? If he really was a cold-blooded killer, why not murder her instead of bringing her back here? He could have abandoned her to the scorpions and coyotes.

Instead, he'd protected her.

He's a killer. You saw his face. You know his legend.

True. Her research of his human past had shown him to be the worst sort of humanity. Scum so foul that even bounty hunters and law enforcement had feared him.

But her personal experience with him refuted that.

What if she were wrong? She'd been so little at the time of her parents' deaths. Did she remember that night correctly? She could still see him so clearly in her mirror. And yet there were differences between the man on the floor and the one in her memory.

Why would he seem larger now than he had when she was a kid?

Even though she needed to sleep, she wanted answers.

Before she could stop herself, she asked the one that bothered her most. "What did you and my dad fight over the night they died?"

Jess fell quiet as her whispered question stirred old memories that cut him up deep inside. Things he'd tried not to think about. Things that had haunted him for years. As bad as those memories had been for him, he could only imagine how much harder they'd been for her. Damn shame for a mite to see such a thing as what had happened to her parents.

A part of him wanted to lie, but in the end, he spoke honestly. "Your mother."

She sat up in the bed to stare at him. "What?"

Lowering his arm, Jess sighed at the inevitable confession she deserved to hear. "Your pa thought I was trying to steal her affections away from him."

"Were you?"

"Hardly. Me and her were friends and nothing more."

"You're lying," she accused.

If only it'd been that simple. "No, sweet. I'm telling the truth. No need for me to lie about this."

"Why would my father think that unless you gave him reason to?"

'Cause he was fucking loco, but Jess would never say that to her. The man was her pa, and the last thing he wanted to do was taint her memory of him. The truth, though—her pa had been insanely jealous of any male in Laura's life who was over the age of five. He assumed every man was eat up with lust for her, and in his world someone couldn't just want to talk to her because she reminded him of someone else. Nah, and the worst of it was that he'd accused her of cheating on him. Something Laura would die before she did.

Since Jess couldn't say any of that, he went with the other simple truth. "'Cause I loved your mama, and there was nothing in the world I wouldn't have done for her or you."

Abigail felt tears sting her eyes as she remembered the beauty of her mother's face. She'd seen her as a wonderful angel with a smile that was filled with more warmth than the sun itself. Most of all, she remembered how safe and loved she'd felt every single time her mother wrapped her arms around her. God, to have one more second with her . . .

"If you were in love with—"

"Not *in* love, Abby. That's what your pa couldn't get through his thick skull. What I felt for her wasn't that. I just wanted to make her happy and keep her safe."

"Why?"

Jess felt the tic start in his jaw as a wave of agony swelled inside him. Laura had been a perfect physical copy of Matilda. Even some of her mannerisms. But she wasn't Tilly, and he'd known it. "She reminded me of someone I used to know." *Someone I once loved more than anything on this earth.*

"I don't understand."

And it was hard to explain. "I met your ma not long after she moved to Reno. She was a waitress in a restaurant where I used to go and eat sometimes." He hadn't been paying a bit of attention to the occupants as he took his usual seat in the small diner. He'd been staring out the window, skimming the crowd as people outside walked by, when a cup of coffee appeared on his table.

"Much obliged," he'd muttered, expecting it to be his usual waitress, Carla, who always brought him coffee the minute he sat down.

"You're welcome." The soft lilt of that unfamiliar voice had dragged his attention to her face. Even now, he could feel the shock of looking up and being sucked back in time.

"Are you all right?" she'd asked.

He'd sputtered and mumbled something back at her that was probably as stupid to her as he'd felt when he said it. Over the next hour, he'd coerced enough information out of her that he was able to get Ed to run a thorough background check on her.

That report had stunned him as much as seeing her in the diner. Laura was the great-great-granddaughter of the child Bart had fathered the day he raped Matilda.

A child Matilda had given up for adoption.

By the time the Squires told him about the infant a few years after it'd been born, he'd been unable to locate it. Records weren't kept the same way then as they were today. Until the night he'd stumbled across Laura and Ed had run his own check, he didn't even know that child had been a boy.

At first, he'd been livid with the discovery and angry at fate for dropping that living reminder slap-dab in the middle of his territory. Since he knew he'd never dishonored Matilda by taking her before their wedding, there was no doubt about the paternal sperm donor for Laura's line.

But by the next night, he'd chosen to focus on two things. One, it wasn't the baby's fault that he'd been conceived by violence, and there was no reason for Jess to hold that against the boy's descendants. Two, they were every bit as much a part of the woman he'd loved as the children she'd kept and raised, and the descendants he had the Squires watch over. It was only fair he take care of Laura, too.

In Laura, he'd only seen Matilda's genteel face.

In Abigail, he saw both. The woman he'd loved more than his life and the man he'd hated with every part of his being.

It was one hell of a combination.

"And?" Abigail prompted. "She was a waitress . . ."

"We became friends," he said simply. And it was the absolute truth. "I'd go in a few times a week, and we'd chat for a bit." He smiled at his bittersweet memories. Like Matilda, she'd been sweet and unassuming. "She was highly intelligent and quick-witted. Funny as all get out. I used to love listening to her banter with her friends and the other customers."

"Did you ever go out with her?"

"Never. Dark-Hunters aren't allowed to date, and I knew I had nothing to offer her. I just liked being in her company. She was a good person, and there's not a lot of those around. I left big tips, and she threatened the life of anyone who dared try and wait on me anytime she was working."

"Then why was my father angry at you?"

He was a psychotic idiot.

But Jess didn't say that. "I made the mistake of giving your mother a butterfly necklace that I'd seen in a local shop on her birthday. I thought it was pretty, and the blue diamonds in it reminded me of her eyes. I meant nothing by it, but your pa didn't see it that way. Even though I'd known her long before she met and married him, he accused her of cheating on him with me, and I left before I physically hurt him."

Abigail searched her mind for some memory to either refute or sustain his words. All she could remember was the loud sounds of shouting voices. Her parents didn't fight a lot, but it'd been enough that she knew to hide whenever they did.

Her hiding over it was the very thing that had saved her life.

Sundown sighed. "I went out on my patrol, but I couldn't shake the bad feeling I had. I didn't want to leave her with him so mad. But I knew if I'd stayed, I'd have rearranged a few of his organs, and that would have only upset her more. I figured if I left, he'd calm down and everything would be all right. . . . At ten, I tried to call and got no answer. That worried me even more. So I headed back and . . ." He hesitated before he spoke again. "The police were already there and they wouldn't let me in. I looked around for you and asked about you, but there was no trace. They assumed that whoever killed your parents took you as well. We searched for you for a long time, but no one ever saw you again." He scowled at her. "So what happened to you, anyway? Where did you go?"

Abigail tried to recall when her adoptive father had shown up. But all she saw was Sundown walking out of her room. And then it'd seemed like forever before she heard a familiar voice call her name. "My adoptive father took me home with him. I don't remember seeing the police or really anything much about that night except you."

"What made you think I killed them?"

"I saw you in my room."

"I wasn't there, Abigail. I swear to you." There was so much conviction in his tone that he was either the best liar in the world . . .

Or he was telling the truth.

"He looked just like you. He even had on cowboy boots."

"A pair of shit-kickers in Reno is normal footwear. That don't mean nothing."

That much was true. Still . . .

"My adoptive father confirmed it. He said you slaughtered my parents because they were allies to the Apollites."

"I had no idea they even knew what an Apollite was. It's not something I normally talk about to anyone outside of the Dark-Hunter network, you know?"

That made a little too much sense. Abigail rubbed her forehead as she tried to discern the truth. Her feelings were so conflicted.

"So what do you believe now?" he asked.

Overwhelmed by everything, she lay back against the headboard. "I don't know, Sundown. I don't." Oh, how she hated being this tired. It made her an emotional wreck, and everything was so much worse right now. Tears started streaming quietly down her cheeks as everything crashed in on her. Her life had never been simple or easy.

But all of the past was like a ride on a merry-go-round compared to what it was right now. It was confusing and terrifying.

And if Choo Co La Tah was right, she only had an extremely short amount of time left to live.

Or the world would end.

What have I done?

What was she going to do?

Suddenly, Sundown was there, sitting on the bed. "Don't cry, Abby. It's all right."

It wasn't and they both knew it.

He gathered her into his arms and held her close. Something no one had done in a very long time. God, it felt so good. . . .

Abigail buried her face into his chest. His heartbeat was strong and sure, and in this moment, she needed that reassurance that she wasn't completely alone—even if it meant cuddling against her enemy. "I'm so sorry. I don't normally do this."

"Don't apologize. My ma used to say that crying is good for you. Tears are the path that free your mind of sorrowful thoughts."

"You sound like Choo Co La Tah now."

He nuzzled his face against her head while a gentle laugh rumbled deep in his chest. "He is kind of like Yoda. . . . 'There is only do or do not. There is no try.'"

That actually succeeded in making her laugh through her tears. "You're a *Star Wars* fan?"

"Oh yeah. May the Force be with you."

She sobered. "If what Choo Co La Tah said is true, I think we're going to need something a lot stronger than the Force to win this."

"Don't worry, we'll find a solution. There's always a way."

His positive attitude amazed her. "How can you be so sure?"

He shrugged. "You're talking to a man who came back from the dead just to even a score. You think I'm going to let something like Coyote win this? Hardly. One thing about Bradys . . . We don't run and we don't lose. Come hell or high water, no one gets the best of me. And I'll be damned if I let them take you. We'll find a way to keep you safe and save the world. You have my personal guarantee on that, and that's not something I give lightly."

His conviction stunned her. "Why do you even care? A few hours ago, I was trying to kill you."

"And not that long ago, you saved me from stepping into daylight. I haven't forgotten that either. Besides, I understand wanting retribution. Spent my whole human life in search of it. I won't hold that against you or anyone else."

That was so different from the things she'd read about him. Was it possible he wasn't as soulless as they claimed?

"But," he continued. "I would ask that if we do manage to save your butt and the world's that you find another hobby besides killing us."

How easy he made that sound. "Do you really think they'll let me live after what I've done?"

Jess paused as he considered it. She was right. The final decision wasn't his to make. The Powers were even more vengeful than his brethren were. Blood for blood. Tit for tat.

Still, things happened all the time that didn't make sense. And the Powers . . .

They were downright unpredictable.

"Have faith, Abigail. Sometimes the world surprises you."

Abigail swallowed at his words, wishing she could put

her faith in them. "Yeah, but it's never done so in a pleasant way. At least not for me."

And deep in her heart, she knew the truth. This wouldn't end until she'd paid for her actions.

She was going to die, and not even the infamous Jess Brady could stop it.

8

Abigail woke up to the sensation of someone cradling her against an impressively hard chest, as if she were unspeakably cherished. She honestly couldn't remember the last time a man had held her like this.

If ever.

He was wrapped completely around her.

Warm. Seductive. Inviting. Protective. It was the kind of sweet, loving embrace people dreamed of finding themselves in, but seldom did. For a full minute, she lay there in complete satiation.

Until she remembered who *he* was.

Sundown Brady.

Outlaw. Dark-Hunter. Killer.

Enemy.

She jerked involuntarily, which immediately caused him to awaken and push himself up on his arms to look around, as if expecting more coyotes to leap out of the walls and devour them.

When he didn't see an immediate threat, he scowled down at her. "Everything okay?"

Yes . . . He was so incredibly sexy in that pose. His hips were pressed intimately against hers, and his arms bulged with his raw strength. It made her ache for the very thing she would die before she gave him.

"No, you're on top of me." She pushed at his chest.

He rolled off her and onto his back with a taunting grin as he wiggled his hips to settle into his new position. "Now, that's not normally the way a woman reacts when I'm on top of her. I usually get a little more enthusiasm and welcome than that."

She gave him a withering stare to mask how incredibly yummy she thought he was right then. No need in feeding that ego. "Well, that's what happens when you pay women for sex."

To her surprise, he laughed good-naturedly. Damn, he was devastating when he did that, and he made it hard to remember she was supposed to hate his guts.

Stretching like a languid cat, he yawned. "Sorry about crushing you all morning. I think we fell asleep in the middle of a conversation."

They had. One she could barely recall now. What she did recall was how comforting he'd been while she'd cried, and that was the last thing she needed to think about. "Yeah, but I'm not sure which of us fell asleep first."

"I'm pretty sure it was you."

She had a suspicion he was right, and this was getting a little too familiar for her tastes. She wanted to keep a gap between them. A nice safe chasm that protected her from caring about anyone, especially him. So she changed the subject. "Your gun's still on the floor."

He scratched at the manly shadow on his cheek in a way that was boyish and somehow endearing. He was so nonchalant with her and she should be aggravated by that, not charmed. "Glad I didn't need it, since it's all the way over there."

No kidding. That could have been a bloody disaster. "So what time do you think it is?"

"Feels like it's still daylight. Not sure of the exact time, though."

"What do you mean it *feels* like daylight?"

He yawned before he answered. "Wicked power we have. We can sense when the sun's up. Which it still is."

No doubt they'd been given that to help keep them alive, since Apollo would kill any Dark-Hunter or Apollite he found in his domain. The Greek god was a real bastard that way.

And you killed two of Jess's brethren by trapping them in daylight. She didn't even want to think about how the others died.

Please, please don't let me have killed a protector. . . .

Trying not to think about that either, she got up and went to the bathroom.

Jess didn't speak as he watched her plod across the room. She had the most seductive walk he'd ever seen on any woman. Slow and sensual and full of sass. It was the kind of walk that made men turn and stare. Most of all, it made him ache to take a bite out of that hot little body of hers, especially that well-shaped ass.

Man, to have *that* naked and wrapped around him . . .

Uh, hello, cowboy? You're not supposed to have those thoughts about a human who's been offering your friends up as sacrifice to the dark gods.

Maybe not, but he was a man, and his body wasn't about to listen to his brain, especially since all the blood was now gathered into the part of him that craved her most. It wanted what it saw, and she was definitely worth an ass-whipping or two dozen.

Pushing that out of his mind before it got him into some serious trouble, he closed his eyes and used his powers to sense Ren. He knew the moment he made contact. Ren pushed back with his own telepathy.

"What, cowboy?"

He shook his head at Ren's surly tone in his head. He didn't like anyone near his thoughts—not the Jess blamed him. Mind readers weren't his favorite thing either. *"Wanted to see if you were awake yet."*

"I've been awake and meditating. And to answer your next question, it's almost four, so you have plenty of time to grab ass if you want."

Jess quickly blocked the image in his mind that those words conjured. Grabbing Abigail's ass was a lot more appealing to him than it should be. *"Stay out of my thoughts."*

"Believe me, I'm trying to. I don't want to throw up right after I brushed my teeth."

Bastard.

"By the way," Ren continued, ignoring the insult that questioned his parentage, *"I'm about as weak as I've ever been. Other than the telepathy, which I obviously know is working, how are your powers doing?"*

Jess winced as he realized his were down, too. *"Probably drained as much as yours are."*

"Guess we're going to pretend we're human for a bit."

Jess snorted. There were many folks, including Abigail, who would say that he'd never been human. *"Can you shape-shift at all?"*

"*Never a problem.*"

Now, that was interesting. "*Care to tell me why that one isn't malfunctioning?*"

"*It likes me best.*"

Jess shook his head. Smart-ass.

His attention shifted as he heard the water in his bathroom come on. Abigail was taking a shower. . . .

"*I'm going to leave you to the thoughts of her naked, since I have no interest in being a voyeur to your fantasies, especially with a viper. Check in with me when you're focused on fighting and not—*"

"*Gotcha, Ren. I'll powwow with you later.*"

Jess lay alone on the bed, listening to the water run in the other room. In his mind, he had a perfect image of what Abigail would look like as she soaped her naked breasts. His body roared back to life with a vengeance. His hunger for her was unlike anything he'd ever experienced before. And it wasn't just because she was a beautiful woman.

There was something else. Something he hadn't felt since the first time he met Matilda. It was a deep-seated ache. An urge he had to be near her. To protect her.

To hold her.

It took every bit of his control not to go in there and make her slap his face. One corner of his mouth lifted as he imagined her outrage if he did.

Definitely worth the slap. But he wouldn't do that to

her. He was too much of a gentleman to horrify a woman. No matter how horny he was.

That being said, his thoughts of her were killing him.

A*bigail was trying* to sort through all the information she'd been given. She wanted to believe her family. She did.

But it was hard to refute what she'd been shown, and the fact that Sundown didn't act like a psychotic killer.

If only she knew the real truth of everything. Were there rogue Apollites who preyed on humans? It seemed preposterous, and yet so did the existence of Apollites altogether. If one was possible, wouldn't it stand to reason that so was the other?

But why had no one in her family ever mentioned them?

The only thing she knew for a fact was that she was being hunted by something she'd accidentally unleashed. And that she didn't doubt at all.

How could she have been so stupid?

Sighing, she reached for the soap, only to feel a vicious stabbing pain rip through her abdomen. It was a thousand times worse than the most wretched menstrual cramp. She tried to move, but it slammed her down to the ground as it continued to twist in her stomach. Her skin burned like it was on fire. The water was no longer soothing. Now it tore at her flesh like a razor. Tears gathered in her eyes.

Oh my God, I'm in an Alien *movie. . . .*

That was what it felt like. Some creature trying to claw its way out of her belly. Light and sound tortured her. Images flashed through her mind as if controlled by a psychedelic strobe.

Help me. . . .

She couldn't speak the words. They were frozen in her throat.

Suddenly, the shower door opened. Her breathing ragged, she looked up to find Sundown there.

"Abigail?" His tone was filled with concern.

"Help me," she choked out as tears coursed down her cheeks.

He turned the water off, then scooped her up in his arms to carry her back to bed.

Had she been able, she'd have protested his carrying her while she was wet and naked. But right now, she didn't care and he didn't seem to notice about either one.

She groaned out loud as more pain lacerated her.

"I've got you," he said comfortingly. He wrapped her in a blanket, then brushed her hair back from her face with a tenderness that was completely unexpected. "What's going on?"

"I—I don't know. It hurts."

"Where?"

"Everywhere. But my stomach's the worst of it."

Jess touched her stomach, and she screamed in agony.

He thought it might be appendicitis until he met her gaze. Her eyes glowed red. "Um, honey, is there something you want to tell me?"

"What? That I feel like I'm giving birth to a fire-breathing dragon?"

"Nah, more like . . . any idea why your eyes would be demon red?" They were the same color they'd turned when she was unconscious.

She opened her mouth as if to respond, but before she could, her incisors lengthened.

Holy shit.

Had she made a pact with Artemis? She definitely looked like a Hunter, but none that he knew of had red eyes. . . .

"Get away from her, Jess."

He glanced over his shoulder to see Choo Co La Tah there. "What's going on?"

Abigail went for Jess's throat with a force so fierce, she forced them both off the bed.

Jess caught her, but it was a struggle to keep her from biting him. Dang, she was strong. Inhumanly strong. He had to turn her around in his arms, and he held her there with her back pressed to him while she shrieked in outrage.

Choo Co La Tah crossed the room and took her face in his hands. He began chanting something Jess couldn't understand while Abigail fought him with everything she had. She slammed her head back into his, knocking him senseless. Still, he held on to her even while his jaw burned.

Her struggles increased until she let out another fierce scream. An instant later, she collapsed.

He lifted her up into his arms and cradled her against him once more. Her skin was suddenly so cold, it scared him. *Was she all right?* He returned her to bed while Choo Co La Tah continued with his melodic chant.

Her breathing was coming in short, hard gasps now.

Choo Co La Tah forced him away from the bed so that he could place one palm on her forehead. After a few seconds, she calmed down and appeared to sleep.

With his hands on his hips, Jess scowled. "What was that?"

"They have merged her blood with a demon's."

That hit him like another blow to the head, which was the last thing he needed. His senses were rattled as much as if he'd taken a header off a bronco onto a fence. "Come again?"

Choo Co La Tah nodded. "One could surmise that they thought to strengthen her abilities by combining her DNA with a demon's."

Now, that was about dumb. But then, most people weren't rocket scientists, and he could see an idiot Daimon thinking they'd found an upper hand by using her that way.

But damn, he'd have figured Abigail for having more sense than to try something so boneheaded.

Obviously not.

"So the demon's controlling her?"

Choo Co La Tah shook his head. "The demon is dead. Demons can control someone only when they're alive, and normally when the demon dies, the control over the person is broken. But this . . . They did something else to cause her to have the powers, and I don't know what it is."

"Beautiful." Well, at least that explained how she had the power to kill a Dark-Hunter. "Can she convert one of us if she bites us?"

Choo Co La Tah nodded grimly. "If her fangs are showing and she mixes her blood with anyone, it will bring them under her complete control. And the demon inside her will crave that control. The longer it's in there, the hungrier she'll become for a victim."

That was the scariest thought of all. "So what do we do?"

"We must get her to the Valley as soon as we can and perform the ritual."

"Then she'll be all right?"

Choo Co La Tah refused to answer—which could mean only one thing.

Abigail would die.

9

Abigail felt her heart rate slow down as she fell through a dark mist. Images flashed through her mind. She saw her parents again. Heard them laughing.

Suddenly, she found herself as a small child on the floor with Sundown, who was smiling at her. Dressed in a black button-down shirt and jeans, he wore his hair shorter, and he was freshly shaved. Still, he was devastating to look at, especially when he smiled.

"Now, look, Abby, you send the bunny under the bush and then down around the rabbit hole. Like this."

She watched in awe as he tied her red princess ballet bedroom shoe. "That's not a bunny, silly, that's a lace."

His smile widened but not so much that he showed his fangs. "Yeah, but we're pretending," he whispered like it was a big secret.

"Oh." She tried to repeat it with the other shoe.

"You need to find you a woman and settle down, Jess. You'd make a great father."

She saw the pain in his eyes that her mother's words evoked. His smile died instantly as he reached to pull his hat, which was filled with her Little Ponies, closer to them. "I don't believe in settling down. That's for folks like you." He held his hat out so that Abigail could take her ponies back.

"Yeah, but you don't want to grow old alone, do you?"

As a child, she'd missed the torment that flared deep in his black eyes while he faced her and had his back to her mother. But as a woman, she saw the demons that tortured him, and it made her ache for him. He ran his hand along the brim of his hat and swallowed before he answered. "Believe me, Laura, there are a lot of worse things in this world than growing old alone."

Abigail had looked up with wide eyes. "Like what?"

He gave her the forced smile that adults often give to kids when they don't want them to feel their pain. "Cookie monsters who sneak past you when you're tying your shoes and eat your chocolate chip yummies." He feigned a reach for the cookies on the floor next to her. Squealing, she threw herself over his arm to keep him from taking them.

He curled his arm, lifting her and bringing her straight to his chest so that he could catch her in his arms and swing her up. In one graceful move, he rose to his feet, then twirled her around.

"Airplane, airplane, airplane," she started chanting while Jess turned faster.

Her mother gaped at them. "You're going to be wearing those chocolate chips soon if you don't stop, Jess."

He laughed. "It'd be worth it to hear her laugh."

And Abigail did. . . . She laughed and squealed in delight.

How could she have ever forgotten how much she once loved that man?

"What's going on here?"

Jess stopped moving as her father's angry voice cut through their joy. He cradled her to his chest while she begged him to keep going. Patting her on the back to soothe her, he faced her outraged father. "I was just teaching Abby how to tie her shoes."

Her father forcefully yanked her out of his arms. "That's not *your* job, now, is it?"

She saw the anger in Jess's eyes, but he quickly hid it. "Nah, guess it's not."

Her mother stepped forward. "Baby, c'mon. Jess just stopped by for a second on his way to work to say happy birthday to me."

Her father's gaze narrowed on her mother's neck, where a beautiful diamond butterfly glittered in the light. Abigail reached to touch it, then protested when her father's grip on her tightened to the point of causing her pain. She cried out in protest and tried to squirm out of his hold.

Her father ignored her attempts to get free. "Long enough to give you *that*, huh? What? You think I can't afford you gifts like that? Is that it?"

Her mother's jaw dropped in shock and outrage as she took Abigail out of her father's arms and held her close to calm her. "What in the world is wrong with you?"

Jess stepped forward to wedge himself between her parents so that he could protect her and her mother from her father's anger. "Look, Stan, I wasn't trying to offend you. It was real pretty and all, and I just thought she'd like it. That's it. No slight to you was ever intended."

Even though her father was a full head shorter than Jess, he shoved him back, forcing her mother to step away from the men. Abigail saw the panic on her mother's face. She might not have known about Sundown's brutal past or his Dark-Hunter status, but it was obvious that he dwarfed her father, and that in a fight, he'd definitely be the victor.

Her father shoved him again. "You need to quit sniffing around my wife every time I leave."

Jess curled his lip and stood his ground. His expression promised a serious ass-whipping if her father didn't stand down. "I wasn't sniffing around her. We're friends. That's all."

"Then I suggest you go be friends with someone else's wife. My family is off-limits to you."

An angry tic beat a frenetic rhythm in Jess's jaw. It was obvious he was straining to ride herd on an urge to beat her father down. He glanced across the room to her mother. "I have to get to work. I'm sorry I caused you any trouble, Laura. I hope I didn't completely ruin your birthday, and I'm real sorry about the gift."

His words only enraged her father more. "Yeah, that's right. Rub it in how much better you are than I am at providing for her. We can't all be international investors and make millions doing it, can we?"

Jess paused, and Abigail saw the grim look on his face that said he was one step away from slamming her father's head through a wall. Instead, he pulled his Stetson off the floor and gently dumped her ponies on the coffee table. He picked up her favorite purple one and crossed the room to hand it to her. "Y'all have a good night." His eyes were dark and sorrowful as he met her mother's gaze. "Happy birthday, Laura." And then he put his hat on his head and walked out.

"Stan," her mother growled the moment he was gone. "That was unbelievably rude. What is wrong with you?"

He sneered at her. "How would you feel if you came home to find a woman in here alone with me?"

"I have many times. Tracy. Remember?"

He scoffed. "She's the babysitter."

"She's a very attractive woman."

"So?"

"That's exactly my point," her mother said in a disgusted tone. "I'm sorry you lost your job, but that's no reason to start hating a man who's been a good friend to me since before I met you."

"Yeah, right. I think it's more than friendship with you two."

Her mother gaped. "Are you completely out of your mind?"

Abigail covered her ears with her hands. "Please don't fight anymore. I don't like loud voices."

Her mother kissed her cheek and gave her a soothing cuddle. "Sorry, baby. Why don't you go play in your room?" She set her down.

Abigail ran to the hallway, then paused as her father grabbed her mother's arm and jerked her closer.

"I want you to give that necklace back to him," he said between clenched teeth.

"Why?"

"Because I don't want to see my wife wearing another man's gift. You hear me?"

Her mother rolled her eyes. "He's like a brother to me. Nothing more."

"Nothing more, huh? Then tell me why he carries a picture of you in his watch?"

Shock etched itself across her mother's face. "What?"

"You heard me. I saw it the last time he was over here. It's a photo of *you*. No man does that for his sister. Trust me."

"I don't believe you. He's never, ever said or done anything to act like he was interested in me in any way."

"And I know what I saw."

She wrested her arm out of his grip. "You're wrong about him."

"No, I'm not. It ain't natural for a man to want to come around someone else's family like this."

"You never had a problem with it before."

"I never saw that damn watch before."

Abigail frowned as she saw a shadow moving along the wall. It lifted up and crawled slowly toward her parents. Where was it coming from? There were no windows, and nothing that could cast it. It slinked down the hallway slowly. Methodically. But as a child, she was easily distracted, especially since her parents were escalating their argument. She scurried to her room to find her Scooter doll and hide.

She'd made a nest beneath her bed for just such occasions. It was where she felt safest. Her mother called it her princess hidey-hole. Abigail called it wonderful. With her blanket and dolls, she stayed there and lost track of time until she heard another familiar voice in the middle of their ongoing fight.

Jess's.

"You don't deserve her, you bastard."

"What are you doing here?" her father snarled, startling her from her play. "I told you not to come back."

"You don't tell me what to do."

Her mother's tone was much more reasonable. "Maybe you should go."

"So that's it, then?" her father shouted. "After all these years and everything I've done for you? You're just going to throw me out for this piece of random shit?"

Abigail covered her ears as the shouts grew louder and louder.

Her mother's scream rang out. "Stan! Put down the gun!" The next thing she heard was breaking furniture. Terrified, she dug deeper into her safety blanket and held her breath. She didn't know why she wasn't crying. But something told her not to even breathe audibly.

Four loud, deafening gunshots rang out.

Wide eyed, she'd been frozen in terror. *Mama . . .* That single word hovered in her mind as tears welled in her eyes. *Go check on her. . . .*

She couldn't. It felt as if someone or something held her down and kept her quiet.

Then there was the sound of lone boot heels clicking

eerily down the hallway toward her room. Chills raised on her arms.

Don't move, Abby. It sounded like her mother talking to her. *Whatever you do, stay silent and still. Pretend you're invisible.*

Her door opened with a slow arc.

Holding her breath, she peeped from beneath her bed to watch the boots move across her floor.

"Where are you, you little brat?" Jess snarled. He searched the room for her.

He's going to find me. . . . Every part of her seized with that fear. *I don't want to die.*

"Abigail!" he shouted as he searched through her closet. "Where are you?"

The sound of sirens filled the air, which made him tear through her room as he did his best to find her. She covered her head, terrified he'd overturn her bed.

"We need to go. Now!"

Abigail frowned at a voice that sounded familiar to her. Not as a little girl, but as an adult.

Whose was it?

"I can't find the brat."

The sirens were getting louder and louder.

"I'll take care of it," the voice whispered again. "But you need to go."

"Why? It might be better if they find me here."

"I have a better idea."

He let out a sound of extreme frustration as pulsating lights flashed through the windows. "Fine," he snarled. "I'll trust you, but if you're wrong, you'll be joining the other two in the living room."

"Don't worry, I have your back."

She watched as Sundown stormed out of the room, leaving nothing but bloody footprints in his wake. . . .

Abigail jerked awake to find herself in Sundown's house.

The memory of the night her parents had died lingered heavy in her heart as the sequence of events was clarified.

Sundown had killed her parents. He'd been lying to her when he denied it.

How do you know that?

Hello? I was there.

Still, there was a tiny part of her that doubted it. Her mind couldn't reconcile the two sides of Sundown that she'd seen. The fierce protector and the lethal killer.

You've killed, too.

But for a reason. Her parents hadn't deserved their deaths.

"You're awake."

She glanced over to the door where Sundown was standing. A wave of fury swelled through her, but she fought it down. The last thing she wanted was to warn him of her intentions.

"Yeah." Licking her dry lips, she glanced down to his right front pants pocket, which caused him to arch an inquisitive brow. Her face turned red as she realized he thought she was staring at his crotch and not the other, much smaller bump. "Not on your life, cowboy."

"Dang. Just when I got my hopes up, too."

For once, she didn't let his charm infiltrate her suspicions. She sat up on the bed. "Do you have the time?"

He pulled an old-fashioned pocket watch out and opened the cover to check it.

Before he could answer her question, she was off the bed and had it in her hand. Her breath caught as she saw the photo that had set her father off.

It *was* her mother.

"What are you doing with this?"

His face turned white. "It's not what you think."

She glared at him as she clutched the watch, wanting to strangle him. "What I think is that you're a liar." She held it up for him to see the picture. "This is my mother."

"It's not your mother."

"Bullshit. I know what she looked like."

Still, he shook his head in denial. "Look at it again. Your mother had short hair and never wore a dress like that one. Ever."

She turned it back toward her to study it.

He was right. The woman in the photograph had her hair piled up into an extravagant braided bun like a woman would have worn in the late 1800s. Her high-collar, white lace blouse was adorned at the neck by an antique cameo.

Like her mother's, the woman's eyes glowed with warmth and kindness.

But the most startling fact was that their features were eerily identical. The same sharp cheekbones and dark hair. Eyebrows that arched at an angle above kind eyes. But her mother's eyes had been blue. The woman in the photograph had dark eyes. Even so it was like staring at her mother all over again.

"I told you your ma reminded me of someone." Jess covered her hand with his. "Now you know."

That touch sent a chill down her spine. "Who is she?"

"Matilda Aponi." There was a catch in his voice that told her the mere mention of the name pained him.

"And what was she to you?"

He took the watch from her and closed it. "Does it matter?"

Obviously the woman had mattered a lot to him. "You loved her."

"More than my life."

Those heartfelt words actually made her ache. She'd never seen so much love in a man's eyes for any woman. It was so intense and unexpected that a part of her was actually jealous of it. She'd give anything to have a man love her so much. "Are we related to her?"

He started to turn away, but Abigail wouldn't let him. She reached out and touched his arm as a creepy suspicion filled her. *Please let me be wrong.*

"Am I related to you?"

"Oh God no," he said, his eyes widening in horror. "I'd have never let you kiss me like you did if you were."

That was a relief. "She married someone else, then?"

He inclined his head to her. "It wasn't meant to be between us."

Abigail didn't miss the way he stroked the watch as if it were a part of Matilda, or the agonized grief in his eyes as he talked about her.

"She was too good for me anyway. I'm just glad she found someone who made her happy." He slid the watch back into his pocket, then changed the subject. "Andy has some food for you. I'll go ring him to bring it."

Abigail didn't try to stop him from leaving this time as she digested everything.

Could a man capable of that much love for someone else be the monster she thought he was?

While she had no doubt he was more than capable of killing her father, she seriously doubted he would have slaughtered her mother. Not with the feelings he'd had for Matilda. It didn't seem to fit.

Could it have been a shape-shifter? There were plenty who could have worn his skin.

But who and, most important, why? What would anyone have to gain by framing him and not turning him over to the authorities? And why kill her parents?

Her head ached from trying to decipher it.

I have to find out the truth and make whoever killed them pay. She owed her parents that much.

She turned back toward the bed to get her shoes, when a disgusted sound made her pause.

"What do you mean I can't go?" It was a voice she was unfamiliar with that sounded like someone standing not too far from her room.

"I thought we'd settled this, mite," Jess said sternly.

"Ah hell no, we didn't. You let me go up to Alaska with you, and I was a lot younger then."

"And there were other Squires there to watch your back. Not to mention, I was dumb enough not to know how much danger was there. This time I know, and you're not going."

"I hate you, you decrepit bastard."

Sundown scoffed. "I hear you. Now take that to Abigail and mind your manners, pup."

"Yeah, yeah, yeah." A few seconds later, he knocked on her door.

"Come in." She couldn't wait to see Sundown's Squire.

Andy walked in with a tray that carried a bottled Coke, water, and a plate filled with chicken, roasted potatoes, and green beans. He paused to eye her suspiciously. Dressed in jeans and a red T-shirt, he appeared to be around her age and extremely cute. Except for the slight curl to his lip, as if it made him ill to be in her presence.

"You must be Andy."

"Yeah, and if you hurt Jess, so help me, I will hunt you down to the farthest corner of hell and make you wish to God you'd never breathed air. You hear me?"

Well, that was most unexpected. "You greet everyone this way?"

"No. I'm usually very nice. But you . . . you have no idea how much effort it's taking for me not to kill you where you stand."

She returned his sneer with one of her own. "Bring it, punk."

"Don't tempt me." He moved to set the tray at the foot of the bed. Closer to him now, she realized he was almost as tall as Sundown. Though without the massive muscles and aura of I-can-kick-the-crap-out-of-you, it wasn't quite so apparent at first glance. Unlike Sundown, he didn't dominate the room or her senses.

Andy started for the door.

"Why are you so protective of him, anyway? I thought Squires hated their Dark-Hunters."

He paused to give her a look that asked are-you-effing-nuts? "Our Dark-Hunters are our family. There's nothing we wouldn't do for them. Even die for them if we had to."

"That's not what I've heard."

He scowled at her. "From who? Daimons? Apollites? If the DH are so bad, explain to me why some of the above have been known to work and live with Dark-Hunters themselves."

She rolled her eyes. "Now I know you're lying to me. There's no way an Apollite would *ever* work for a Dark-Hunter."

Crossing his arms over his chest, he gave her a droll stare. "Babe, I know two of them who married one." He jerked his chin toward the door. "Ishtar Casino, here in Vegas, has a whole staff of Apollites who work for Sin Nana . . . who up until about four years ago was a Dark-Hunter, and he was doing his duties while they worked for him. Hell, half of them helped him, and when he was attacked, they and even a Daimon fought to protect him."

Abigail would argue, but she knew Apollites who'd worked there, and she knew Sin owned it. "How do I know Sin was ever a Dark-Hunter?"

"Why would I lie?"

"It could be pathological."

He rolled his eyes. "Whatever. I'm not going to argue with you. Don't like you enough to bother. But like I said, you hurt one hair on his head, and you will regret it. Jess *is* my family, and he's been through enough damage in his life. And in spite of all the shit people have done to him, including his best friend shooting him in the back and in his head on the day of his wedding at the feet of his fiancée, there's not a more decent human being ever born." He turned and was out the door before she had a chance to say anything else.

Stunned, she stood there as that last bit hit her like a fist.

Shot in the back on his wedding day? An image of Matilda and her mother went through her mind. For a full minute, she couldn't breathe. She could see it all in her head so clearly.

It wasn't meant to be. Sundown's words echoed in her ears. No wonder he'd been so sad when he talked about her.

To be with her mother, who looked so much like Matilda, must have killed him.

It's why he killed her and your father. He couldn't take it any more.

A psychotic break would make sense.

Andy and Jess were lying.

She wanted to believe that. It would be the easiest. Not to mention, it was the option that didn't leave her with a conscience that would flog her for the rest of her life.

However long that was.

Rubbing her hand over her eyes, she sat down on the bed and looked at the food. It turned her stomach.

No, not the food. What she'd done. The one thing no one had ever told her about was how to cope with the lives she'd taken. Even before Sundown had kidnapped her, her conscience had been there, telling her that she'd taken someone's life. Her anger kept her going, but it wasn't enough to drown out her actions.

"They deserved it. Think of how many of us they've killed over the centuries. Do you think they ever have a minute's worth of compassion when it comes to us? No, they don't. Kill the Apollite. We're animals to be butchered

to them. Wasn't it bad enough Apollo cursed us? Then his damned sister had to go and create a race to hunt and kill us as brutally as they can. They stab us in the hearts, Abby. And stand over our bodies while we die. Where is fair in all of that? We live twenty-seven years and hit full puberty at a time when most humans are still in grade school, learning their ABC's. Our lives are horrifically short, and you were there when my mother withered into dust. At twenty-seven. Remember that? Did you ever even hear her speak a bad word about anyone? No. She was kindness incarnate. We took you in and you've seen it firsthand. We don't hurt anyone. We are the victims." Kurt's indignation had fueled her vengeance quest, along with Perry and Jonah.

Even Hannah.

Kill the Dark-Hunters, Abby. That had been chanted to her since the moment Kurt's mother died. Even her adoptive father, on his deathbed, had begged her for retribution.

"You're our only hope, Abs. Don't let us down. Remember what they did to us. What that animal did to your parents. Never forget it."

But her memories . . . Something in all of this didn't feel right. There were too many missing pieces.

If only she knew the truth.

You do know the truth. You were there.

Unable to sort through it, she looked up at the ceiling,

wishing the real answer would fall down and smack her hard enough to make her listen.

"Your *coyotes just* came slinking back in the door with tucked tails. I would have killed them, but figured you'd want the honor. They claim there's a wolf helping your enemies now. But they don't know who he is, or if he's one of ours or from another pantheon. My guess is he's not one of ours."

Coyote narrowed his gaze on the huge bear of a man who dared to enter his den with such unwelcome news. And there was only one who would be so bold. Snake was a full head taller, which given the fact that Coyote was six feet two was impressive. While his own hair was short and black, Snake's was shaved bald and an intricate snake tattoo started at where his hairline would be on top of his head. It coiled down his neck and both of his beefy arms into a symbolic pattern that only one of their people could read. To most, Snake would appear like a criminal. But Coyote knew him for what he really was.

An ancient warrior who, like him, had lain dormant for far too long. Who would have thought when they agreed to their duties centuries ago that they, who had once made the very earth tremble in fear of their strength and skill, would be relegated to a role that was only one step above nursemaid?

"Did you hear me, Coyote?"

He gave a subtle nod. "They've grown fat and lazy. Unable to hunt. I weep for what has become of our people." Most of all, he wept for what had become of them.

"With Choo Co La Tah weakened, we'll have better luck after this."

He wished he were so optimistic. Choo Co La Tah had turned back his scorpions faster than he'd expected. But it'd drained the old man. With luck, his next plague would weaken him enough that they could kill him, too.

With Choo Co La Tah out of the way, there would be no stopping them.

He could almost smile at the unexpected gift the human had given them. He'd hoped she would kill Renegade and Brady. Taking out his other enemy was a bonus.

It'd been centuries since he stood this close to his goal. So close, he feel the breath of it on his face.

But nothing was certain. Nothing should ever be taken for granted.

And never, ever underestimate Choo Co La Tah. Even though he and Snake outnumbered the old man, they still had the problem that while Coyote was the Guardian for the East, he'd only obtained it by trickery.

It wasn't his right.

The legitimate Guardian still lived, even though it was as a Dark-Hunter and so long as he did, there was always the possibility that he'd step forward to claim his station and kill Coyote where he stood.

I would gladly step down. But the true Guardian had made it clear that he wouldn't allow it. Not at the price Coyote demanded.

Snake looked up at the sky above them. "The cycle is drawing close."

At last. He didn't say it. He didn't have to. They'd both been waiting for the Time Untime for far too long.

If the Butterfly and the Buffalo were to unite during the Time Untime, he and Snake would be destroyed. And all the Guardians replaced by those *they* chose.

But if he could stop it, he could rise on the eve of the Reset, and then he would have the power to select the new Guardians himself. With them under his control, they could unite their powers and return the world to their people. The Pale One would be defeated for once and for all.

The reign of the Coyote would be absolute. Uncontested.

Their enemies would be driven back into the sea.

And the elders and earth would weep for the wrong it had done to him. Blood would rain from the skies, and the Coyote would eat the sun and cover this earth with his vengeance.

He could already savor the taste. Soon this world would be his, and with his raised army, he would subjugate everyone.

The one thing he wanted most would then be his. No one would ever remove it again from his possession.

All he had to do was destroy one more Guardian.

So simple . . .

So damned hard.

But he wouldn't fail this time. This time, he would succeed and the world of man would finally understand what true misery meant.

The Reign of Coyote was about to begin, and the world would never be the same.

10

"You know, Jess. If something breaks in and eats me while you're gone, you're going to feel real bad about it. You've seen the movies. Read the books. You know it happens. Sidekick and girlfriend always get kidnapped, snuffed, or usually both by the bad guys after the good ones."

Jess rubbed his brow, trying to soothe the migraine Andy was causing. Not that Dark-Hunters could get migraines, but the boy was definitely putting that theory to the test.

It was either that . . .

Or a tumor.

Can't get those either.

Then what was the painful throb that wouldn't let up?

Oh yeah, it was Andy.

Jess sighed. "You're right, pup. So I'll be sending you over to the Ishtar for Sin to babysit until I get back. That'll make sure nothing bad happens to you."

Now, that was a nice shade of indignation mottling the boy's skin. Quite impressive, really. If he were tea kettle, he'd be whistling like a train. "I can take care of myself."

"Not what you just said."

"That don't mean—"

"Jess, we have a problem."

He glanced past Andy's shoulder to see Ren looking as flustered as the kid. Ren joined them in the kitchen.

A huge weight of dread fell right on top of Jess. "What's wrong?"

"Abigail's gone."

There was something Jess didn't want to hear. "Excuse me?"

Ren nodded. "I went to get her from downstairs, and there's no trace of her. She must have snuck up and out while we were preparing. Damn you for a house this big. Really, folks? Was it necessary?"

Andy snorted. "You try finding a house to accommodate a dozen horses with a large basement in Vegas that's not haunted, and that you can close on in two weeks and move in. I think I did pretty damn good."

Ignoring Andy's ornery outburst, Jess cursed. Both he and Ren were still plagued with their waned powers. And he could kick himself for not watching her closer. How could he have lulled his brain into forgetting she was a prisoner they intended to sacrifice?

Hell, he'd have run, too.

Andy arched a brow at them. "Why are you two freaking out, anyway? If she's in one of your cars, which I'm sure she is, she's LoJacked."

Jess scowled. "Come again?"

"I LoJack your ass every minute of the night, cowboy. Just in case." Andy went to the wall security monitor that tapped into all their camera feeds and pulled up the garage surveillance. Then he cursed even more foully than Jess had. "Forget yours, that bitch has taste. She's in my Audi R8 Spyder."

Jess growled at him. "Watch your mouth, pup. That's a lady you're talking about."

He grumbled under his breath, questioning that category. "You wouldn't feel that way if she'd run off on one of your stinking horses."

Ren crossed his arms over his chest. "Is it LoJacked?"

"Of course," Andy said indignantly. "That's my baby. I even have a kill switch on her."

"Then stop the engine."

Andy appeared downright horrified by Ren's suggestion. "Are you out of your mind? What if someone hits it for stalling? I had that thing on order for over a year. Custom hand built. The epitome of German engineering. I even paid extra for the paint on her. Ain't no way I'm going to chance someone denting my baby. Or, God forbid, totaling it."

Jess rolled his eyes at the boy's hissy fit. If he kept that up, he'd be putting Andy back in diapers.

He turned to Ren. "You take the air. I'll get a bike." Then he focused his attention on Andy again. "And you—"

Andy held his cell phone out to him. "Have an app. Track her down, get my car back, and beat the hell out of her. . . . In that precise order."

Jess would laugh if the entire fate of the world didn't hinge on his finding Abigail. Shaking his head, he went to the garage to get his red Hayabusa. It was the fastest thing he owned. Plus, it would synch to the tracker in Andy's phone—had to love the Squires and their toys.

He grabbed a full face helmet off the rack, along with the keys, and was on it in record time. While the garage door opened, he synched the phone. As soon as it was complete, he peeled out, leaving the stench of smoke and rubber behind him. He ducked to miss the door that hadn't gotten out of his way fast enough.

Opening the throttle, he shot through the gates that were also only partially parted and turned on to the street, heading south. The best part about the tracker was that it told him the speed the car was traveling. She didn't appear to be going too fast—she probably thought she was home free and didn't want to attract the attention of any police. Smart on her part.

But it wouldn't be enough to keep him from finding her.

Abigail regretted her choice of cars as she tried to navigate traffic. She'd thought the Audi, with its V10 engine, would be fast, but she couldn't have been more wrong. People actually cut her off or boxed her in so that they could slow her down to take pictures of the car with their camera phones. Good grief. She'd never seen anything like it.

Really people, it was a car with four tires like any other. She'd never understood how anyone could become so enthralled by a piece of metal transportation.

How did Sundown ever get anywhere with this much attention? It was so frustrating. She'd never been in a car before that affected traffic and drivers like this.

"I should have found something generic." Unfortunately, her choices had been limited to a Ferrari, an old classic Ford pickup from the 1940s, a Gator and this. The Audi was the only one that was street legal and wasn't a stick shift—something she couldn't drive.

The rest had been motorcycles, and since she'd never ridden one before, she didn't think her escape attempt should serve as her first learning experience. With her luck, she'd have wrecked it in the driveway.

Her heart raced as she habitually checked her rearview mirror, expecting to see Sundown catching up to her any second.

Don't discover I'm gone for a while. Please.

At least not until she had a chance to find out some truths. She wasn't running from what she'd done. She just wanted to understand her memories.

Who was lying to her?

She hated to be so confused. All her life, she'd had one clear-cut goal.

Kill Jess Brady.

Now . . . her emotions and memories were tangled into a knot she wasn't sure she could ever undo. If that wasn't bad enough, there was a bitter hunger inside her for . . .

She didn't know. The demon blood they'd mixed with hers was causing all kinds of problems. At times her senses would sharpen, then fall back to normal.

Beware the pathway that vengeance will take you down.
The voice in her head sounded a lot like Sundown's.

His name had no more crossed her mind than something akin to lightning flashed behind her eyes. In that moment, she saw the past so clearly that it stole her breath.

It was Jess.

He kicked open the door to an old-fashioned room. The low, burning fire cast shadows across the cornflower blue scroll wallpaper that covered the walls. A man shot up from the old-fashioned sleigh bed with a gun in his hand. But as soon as he focused on Jess's face, he hesitated.

"I killed you."

Jess wore the mask of stone cold killer. Fierce. Terrifying. Gut-wrenching. "Yeah, you did, Bart. And I told you, you son of a bitch, that I'd be back for you." He spread his arms wide. "Here I am."

Bart came to his senses and unloaded all six of his bullets straight into Jess's body. The rounds left small puffs of smoke as they embedded in his chest without hurting him. He didn't even bleed that much.

Even with the chamber emptied, Bart continued to uselessly pull the trigger.

Jess laughed evilly as he stalked across the room to jerk the gun out of Bart's grasp with one hand. With his other, he grabbed him by the throat and held on so tight that Bart's eyes bulged while he knelt on the bed. Jess pulled him closer so that he could growl into his reddened face. "It was bad enough you killed me. I might have spared you for that. But you had no right to rape Matilda and kill her father in front of her, you worthless bastard. It's what you've done to her that will cost you your life. She was the only decent thing I've ever known. Damn you to hell for hurting her. You had *no* reason for it."

He waited until Bart was almost dead before he released him and slung him to the ground. Bart lay on the floor, wheezing while Jess went to the wooden washing stand in the corner and pulled the ceramic pitcher up and emptied it over Bart's head.

Now completely drenched, Bart sputtered and coughed.

Jess kicked him onto his back and planted his booted foot on his chest. He slammed the pitcher down on the floor, shattering it near Bart's face. Bart jerked, closing his eyes as shards rained down on him. Some of them even caught in his tousled hair.

"You didn't think I was going to kill you that easily, did you?" Jess taunted. "For what you did to her, you are going to suffer every second between now and dawn. I'm going to give you pain the likes of which my mama's people were famed for. And when I finally end your life, you will thank me for it."

"Go to hell!"

Jess scoffed. "You already sent me there. It's your turn now. Give the devil my regards."

Abigail jerked out of the memory as the sound of a horn blared. Blinking, she realized she was about to plow into an oncoming truck. She jerked the wheel and headed back into her lane.

Her breathing ragged, she rubbed at her forehead. Why was she seeing Jess's memories? And she knew that was what they were. It was too vivid to be something she created. She could still smell the fire and the stench of Bart's breath mixed with his sweat.

Jess had sold his soul not to avenge himself. He'd done it for Matilda.

Her gaze clouded as she saw another image. This one was a few years later. It was just after midnight, and Jess stood inside what appeared to be a lawyer's office. A man with a handlebar mustache and parted black hair sat behind a huge mahogany desk. He wore a dark gray suit over a bright burgundy brocade vest. Over his head was a large clock that ticked so loudly, it hurt Jess's hearing.

"I'm breaking all kinds of rules here," the man said as he passed a piece of paper across the clean desk to Jess. "But I did what you asked."

"She's happy?"

The lawyer nodded. "I transferred another half million into her account so that she could buy that house and land she wanted. She now has enough to do anything she wants for the rest of her life."

A tic worked in Jess's handsome jaw. "It's not enough. Keep adding to it every year like I said originally. I don't ever want her to have anything to worry about other than what dress looks best on her."

He inclined his head to the paper Jess held. "That's an

extra photograph I talked the photographer into making of her. Thought you'd like it."

There was no missing the love in his eyes, even though he kept his features completely stoic. "Does she need anything else?"

"No. She's married to a good man who owns the local mercantile."

Jess frowned as if the lawyer had said something wrong. "But?"

"I didn't say there was a but."

"She sits at her window at night and cries." Jess's tone was hollow.

"How did you—?"

"I can read your mind." Jess swallowed hard. "Thank you, Mr. Foster. I appreciate everything you've done." He went to the door and put his hat on his head before he left.

Outside, he tucked the photo into his jacket, and it was only then that she saw the moisture in his eyes.

He quickly blinked it away, then headed for his horse.

Abigail ached as she felt his pain like it was a part of her. He really had loved his Matilda.

"Stop it!" she snapped at herself. This was ridiculous. She didn't want to see Jess. Not now. She had more important things to do.

Slapping herself on the cheek, she focused her attention on the road that led her home. . . .

. . .

*J*ess *cursed as* he lost all trace of Abigail. The GPS literally flashed bright, then vanished altogether. It looked like something had burned it out.

What the hell?

He started to dial Ren, then remembered he was in crow mode so he wouldn't be able to answer. Instead, he rang Sasha, who picked it up immediately.

"Yell-oh?"

"I've lost her," Jess said without preamble. "Can you give me any guidance?"

Sasha snorted. "On what? A new personality? Car buying? I'm a Wolf, cowboy, not a life counselor."

That sarcasm snapped at his tolerance. "Can you track her, Scooby, or am I asking too much of you?"

"Now, *that* I can do. But it would leave Choo Co La Tah unguarded. Send birdbrain back, and I'll swap off."

"Fine." Jess hung up and mumbled under his breath how much he really hated shape-shifters.

Changing lanes to avoid a slow-moving Toyota, he used his powers to talk to Ren. He'd never tried to do this before when Ren was in crow form, so he had no idea if it would even work. While his powers were starting to re-cover from being in the house with Ren all day, they still weren't up to their usual strength.

"Talk to me, *penyo*. You there?"

Luckily, Ren came back fast. "I'm here."

Jess breathed a sigh of relief. "You wouldn't happen to know where Abigail got off to, would you?"

"No. I can't track her scent and I haven't had a visual on her yet."

Figured that would be too much to ask. "Then I need you to swap duties with Sasha so that he can track her down."

"Why isn't the GPS working?"

"Twenty-million-dollar question. No answer, and I have no idea who to call to get a clue. I'll keep heading in the direction she was and hope she doesn't turn off anytime soon."

"All right. I'm flashing back. Will get Sasha to you ASAP."

Jess slowed down and tried to use his own abilities to track her. He didn't really have that power, but . . . At this point, he was willing to try most anything.

Why? The bad feeling in his gut that said if he didn't find her quick, something awful would happen to her. It had nothing to do with needing to get her to the Valley to save the world. This was something else entirely. Something that made him desperate to locate her.

"Hang on, Abby. I'm coming."

Abigail slowed as she reached the modest home she shared with Hannah in Henderson. She cringed a bit as she scraped the front of the car on the angle of the aggregate driveway. *Hope Jess doesn't love this thing.*

He might kill her after all.

She parked outside and headed for the front door. But as she neared it, a strange red haze seemed to drop down over everything. It was like she was staring out of a pair of red glasses. She heard that strange thrumming sound again—the same she'd heard when they put the demon blood in her.

Like she was listening to the heartbeat of the world.

Shaking her head, she forced herself forward.

"If something's happened to her, Kurt, I swear I'll never forgive you."

"Shut up, Hannah, and sit down."

She knew they were inside the house, but she could hear them as clearly as if they were standing beside her. More than that, she could see them sitting at the table with Jonah.

"We know where Sundown lives," Hannah said. "Why can't we go get her?"

Kurt curled his lip. "Are you out of your mind? We march into a Dark-Hunter's home and do what? Tell him to hand her over?"

She lifted her chin defiantly. "Yes."

Looking up from the laptop where he was working, Jonah rolled his eyes. "I'm really sick of you two fighting. Take your sister out of here while I do this."

His voice . . .

There was something about it that tugged on the edge of her memory. But what?

Kurt grabbed Hannah by the arm and hauled her out of the room. As soon as they were gone, Jonah pulled out his phone and dialed it. "Hey. I've got her heartbeat on the monitor so we know she's still alive. Yeah, I think it's a good sign that the Hunter hasn't killed her yet."

At the sound of those words, Abigail felt a surge of some odd emotion throughout her entire body. Her teeth elongated. It was the demon again. It was reacting to being here.

Why?

Raw, unfettered rage followed the wave. The demon wanted to taste Jonah in the worst sort of way.

I can't do that.

Yet she salivated. The taste of warm, sweet blood filled her mouth, making her ache to take some from someone else. The haze turned brighter. She walked through the door without opening it. With no real understanding of moving, she found herself in the kitchen with Jonah.

He looked up and blanched. He dropped his phone straight to the floor, where it landed with a thud. "What's wrong?"

She licked at her fangs. *Taste him. . . . You know you want to.*

Strangely enough, she did.

Abigail reached for his throat, but he jumped to his feet and put distance between them.

He kept backing away from her. "What did they do to you, Abby?"

Abby . . .

No, that didn't seem right. She was . . .

Caught in a maelstrom. She could feel the winds whipping, howling, and tearing at her. The room spun around as more images flashed. She saw the past, the present, and a future filled with horrors that were indescribable.

But the one thing she saw clearest . . .

The night her parents died. And this time she knew why that voice had been familiar. Who had been there with "Sundown."

"You were there." She pointed her finger at Jonah, who stood before her, gaping.

"What are you talking about?"

She didn't answer as the demon swallowed her whole. Before she knew what she was doing, she was on him, biting into his neck. The moment she tasted his blood, she knew the truth.

Jonah was a Daimon. It was why the demon in her wanted to annihilate him.

The souls of his victims screamed in her head with a chorus that was deafening and sickening. They wanted their freedom.

And she wanted his blood.

"Abby! Stop!"

She recognized Kurt's voice, but there was no way she would listen to him. Not now. Not when the demon had her.

Kurt ran at her back and tried to knock her away. She turned on him and hissed, while she maintained her grip on Jonah, who was crying and begging for mercy.

Really? After all the people he'd ruthlessly killed to live, he had the nerve to beg for his own life? The hypocrisy sickened her even more.

"Coward," she breathed in his ear. "You could have saved my mother, and you didn't." He had swallowed her soul so that he could live. Damn him! Agony and fury bonded inside her to such a level that it was all she could do not to rip him apart.

Instead, she reached down to his boot, where he always kept a knife hidden. In slow motion, she saw Kurt lunging for her back. Before he could reach her, she stabbed Jonah in the heart.

He gasped, then burst apart into a shower of gold dust.

"No!" Kurt drew the word out, but it was too late.

Jonah was dead. She'd killed him.

Numb and dizzy, she stared down at her pristine hand. There was no blood there. Nothing left of Jonah except a shimmering film that graced the floor. Iridescent like the wings of a summer butterfly.

She could hear the laughter of the human souls as they

finally ascended to their rightful places. But more than that, she heard their gratitude. At least she had saved them. Too bad no one had saved her parents.

"What have you done?" His eyes wide, Kurt stared at her as if she was a stranger.

And she was. She didn't know herself any more than he did. "What have you made me?"

"You were supposed to be stronger. Not . . . not—" He gestured wildly at her. "—*this*."

A weird odor filled her head. It was like sulfur, only stronger. It was . . .

"You took demon blood, too," she accused him as she understood what the demon was telling her.

He didn't deny it. "What was I supposed to do? I'll turn twenty-seven in a few months. I don't want to die any more than you do. At least it's better than killing a human."

Was it?

Hannah came out from the back of the house. She stared at Abigail with horrified eyes before she let out a shrill scream.

Abigail covered her ears as pain split her skull. She glared at her "brother." "You lied to me. *All* of you. You didn't tell me about Daimons."

Kurt narrowed his gaze on her. "You didn't need to know about them."

Oh, now there was an award-winning answer. "You told me the Dark-Hunters were our enemies."

"They are our enemies. They hunt and kill us."

It wasn't that simple. Not anymore. Jess had been right. They had lied to her. Used her. "You have no idea what you've done. What you've set into motion."

You will be known forever by the tracks you leave. Her mother's words haunted her now.

I will be known as the woman who ended the world. She felt so sick. Lost. Confused.

Betrayed.

Kurt grabbed her arm. "Abigail, listen to me. We're not your enemies. We took you in when no one else would have. My parents raised you like one of their own."

But there was more to it than that.

The truth hovered around the fringes of her mind like a ghost she could neither see nor touch. Only feel.

She stared at him as her conscience shredded her over her actions. "I don't trust you anymore."

Hannah stepped forward. "Abby—"

She moved away from Hannah's grasp.

I need to go. She didn't want to be here. It no longer felt like home.

It felt like hell.

She'd taken innocent lives. Killed an elder Guardian. Her life would never be the same. And it shouldn't be. Not after what she'd done. She stumbled back toward the door and went outside. The sky above twinkled with stars. It looked a thousand times brighter tonight than it ever had before.

Why?

Why would it be that way when everything was so wrong? Surely it should be storming. But it wasn't. The world appeared completely ignorant of the horrors to come.

"I have to fix this," she whispered. Before it was too late.

She would go with Choo Co La Tah to the Valley.

And there she would die.

11

Jess followed Sasha's directions as they sped toward Abigail's location. His stomach was knotted tight, and he had no idea why. It wasn't just that she was gone. He had a tangible need to find her and make sure she was all right.

To make sure no one hurt her.

He came around a corner right as a car rolled through the stop sign—straight into his path. Biting his lip, he tried to swerve to miss it, but because of the car's speed, it still managed to clip his back tire. His motorcycle came out from under him and dragged him down the street at a deadly pace.

Crap! The asphalt tore at his clothes and skin, reminding him why he wore a duster when he rode and why he was glad he was no longer mortal. Still, it hurt to kiss pavement, and his body was extremely unhappy with this predicament.

Abigail's heart stopped beating as she realized in her dazed stupor that she'd just hit someone. She slammed on the brakes and looked back to see the motorcycle and rider on the street, skidding sideways toward the curb.

Oh my God! What have I done now?

It wasn't until she'd put the car in park and opened the door that she recognized the sprawled-out man.

"Jess!" She ran toward him as fast as she could. She cringed at the length of how far he'd traveled over the road on his back. *He's a Dark-Hunter. A crash won't kill him.* In her mind, she knew it was the truth.

But her emotions weren't listening. Panic filled her as she drew closer and didn't see him moving.

Jess lay on the street, looking up through his helmet,

trying to figure out if he'd broken something other than his pride. Gah, it hurt to breathe. To move. He felt pretty banged up, but it was hard to tell just how bad.

And the damned billion-pound motorcycle was lying on his foot. That was going to leave a limp.

"Jess!" Out of nowhere, Abigail appeared, her face a mask of terrified fear. Before he could answer, she sank down beside him. "Oh my God! Oh my God! Oh my God! Are you all right? Are you alive? Did I hurt you?" She clutched at his body as if trying to find an injury. "Jess? Can you speak?"

It was so wrong, but he couldn't help grinning at her panic. No woman had been this scared for him in a long while. "Yeah, I can talk. But I kind of like the attention you're giving me. You want to grope a little lower, it'd be even better."

"Oh, you . . ." She shoved at him.

Pain cut through his body. "Ow!"

Her panic returned instantly. "Are you all right?"

He laughed. "Dang, you're easy."

"And you're completely evil."

Jess pulled his helmet off to stare up at her. The streetlights played in her dark hair, making it shimmer. Her eyes glowed with warmth, concern, and anger. It was a heady combination. "And you're completely beautiful."

Abigail's breath caught at those unexpected words. They settled something deep inside her. Made it calm in a way she'd never been calm before. And at the same time, her entire body was on fire from his nearness. A strange dichotomy that made no sense whatsoever.

He wrapped his arms around her and pulled her lips down to his so that he could give her the hottest kiss she'd ever received. One so unsettling that it made her entire body burn and caused her to forget where they were and what had happened. Nothing mattered in this moment except the sensation of his tongue sweeping against hers. Of his arms holding her close to his hard body.

Nothing had ever felt better.

"Excuse me, people. You're both lying in the middle of the street. Might want to move before someone else runs over both your damn fool selves."

Abigail pulled back, then turned to glare at Sasha, who stood on the curb, under the streetlamp, giving them an irritated grimace. She started to smart off, when all of a sudden, she heard a peculiar sound. It was like someone had let loose a herd of angry chainsaws.

Scowling, she looked back at Jess. "What is that?"

Sasha's face blanched. "Wasps . . . A shitload of them." He pointed down the street.

Following the direction of his arm, Abigail gaped at the sight of what appeared to be a thick, dancing cloud rolling toward them.

"Next plague." Jess jumped to his feet and pulled her up. He met Sasha's gaze. "Can you get the bike home?"

"On it. I'll see you back in your compound."

Jess inclined his head to him before he took her hand and ran with her back to the Audi. Abigail was still gaping as she watched the wasps draw closer and closer at an abnormal pace. The cloud rose and dived like some giant, lumbering, solid beast.

She ran to the passenger side while Jess wedged himself into the driver's seat and moved it back.

"I really hope you didn't damage this thing."

She slammed the door shut, grateful she'd left it running, then buckled herself in. "You that attached to it, cowboy?"

He put it in gear. "Nope. Not mine. It's Andy's pride and joy. If there's so much as a scratch on this thing, I'll never hear the end of it."

Great. Now the Squire had another reason to hate her. "I can't win for losing with him, can I?"

Jess didn't answer as the wasps literally enveloped the car. They landed on the windshield so thick that he had to turn the wipers on to try and dislodge them.

It didn't work. All it did was piss them off.

Disgusted and scared, Abigail hissed as she realized they were also crawling in through the vents.

"Close them quick," Jess said, snatching his shut.

She complied and held them in place to make sure the wasps didn't push them open again. "This is getting ugly."

"Like my great-aunt's underpants."

She arched a brow at his strange and unexpected comment. Okay . . .

Jess tried to navigate the streets, but it was far from easy going. Cars were swerving everywhere, trying to avoid the wasps. Horns blared and people screamed so loudly that it was deafening. She'd never seen anything like it.

What were they going to do?

She sighed. "I'm getting a little tired of this."

Jess flashed a fanged grin. "Not my fave thing either, I have to say. You wouldn't happen to have a can of Raid, would you?"

"I wish. What else don't they like?"

"Apparently us . . . and a little brown Audi."

She shook her head. "How can you find humor right now?"

"Damned if I know. I must be one sick SOB. There's definitely something in my noodle that's shorted out."

And how could she find that charming?

More than that, her entire life was falling apart, and the only comfort she had was him. Maybe he wasn't the sick one after all.

Maybe it was her.

Yeah, there's definitely something wrong with me. And it wasn't just the wasps trying to break into the car and sting them or the demon that had made her eat a friend. "This is definitely one of those days when you're praying it's a dream. Only you never wake up from the nightmare."

"I've had a few of those in my time. But this one here's not so bad."

"How do you figure?" she asked, flabbergasted by his words.

He flashed a fanged grin at her. "I might have lost some skin, but I got kissed by a beautiful woman who was happy to see me. I gotta say that's pretty epic in my book. Definitely not a worst-case day here."

Given what she'd seen of his past, she knew that for a fact. Still . . .

"Thank you."

He frowned. "For what?"

Being here.

Being you. Things she couldn't say out loud without embarrassing herself to the deepest level. But she felt that gratitude so much that it made tears prick at her eyes.

After a few seconds when she didn't respond, Jess looked over at her. She was staring at her hands as if they belonged to a stranger. A cloak of sadness enveloped her. "You okay?"

She nodded. And still she looked at her hands. "I killed a . . . Daimon tonight."

"What?"

Swallowing, she glanced over at him. "You were right. They'd lied to me my whole life and kept that knowledge from me. I don't know what to believe now."

"Believe in yourself. Trust your instincts."

"Is that what you do?"

Jess snorted as old memories burned. "No. Not doing it is what got me shot in the back by a man I thought was my brother. I like to think I learn a little as I go."

But sometimes he wondered. Like right now, there was a part of him that wanted to trust her, and if ever someone should know better than that, it was him. She'd already proved that she was willing to hurt him to get what she wanted.

And she'd also run to him when he was hurt to make sure he was still alive.

After she hit him with a car, of course. Yeah, okay, so that part sucked. But she *had* come back when she didn't have to. It was more than a lot of people would do.

"We're not going to make it back to your house, are we?" He heard the fearful undercurrent in her voice.

"Don't get maudlin on me. We're not dead yet . . . any chance those demon powers of yours have anything to help with this?"

"Not that . . ." Her voice trailed off as if an idea suddenly occurred to her. "Don't wasps hate bad smells?"

"I'm not fond of them neither. Is there something you need to tell me? 'Cause right now, I really can't open a window."

She made a sound of disgust at his offbeat humor. "Whenever the powers surge, they put off an awful smell. I was thinking—"

"I prefer the idea of me driving through the worst BOB ever than having you smell up the car with demon funk to choke us down. No offense, my sight and hearing aren't the only things my Dark-Hunter powers boost."

"BOB?"

He loved that out of all that, she'd gotten only one word. "Baked on bugs. Or in this case, I guess I should have said BOW—baked on wasps."

She started to laugh, but something slammed into them so hard, it snapped her forcefully to the right.

Jess cursed as he lost control of the car and they spun around. He wasn't sure what had struck them, but it felt like a semi.

On steroids.

All of a sudden, there was a lone howl.

Coyote. He'd know that sound anywhere. The only question was if he meant it as a taunt or an order for his servants. When the car finally stopped moving, it ended up embedded against a pole.

"You all right?" he asked Abigail.

She nodded. "I think so. You?"

"Brain's a mite rattled, but that's nothing new for me."

She jerked up in her seat as if someone had shocked her. "You hear that?"

He strained, then shook his head. The only sound in his ears was a bad inner buzzing and the wasps outside. "Hear what?"

"I can't make out the words, but it sounds like some-one whispering."

He tried again, and again he heard nothing. "I only hear you."

"You really don't hear that?"

"Sorry. My medium powers are on the fritz, and I can't channel spirits or bells right now. I'll get them worked on later. For—"

"Shh," she said, touching his arm with her hand. "The wasps are talking to someone. I hear them so clearly."

Okay, time to get someone to a psych ward.

"It says to kill the buffalo."

His scowl deepened. "There's no buffalo in Vegas. At least not that I know of."

"That's what they're saying, though."

Maybe what she heard was that weird tendency people had to make ambient noise and other obnoxious things tolerable by incorporating them into understand-able sounds and syllables. He didn't know for sure.

At least not until he felt something else strike the car and land on the hood. It struck the windshield repeat-edly.

The wasps pulled back enough for them to see a giant mountain lion. It was trying to break through the wind-shield to get them.

"Oh, this ain't good," Jess muttered under his breath. He put the car into reverse and backed up at a scary pace.

Cutting the wheel, he sent the mountain lion flying. Then he put it in drive and floored it.

Abigail held her breath as panic seized every part of her. She didn't see any way out of this. "You think Choo Co La Tah can save us again?"

"Eventually, he can stop it. I just don't know how long we have to hold out. Not to mention, the mountain lion is new. Man, what I wouldn't give for some catnip right now."

Cars were still running off the road as their drivers were swarmed.

As Jess passed a gas station, an idea hit him. It was lunacy, but . . .

It was all he had. He headed for another gas station down the street.

Abigail cringed as they pulled into the station and she saw the bodies on the ground of people who'd been caught outside by the wasps and who were now dead from their stings. There were others trapped in cars who screamed for help while the wasps continued to swarm, looking for new victims.

"Is there anything we can do for them?"

"Yeah. Stop Coyote."

That was much easier said than done.

Jess took them to the carwash and pulled inside. She started to ask him what he was doing when all of a sudden, the doors closed, sealing them in. The mountain lion slammed into the door, but couldn't reach them through the tough plastic.

Waving his hand, Jess appeared to make the water come on.

The wasps around their car went crazy as they were sprayed.

Her heart lightened. It was a brilliant idea. They were going to drown the wasps.

Laughing, she turned to Jess and kissed him on the cheek. "You're a genius!"

"Ah now, don't be going on like that. I might actually think you like me, and where would we be then?"

He was right. That was even more terrifying than being assaulted by killer wasps and angry mountain lions. And as that thought went through her head, she was struck with another realization.

"You have telekinesis."

He nodded. "A little, but it's not always reliable."

"How so?"

"I've had a few mishaps with it. I used to try and control it more, but after an embarrassing incident, I learned to leave it be."

This she wanted to hear. "What embarrassing incident?"

He actually blushed. "Really don't want to share or relive it. Suffice it to say, it learned me a thing or two that I've never forgotten."

All righty, then. She leaned back in the seat while the water and suds took care of their menace for them. It slid the wasps around and made a nice thick ick on the ground. And as she sat there watching them go down the drains and fall away, the horror of her actions hit her fully.

She'd killed a friend tonight.

And she'd lost her family.

I'm alone. But it was so much worse than that . . .

Jess felt her sadness as if it were inside him. He watched her in the dim light while emotions flitted across her face and darkened her eyes. "It'll be all right." He tried to reassure her.

She shook her head in denial. "No. Everything I've ever known. Everything I've been told by the people I loved was a lie." She held her hand up, grateful it was human and not demon, and yet she knew the truth. . . . . "I let them mix me with a demon and my adoptive brother did the same, too. I don't know what I am now. I don't know what he is. It was all so clear before. Kill you. Avenge my parents, and then protect my family and the Apollites and humans from the Dark-Hunters." A single tear went down her cheek as she met his gaze. "I'm a monster, Jess. I've destroyed myself."

Those words tugged at his heart and reminded him of the day he'd come to that same realization. It was so hard to see the truth in yourself.

Harder still to face it.

"You're not a monster, Abby. Confused, I'll give you. But not a monster. Believe me. I've seen those enough to know."

"Yeah, right."

He cupped her cheek and turned her head to face him so that she could see his sincerity. "Look at me, Abby. I know what it's like to wake up every single day, angry at the world. Angry at God and humanity for what they've done to you and to want to make them pay for it. To feel like the entire world sees you as nothing but its whipping boy. Like you, my mother died when I was a little kid. She was the only thing good I had. The only one who'd ever made me feel like I was human. My father hated me, and he never hid that fact from anyone. He took his own anger at the world out on me, and it left a lot of scars, inside and out. To this day, I can still hear him and that hatred in my head, trying to poison my thoughts. Trying to poison me. I ran away from home after he almost killed me. Thirteen, I was. I tried to find decent work or someplace to stay and call home. What I found out was that people like to kick others when they're down, even when they're just kids. They get a sick thrill out of it. Makes them feel big and powerful while it destroys the heart and soul of their unfortunate victim."

He swallowed as some of his harshest lessons resurfaced and he saw the faces of those who'd wronged him. But this wasn't about him—it was about her.

"I learned human decency is probably the rarest creature out there. And I couldn't find anyone who didn't want to take advantage of me or hurt me even worse than my pa had. And it hardened me even more. By the time I was sixteen, that poison had rotted me from the inside out. It colored everything about me. I justified what I did to other people by reminding myself of how they'd treated me. They deserved whatever I did to them. Do unto others before they do unto you."

"You became a killer."

He nodded. "Until the day I killed a boy, thinking he was a man. He'd wanted to avenge his pa, and for the first time in my life, I saw someone else capable of love and sacrifice. Believe it or not, it was something I hadn't seen except from my mother. And as stupid as it sounds, I'd convinced myself that it was unique to her and that no one else had it in them. But after that, I saw the difference between love and loyalty. Most of all, I saw what I'd become. What my hatred had turned me into."

His dark gaze was filled with torment. "Don't talk to me about monsters. I was one of the worst."

A few days ago, she'd have agreed completely. Hell, a few hours ago, she'd have agreed. Now . . .

"You told me you never killed a woman or child."

"Just that one time, and I never got over it. One stupid mistake that has lived with me every day since. Bart told me I was an idiot to let it bother me. Better he give up the ghost than I be the one lying in a grave. But that boy didn't give up the ghost. Not really. It followed me from town to town, and no matter what I did, I couldn't escape it. Until the day a beautiful woman smiled at me. She didn't see the ugliness I kept inside. For the first time in my life, she saw the man I wanted to be, and she helped me to find him. Because of her, I learned that, yeah, people are selfish assholes for the most part, but not everyone is. That there are some rare beings out there who will help others and not abuse them. People who really don't want anything from you."

He stroked her cheek with his thumb. "Acheron always says that our scars are there to remind us of our pasts, of where we've been and what we've gone through. But that pain doesn't have to drive or determine our future. We can rise above it if we let ourselves. It's not easy, but nothing in life ever is."

Those words haunted her. Like he said, she'd allowed her past to color everything about her and to infect any part of happiness she might try to find. She'd worn her scars like a badge, and her family had used them against her. Not for her best interest.

For theirs.

His warm hand felt so good as he soothed her. "I don't see the monster in you, Abby. Monsters don't care about other people, and they don't care who they hurt. In you, I see a woman who is strong. One who knows what's right and who will do whatever she has to to protect the ones she loves."

"I killed your friends," she reminded him.

"And I'm not happy about that. But your head wasn't

screwed on right. It's easy to let the enemies in and listen to them sometimes, especially when they're pretending to be your best friends who only want the best for you. At least that's what they claim. They're insidious bastards, telling you what you want to hear and using your emotions to manipulate you into doing their bidding. I did it with Bart. I thought he was the only person in the world who gave a shit about me, and I would have protected him with my life."

That was how she'd felt about Kurt.

"Sooner or later, usually out of jealousy, their real colors come out and you see the truth that makes you feel like a fool. I know that betrayal, Abigail. That sting that's so deep inside, it leaves a permanent scar on your soul. But you don't have to be like them. And *you're* not."

She felt her tears start falling at his words. He made her feel so much better, and she wasn't sure she had a right to. Honestly. She'd hurt so many people. Destroyed lives.

Over a lie . . .

Before she realized what she was doing, she had her belt unhooked and crawled into his lap.

Jess slid the seat back so that he could hold her in the darkness. The scent of her hair filled his head as his heart thumped wildly. He held her close, wishing he could take away the pain.

Only time could do that.

And it sucked at it. "It'll be all right, Abigail."

"Yeah, after I sacrifice myself for my stupidity."

"I told you, I'm not going to let that happen."

Abigail wanted to believe him. She did. But she knew better. "There's nothing to be done. It is what it is."

He scoffed at that. "You're talking to a man who sold his soul to a goddess to get revenge on the man who killed him. Really? You think *this* is impossible?"

She smiled against his chest. The way he said that, she could almost believe in a miracle. For the first time, she wanted to. She buried her face against his shoulder, inhaling his scent. Why was it that here, she finally felt safe? Even though there were enemies all around and a vicious mountain lion waiting outside to devour them, she felt safe. It defied all logic and sense.

Jess kissed the top of her head while his own emotions flared deep. He'd forgotten what it was like to look into a woman's eyes and see a future he craved. To be this close to one and to share things about his past that he told to no one.

Not even Matilda had known what he told to Abigail tonight. While he'd loved her, he'd always lived with the fear that she'd find out about his past and be horrified by it. That she'd cast him aside as everyone else had and hate him for the very things he'd done to survive.

But Abigail knew his ugliness.

She felt his scars.

It made him feel all the closer to her. Appreciate her more for not judging him. At least not now. She understood how easy it was to get sucked into a nightmare and how hard it was to get out. To do things you thought were justified and then wake up and realize you'd been duped. Lied to.

Used.

He'd woken up as a Dark-Hunter only to feel like a whore. Like he'd sold his life away for pocket change. And for what? To die alone in the gutter at the hands of his best friend.

He could hide his past from everyone, except himself. That was the hardest part. Even when you tried, forgiveness didn't come easy.

Some days it didn't come at all.

Maybe it would be kinder to let her die so that she wouldn't have to face that agony.

Life ain't supposed to be kind.

True. And God knew, it'd been nothing but a kick in his groin most days. But then there were moments like this one. Perfect moments of feeling close to someone. Of letting their warmth soothe you.

That was what living was about. That was being human. When everything hurt and everything was wrong, to have that one person who could make you smile even when all you wanted to do was cry.

These were the moments that got you through the bad.

Abigail looked up at him. He stared into those clear eyes as her breath tickled his skin.

And in that heartbeat, he knew he would die to protect her.

God help me.

The last time he felt this way, he had died. Leaning his head down, he pressed his forehead against hers and tried to see the future.

If there was one after all of this.

But he knew the truth. He was a Dark-Hunter, and she was . . .

Unique. There was nothing in the Dark-Hunter handbook about this situation.

He looked outside the car wash to see the wasps still swarming as they tried to find a way in. He didn't know how long this wave would last. How much time they had for anything.

Abigail cupped his head with her hand as her thoughts warred with each other. In spite of what Jess said, she couldn't see anyway out of this.

Except for death.

She'd really screwed up this time. In a life marked by mistakes, this had been the mother lode. And she'd dragged a good man into the nightmare with her.

Emotions ripped through her so fast, she couldn't even sort them out. She wanted to feel grounded again. To feel like she had a future.

But the only thing that kept her anchored was Jess.

Her heart swelling, she pulled his lips to hers and kissed

him. This was probably the last night of her life. She'd be lucky if any of them were alive by dawn.

And all because she'd been an idiot.

She owed him a debt more than she could pay for standing by her and saving her life. But it wasn't just obligation she felt for him. There was something so much more. Deeper.

She felt like she was a part of him. And she didn't want to die without letting him know.

Rising up in the seat, she straddled his hips.

Jess frowned as he looked up into Abigail's eyes. There was a hungry fire there he'd never seen before. And as she started unbuttoning her shirt, his breath caught. "Um . . . Abigail—"

She stopped his words by pressing her forefinger to his lips. Then she slid it slowly down his chest, heading south until she reached his fly.

"I know we don't have long, Jess. But this may be the only time we'll ever have. And I don't want to die without making amends to you."

"You don't have to do *this*."

She smiled. "I know. I want to do this."

And all his arguments and thoughts scattered as she slid her hand into his jeans and touched him. Oh yeah, he was lost now.

He knew that after this, he would never be the same again.

12

Abigail had never done anything like this a day in her life. She'd never even fantasized about it. But as they waited here, so close to death and with her mortality breathing down her neck, she couldn't help herself.

Jess didn't love her—she knew that. But it didn't matter. She'd seen inside his heart to the man he'd been and to the one he currently was. And the woman in her wanted to touch that part of him and share it. Once she was gone from this earth, he'd remember her.

For eternity.

She wanted him to remember her as someone who'd been decent and caring. Not the soulless monster she currently felt like.

Please see the real me.

Just once.

No one ever had. She'd always been so strong around Hannah and Kurt. Never let them see her fears. She'd strived to be a perfect sister and to help them with whatever problem they had, no matter what was going on in her own life, no matter how badly she ached inside.

They had come first.

And of course, to be a dutiful daughter to her adoptive parents, she'd learned to bury herself and her emotions and let no one ever see them. Her one fear had always been that they would regret taking a human into their home and turn her out into the streets if she caused them any problem whatsoever.

Most Apollites tried to hide their distaste about her unfortunate human birth, but she saw through the hollow smiles and false offers of friendship, especially her adoptive father's. Like the others, he'd tried to hide it. But he couldn't.

The truth had been forever etched in his eyes, and it had cut her to her soul.

They weren't her people, and they never forgot that fact. No matter how hard she'd tried to fit in and convince them that she was on their side. That she would fight to the death for them. No matter how many Hunters she pursued for them. There was still a wall they kept in place that she wasn't allowed to climb.

You're a human, and that's all you'll ever be to them.

But she'd always wanted to be more. In spite of it all, she'd loved them like the family they were to her. She'd always wanted to be accepted by them. To not feel like that needy child staring through a window at a world that would never welcome her in. That isolation had always stung and hurt.

Until now. Now, for the first time, all that desolate pain was gone.

Sundown made her feel like she belonged. Like she was wanted. It was as if he'd opened the door and finally said that it was okay for her to come inside. That he didn't mind being with her.

That she was welcome here.

For that, she would sell her soul.

Jess lifted his hand to cup her face. Smiling at him, she kissed his palm before she nuzzled the calluses there. His skin was so much tougher than hers. So manly. But that was what she loved about it. She leaned forward to nip at his whiskered chin while she stroked his cock. He was so hard and yet velvety soft.

He watched her from beneath lashes so thick, they should be illegal. "Be a hell of a time for a bee sting, wouldn't it?" he whispered against her lips.

She laughed. "You're so not right."

He kissed the tip of her nose. "Yeah, well, you're pretty damn perfect from where I'm sitting."

Those words made her heart soar. No one had ever said anything kinder to her. Closing her eyes, she leaned into him and held him tight. Why couldn't they have met under different circumstances? He was someone she could have loved. Had he not been a Dark-Hunter. Had her parents not been murdered.

Now . . .

There was nothing for them. If they survived, they couldn't stay together. No hope for any kind of future. This was all they'd ever have.

And she wanted to hold on to this moment forever. To pretend that they weren't who they were. Just two normal people who meant something to each other, who'd met by mere happenstance.

"Why are you so sad?"

She swallowed at his question. "I'm not sad, Jess. I'm scared."

"I won't hurt you."

And that made her ache all the more as guilt stabbed

her hard. Before she knew the truth, she would have hurt him in an instant. "I know."

He captured her lips as he slid his hand beneath her bra. His fingers teased her skin, sending chills the length of her body. It had been so long since she'd been with any man. Her training had always taken precedence, leaving her very little time to focus on something she'd always considered trivial. Relationships had seemed wasted. You never got as much out as you put in. It was a recipe for disaster and heartbreak, and she'd never wanted to waste her time with it.

Jess would have been worth the effort, though. The way he'd cherished Matilda . . .

That was what it was all about. Putting someone above you. Loving them with everything you had. Living for the sole reason of seeing them happy even if it meant you suffering for their well-being.

It was so rare that she'd never once allowed herself to contemplate the fact that it might be real. She'd relegated it to the realm of unicorns and fairies. A nice story to hear, but a total pipe dream.

Why couldn't she have been worth a love like his?

Had Matilda really appreciated what she'd been given?

I hope so. It made the tragedy of their doomed love seem less severe.

Jess cradled Abigail against him. She was shivering, and he wasn't sure why. Yeah, he could read her mind and find out, but he didn't like doing that to people. It was downright rude. And something he reserved for necessary times only.

This wasn't one of those.

A woman's mind was her own. Matilda had taught him that. It was something to be respected, as was her will. Still, it pained him to have her hurting while she was making love to him. It didn't seem right.

"Is there anything I can do for you?"

The look on her face gut-punched him as she traced the line of his lips with her fingertip. It sent chills over him, but not nearly as many as the adoring look in her eyes as she stared at him. "You're already doing it."

"Well, I got a fear here that I ain't doing it right, and I don't want this to be wrong."

She smiled then. A real one that reached all the way to her eyes and warmed him to his toes. Licking her lips, she lifted herself up so that he could undo her pants. "I promise you, it's all good."

Maybe, but wrangling her pants off her was another matter entirely. She actually elbowed him in the eye as he tried to maneuver.

She gasped in horror at what she'd done as she cupped her hands around her mouth. "Oh my God, are you okay?"

He rubbed at his eye and considered knifing his Squire when he got home. "Andy needs a bigger car." Damn it. Why did pain have to intrude right now?

She laughed again. "You poor baby." She leaned forward to kiss his eye, and that drove away most of the pain.

When she leaned into the passenger seat and pulled her pants off, it took the rest of it. She had long, shapely legs that begged for a tongue bath. Another thing he couldn't do in this infernally small car.

I'm torching this thing when I get it home. . . .

She hesitated at the waistband of her black panties. It was sheer torture for him.

"You changing your mind?" *Please, don't change your mind.* That'd be downright cruel, and he wasn't sure he could survive it. Not after they'd come this far.

Shaking her head, she slid them down her legs slowly. Seductively.

Dayam . . .

He thought he was going to die as he saw her naked. She was exquisite. And he was so hard now, he felt like he was about to explode. Before he could catch another thought, she was back in his seat, straddling him again as if she was as eager for him as he was for her.

Ah yeah . . . he could die right now without regret. This was what he'd been craving.

She raised up on her knees and pulled at his shirt.

Gladly, Jess let her strip him. He was as desperate to feel her skin on his as she was. Never in his life had he seen anything hotter or felt anything sexier than her breasts pressing against his bare flesh. He ran his hands through her hair, inhaling the scent of it as it stirred around them.

While he was far from celibate, he'd never been with a woman before who knew him. As a human, because of Bart, he'd been branded an outlaw at age thirteen. So by the time he was with a woman, he'd known better than to let her know his real identity. Or anything about him that she could tell or sell to someone out to put a bullet in him.

Then after he'd become a Dark-Hunter, he'd been expressly forbidden from telling anyone about their existence. He'd had to hide his fangs, his age.

Everything.

Only Abigail knew the truth about him. And it made this moment all the hotter. There was no fear of slipping up by letting her tongue brush against his fangs. Or having to be careful when he nibbled her since she might notice his longer teeth.

For once he could be himself, and that was the most incredible feeling of all.

He ran his tongue over her breast, savoring the ridges in her hardened nipple. Her skin smelled like the sweetest nectar imaginable. And the sensation of her hands in his hair . . .

If he died tonight, it'd be worth it.

She would be worth it.

All of a sudden, she let out a soft giggle. The uncharacteristic sound surprised him. "What are you laughing at?"

Her face turned bright red. "It's too cheesy to even mention."

Yeah, there was something a man didn't want to hear in this situation. *What did I do?* "Now, hon, you can't leave me hanging like that. I have to know."

Please don't be laughing at me.

She bit her lip. The expression was so playful and adorable that it made his stomach flutter. "I was thinking of the phrase, save a horse, ride a cowboy."

He laughed. "Well, baby, you can ride me any time you get the urge." He feigned deadly earnest. "I'm here *for* you."

She wrinkled her nose as she leaned him back in the seat. Damn if she wasn't the most beautiful thing he'd ever seen.

He slid his hand up her thigh until he found what he was seeking. She was warm and wet and she let out a deep moan as he lightly fingered her.

Abigail couldn't breathe as Jess slid his fingers deep into her body. Oh yeah, that was what she'd been desperate for. And it set her entire body on fire. Kissing his lips, she rose up and allowed him to guide her down onto him.

She sucked her breath in sharply at the sensation of him hard and full inside her.

This . . . this was heaven.

Her heart pounding, she rode him slow and gentle, savoring every inch of him. She laved his neck as she ran her hands over his muscled chest. He had a number of scars marring his flesh. Most looked like knife wounds or from barb wire. But a few were obvious bullet wounds.

Anger whipped through her that anyone would hurt him like that.

Until she remembered that she would have killed him, too.

Thank God, I didn't. And she was grateful to whatever power had brought them together. Most importantly to the one that had kept her from hurting him.

Not even the sight of the double bow and arrow mark of a Dark-Hunter on his arm could detract from this moment. Even it looked like it had hurt when he received it.

She'd never thought about that before. Dark-Hunters had their souls stripped from them. How much agony did Artemis put them through when she took it?

Abigail knew from her own experience, when her own soul had withered and died the night she lost her parents, how bad it hurt to lose one. Her scar had never healed.

Neither had his . . .

Jess let her take control of their pleasure as he ran the back of his hand across her breast. He enjoyed watching her love him, watching the light in her eyes that touched a part of him he liked to pretend didn't exist. It made him remember long forgotten things that he'd buried deep inside.

As a human, all he'd ever really wanted was a calm,

peaceful home with a good woman by his side. Someone he could grow old with, who would make him laugh and give him a reason to look forward to the next day.

And the ones thereafter.

A woman like Abigail.

She was a little more challenging than what he'd had in mind. But sometimes, cravings left out important, if not irritating, details. He actually liked her stubbornness. Most of all, her spirit.

More than that, there was a spark inside her. A fire that warmed him through and through.

Abigail smiled as Jess took her hand and led it to his lips so that he could kiss and nibble her knuckles. It was so sweet. Until he nipped her flesh with his fangs. Not too hard, but enough to send a quick rush through her.

There was nothing sexier than her cowboy. Nothing hotter than feeling him inside and outside her body while he held her close and loved her.

It was the headiest of mixtures. One so hot that it sent her straight over the edge. Throwing her head back, she felt her body release. She lost herself to that one moment of sheer perfection.

Jess smiled as he saw and felt her climax on top of him. Her body clutched his, heightening his own pleasure. He lifted his hips, driving himself in even deeper while taking care not to bump her head against the low-hanging roof.

She cried out in ecstasy.

And he quickly joined her there. His head reeled as wave after wave of pleasure rolled through him. Yeah, he needed this a lot more than he'd thought. For the first time in weeks, his head was clear and his body calm.

Right now, he was the happiest man on the planet. *That's right, all you badass punks. Bring it.*

'Cause right now, he felt like he could take on anything or anyone. And he was more than ready to.

Abigail lay flat against Jess's bare chest, listening to his heart pounding under her ear. A fine sheet of sweat covered them both as she slowly came to her senses.

I'm sitting naked in a car wash surrounded by angry wasps trying to kill us . . . with a man I've only known about forty hours.

Yeah, this was one for the books. And she definitely deserved the I-Have-No-Shame and What-the-Hell-Was-I-Thinking Award.

I can't believe I just did this.

But then, she'd have it no other way. She really didn't regret it. *And at least I don't have to worry about getting pregnant or diseased.* The one good thing about a Dark-Hunter was that they couldn't have children or carry any kind of STD or other illness.

Still, it was embarrassing. Anyone could walk in on them. Any minute. *I would die if anyone did.*

Jess kissed the top of her head. "We're all right, Abs. I have the doors sealed, and no one's coming."

That went over her like an ice water plunge. Her entire body locked up in horror.

"You heard that?"

"Um, yeah," he answered without reservation.

She shot up to stare at him as a new terror went through her. No . . . she better be wrong.

Surely . . .

"You can hear my thoughts?"

Now his gaze turned panicked. He glanced around as if trying to access some cosmic database in his head that would funnel a correct answer to him and get him out of this. "Uh . . ."

Good answer . . .

Not. His inner computer must be on the fritz, and her fury was mounting by the heartbeat. She could absolutely kill him! This was awful. Horrible!

Why didn't he tell me?

Abigail curled her lip. Yeah, okay, she vaguely remembered seeing that ability in one of those weird psychotic flashbacks of his past, but it hadn't sunk in and stayed with her.

Now it did.

"Oh my God, you can hear my thoughts!" She was thoroughly humiliated. Anger whipped through her as she returned to her seat and snatched for her underwear. *Oh, don't even get me started on the indignity of this. . . .* She wanted to crawl under the seat and die. *I should throw myself outside and let the wasps have me.*

Oh wait, he can hear me. He's probably listening in right now like some psychic pervert, getting his jollies off my embarrassment.

You suck, Sundown. You. Suck.

That she hoped he could hear.

She glared at him. "Why didn't you tell me you could do that?"

He held his hands up in surrender. "It's all right, Abby." His tone was soothing, but his eyes still showed panic.

And she wasn't ready to listen to any form of reason. She was too humiliated. Gah, if he'd heard everything she'd thought . . .

She couldn't stand it. "It's not all right. How dare you not tell me about this. What kind of sicko are you? I can't believe you'd do that. It's so intrusive and . . . and . . ." She couldn't think of a word bad enough to convey how very bad it was, and she was too angry to have full access to her vocabulary, anyway. "Have you been spying on me the whole time?"

Jess silently cursed as she continued to rant at him and snatch her clothes on. Damn, the woman was hotheaded. Not that he fully blamed her for it. He'd be pissed, too, if someone was traipsing in his mind.

Still . . .

"Abby, listen to me. I can hear thoughts—"

"Little late now, bucko." The last word was said with

such snapping venom, it oddly reminded him of a chicken clucking. She snatched her head up to pierce him with a look that really should have splintered him into pieces. Damn, someone should bottle that. It'd make entire armies drop arms. "I noticed. Thanks for volunteering *that*. Let me give you a Hero Award for your first confession. Big flippin' hairy doo dah . . ." Then she added an extremely sarcastic, "Woo. Hoo."

"But," he continued in what he hoped was a calming tone while he ignored her outburst and go-to-hell-and-roast-your-nuts glare. Now, that was what he deserved a Hero Award for. Took guts to face a woman this angry. "I don't. Not normally. Just every now and again, something comes through and pops into my head like your question. I don't know how it got past my defenses. Maybe 'cause I was in my zone and not thinking of anything other than how good you felt."

She covered herself with her jeans. "Like I believe that. How stupid do you think I am?"

"I don't think you're stupid at all." *He* was the rank idiot who'd opened his mouth when he should have kept it closed. His mama had always said 90% of intelligence was knowing when to shut up.

Other 10% was knowing when to nut up—which he was trying to do, but it wasn't easy.

She finally paused and locked gazes with him. That look paralyzed him because he knew if he so much as blinked wrong, it would set her off again, and that was the last thing he wanted.

Don't smile. Don't sweat. Don't do nothing.

Don't even breathe.

It was like watching a salivating bear you knew would either lumber past and go on its way . . .

Or rip your arm off and beat you with it.

"How do I know you're not in my head right now?"

He ran various answers through his mind. *'Cause I said so.* Nah, that'd get him bitch-slapped for sure. *I wouldn't dare.* Made him sound like a coward.

Think, Jess, think.

Finally he opted for the simple truth. "It's rude, and I wouldn't want anyone to do it to me, so I try hard not to do it to others. Honestly, it ain't my favorite power. You have no idea how sick people are, and I really don't want to know most days. The world can have their thoughts. I got enough of my own to deal with."

Abigail hesitated as she considered his words. For reasons that made no sense whatsoever, she believed him. Not to mention, what he said made a lot of sense. She wouldn't want to look into other people's minds and find out their psychoses and insecurities either.

And he hadn't said or done anything previously that led her to believe he had that ability. Her only clue had been that one snippet with him and the lawyer.

He'd been stressed then, too.

Okay, I'm going to trust him. But if she ever found him near her thoughts again without her permission . . . It definitely wouldn't pay to be in his boots.

"Don't do it again," she warned.

"Trust me, I won't. At least not on purpose. Like I said, I can't always control it, but I do most of the time, and I will definitely be more on guard around you, especially any time you're going near the more tender parts of my body."

She didn't want to be amused by that last bit at all. Unfortunately, she was.

Even so, it didn't mean she had to let him know it.

Forcing herself to stay stern, she nodded. "Good. Now what other evil powers do you have that I should know about?"

"I can roll my tongue," he said proudly.

Gah, he was such a goofball sometimes. Hard to believe a man with such a fierce, lethal reputation who'd been wanted and hunted voraciously by every branch of law enforcement in the Old West, could be so irreverent and playful. She wondered what those enemies would have thought of him had they ever seen this side of his personality. They certainly wouldn't have been so scared of him.

Which made her wonder if he'd been like this as a human. Or had he developed his humor as a Dark-Hunter?

In the grand scheme, it didn't matter. Right now, she

needed to know who and what, exactly, she was dealing with. "I'm serious, Jess."

"So am I. Not everyone can do it. It's a genetic thing, you know."

Abigail let out a tired sigh as she fought down the need to choke him.

He gave her a teasing grin, then finally took mercy on her and answered the question. "I have some telekinesis, which you already discovered. Premonitions. Can see auras and . . . I make a killer omelette."

That was an impressive list—including the omelette tidbit. But what made her sick to her stomach was that she'd stupidly gone up against him without knowing any of that.

Thanks, Jonah, for the extensive research you didn't do. It was a wonder Jess hadn't killed her.

Maybe that had been Jonah's intent all along. *"Believe me, Abigail. I've found every bit of detail on Sundown that's ever been documented or thought. There's nothing about him I don't know. We have all we need and then some to kill him."*

A clue about his powers would have been a nice addition to their arsenal.

Jess leaned forward and kissed her bare shoulder. "Am I forgiven yet?"

Dragging a slow gaze down his lush body, she hesitated. One because she basically lost her train of thought to how much she'd like to take another bite out of him. No man should be so sexy. Even naked, he exuded such power and confidence that it raised a chill on her skin. And two, she did have to think about the possibility of forgiving him. She still wasn't sure she should.

But really, what choice did she have? Could she really hold mind-reading against him when it was something he hadn't asked for?

She made him wait a few seconds more before she answered. "Fine. But only because you look good naked."

His grin turned evil. "I'll take that."

"Good. Now, let's get dressed before we do get discovered by some nosy clerk."

He tsked as he pulled his pants up and fastened them. "Remind me to kill Coyote for rushing this when I'd rather lay naked with you than fight wasps and coyotes and all the other crap he's throwing at us."

"Don't worry. I think we have many reasons to kill him." Abigail finished buttoning her shirt, then looked outside. The wasps were still everywhere. It was a sickening sight, and she was getting tired of listening to them buzz. "What are we going to do about our friends out there?"

Jess had no idea. But before he could respond, his phone rang. He fished it out of his pocket and answered it.

"Where are you?"

He arched a brow at Ren's angry tone. "We got trapped by the wasps. Where are *you*?"

"At your house with Choo Co La Tah. He was trying to chant the wasps into submission when something happened."

That can't be good. Dread ripped through Jess. They couldn't afford to lose him at this point. He was the only guide they had who actually had a clue about what was going on and how to correct it. The only other Guardian around was Snake . . . and he was on Coyote's side.

"What happened?" he asked Ren.

"I don't know. He's in some form of coma. I've never seen anything like this."

Jess winced. If Ren was panicked over this, then there was a good reason to be panicked over it. The man had ice water for blood and wasn't prone to any form of overreaction.

"Can we wake him out of it?"

Ren lost his patience. "Well, you know, cowboy, that's a really good idea. Damn shame *I* didn't think of it, huh?"

"Cut the sarcasm. Are you're sure it's not a vision quest?"

"For the sake of our long-term friendship, I'm not even going to dignify that with the response it deserves."

Because it, too, was a stupid question. Jess had known that before he asked it.

Still . . .

He ran his hand over his face as he tried to think of some kind of plan or action to save Choo Co La Tah and get rid of their current pest problem. "We need someone else who can control the weather. You know anyone?"

"I do." Jess heard Sasha in the background. "Give me a few, and I'll be back with help."

Ren said something muffled to Sasha, then uncovered the receiver so that Jess could hear again. "I have to say, Sister Fortune has ridden out of town on us, and I don't like it."

"Gotta say, I don't blame you. I'm not exactly sending roses to her either." He let out an aggravated breath. "So do we have any intel or insight as to what we need to do for Choo Co La Tah and to stop Coyote?"

"Not really. I don't know what else Coyote will come up with. He's unpredictable at best. A bastard at worst. And when cornered, he's lethal beyond measure and will do whatever he must to win. His heart lives in a place best left untrodden. All I know is we have to get to the Valley by sunrise."

"I know."

"No, Jess. You don't. We have to beat Coyote to Old Bear's magic. If we do, we might be able to keep him from unlocking the next set of plagues."

That would be good. But it wouldn't be easy. "What exactly is his magic? Other than the Grizzly?"

Ren sighed. "You should have listened more to your mother's stories, boy. Your lack of education offends me."

He glanced over to Abigail, who watched him with a

penetrating stare that said she was dying to know what they were talking about. He was grateful she didn't inter-rupt them. That was something he'd always found rude and extremely annoying.

Jess returned his attention to Ren. "My mother didn't talk that much about her beliefs or tell me many stories." She'd been too sick for too long. For the last three years of her life, every breath had been a precious struggle for her. So she'd conserved them for living and not for talk-ing. "And when she did, it was in a hushed tone." Because she'd been terrified of anyone hurting him over their heritage.

Better to blend in than stand out, penyo. *The one who flies against the flock is always flying into opposition. No matter how strong the beast, sooner or later, he tires from his ragged journey.*

And when he falls, he falls alone.

His mother's words were still with him.

Even so, he'd never been one to conform. But all that had done was prove to him how wise and right his mother had been. In the end, he had died alone and he was tired.

Then and now.

He cleared his throat. "So you'll have to forgive me my ignorance."

"A wise man never argues a mother's decision for her child. Not unless he wants to face her claw, and there is nothing sharper than a mother defending her young."

Jess definitely concurred with that.

"You probably want to put me on speaker so that Abigail can hear it, too."

"All right." Jess pulled the phone back to comply. "We're here."

Abigail frowned.

"At the beginning of time when the Code of Order was being established, the First Guardian locked away all the evil he'd found in the world. Things that had been created by the Dark One for no other purpose than to plague man and hurt him. The First Guardian knew that mankind wasn't strong enough to fight it. So he banished it all to the West Lands where the sun lay down on that evil every night and kept it weak."

Ren paused. "But Evil is always resilient and ever resourceful. In time, it bred with Father Sun, and a tiny piece escaped to find an embittered warrior whose heart was blackened by jealousy over his own brother. He took the evil into him and was seduced by its promise that if he hurt others enough, their pain would make him stronger and drive his pain away. It succored him like a lover, and he embraced its insanity with everything he had. And so he went on a killing rage, and he consumed the lands until he ruled all from his bloodied fists."

"The Grizzly Spirit," Jess said quietly. He knew this legend from Choo Co La Tah.

Ren continued. "His war brought him to the realm of

the Guardian, and the two of them fought for a year and a day—a battle so violent, it left a permanent scar on Mother Earth."

The Grand Canyon. It was said the red color came from the blood of the wounds they'd given to each other while they fought.

"Finally, the warrior made a mistake and the Guardian was able to pin him down. He stripped the evil from the warrior, but it was too late. They had sweated and bled so much over that year on the earth that the very fabric of Mother Earth's gown, the granules of sand that carry man on his life's journey, was saturated with it and forever stained by it. There was no way to take all the evil back or to make her gown white again. The damage was done."

"What did he do?"

Jess smiled at the way Abigail was completely absorbed by the tale.

"The Guardian realized his mistake. There was no way to keep evil locked away forever. It's as pure an essence as good, and like good, it can't be denied or held back. And as Night and Day divide the sky between them, so must good and evil divide the world. Only then can there be balance and harmony for humans. Only then can there be any semblance of peace. So the Guardian banished the Grizzly Spirit that had infected the warrior and locked it behind the West Land Gate so that it could rage without harming man. He then took from Mother Earth eight jars to hold the plagues that had helped the Dark One escape and sealed them with his tears so that they could never again be used by the Grizzly. Those jars, he turned over to four Guardian protectors. North. South. East. West. The strongest corners of the earth who could be called on to defend should the West Gate ever be opened. Two of those Guardians were ruled by the Dark and two ruled by the Light. Perfect balance."

"How did he choose them?" Abigail asked.

"All but the East Guardian went through a trial created by the First Guardian to see who was the worthiest. The top three were the chosen ones."

"And the one from the East?"

"He was the warrior who'd been owned by the Grizzly Spirit. The First Guardian thought that if anyone would understand why they had to protect the West Gate, he would be the one. And that he would stand strongest against all threats to keep it from happening again. Not to mention, given their fight, he knew the warrior would be a worthy opponent for anyone who dared to breach his gate."

"That makes sense."

"Once they were given their jars, the First Guardian warned them of how serious their duties were and that they should never waver or falter. They were to stand together and to keep each other in line. Then he retired into the West Land so that he could rest after his battle. They say he still slumbers there even today."

"And the Guardians?"

Ren let out a light laugh. "Each took his jars deep into the sacred land where the Fire touches the Earth and hid them so that no one would be able to use the plagues against them or man."

Jess sighed as it all started coming together. "Coyote released his jars already." The scorpions and the wasps.

"Yes. Coyote has been trying for centuries to find the key to unlock the Gate and free the Grizzly Spirit. He knew as long as Old Bear and Choo Co La Tah were joined, there was no way for him to overpower either of them and open the Gate. Now that one has fallen, he and Snake can join together."

"And screw us royally," Jess said under his breath.

"You've no idea, my brother."

"But why?" Abigail asked. "Why would Snake join him?"

"Snake by nature is, and has always been, a follower. And he's served the Dark One too long. It was something the First Guardian feared the moment he assigned the two Dark Guardians their posts. He knew how insidious the Dark would be and how corruptible even the most noble of heart is. He'd hoped that the East Guardian would watch after and counsel Snake away from the darker side of his personality. But just in case the East Guardian failed, it was why he put a finite limit on the service of the Guardians. Next year, during the Time Untime when our calendar resets, the feathered rattlesnake will bear his color, and on the night when the evening star comes first, new Guardians are to be chosen by the one who holds the key. Old Bear. With him dead, that choice moves to Choo Co La Tah. If Coyote and Snake can kill him, they can choose the new Guardians."

Abigail frowned. "Why is that important?"

Jess answered before Ren had a chance. "Whoever assigns the Guardians, controls them and most importantly, controls the West Land."

"Ultimate power," Ren said. "Your every wish granted. You own the entire world."

Who wouldn't want that?

Well, okay, Jess didn't. He had enough trouble managing his own life. Last thing he wanted was to be responsible for everyone else.

Unfortunately for all the world, Coyote didn't feel the same way.

"Snake is now a loyal servant to Coyote and has been for a long time," Ren continued. "The only thing that kept them at bay was the Light Guardians."

Abigail winced.

And Jess didn't miss the heavy dread in Ren's tone. "What haven't you told us?"

"One of Old Bear's jars contains the Wind Seer which

is the one plague that can open the West Gate and free the Grizzly Spirit."

Crap. Crap. Crap. Jess flinched at the very thought.

Abigail drew her brow together in confusion. "I don't understand. If the First Guardian is there, can't he stop the Grizzly Spirit from escaping again?"

"It's not that easy, Abigail. No one has heard from him in countless centuries. For all we know, the Grizzly might have killed him when he went behind the Gate or he could have possessed him. You have no idea what the Grizzly is capable of. Trust me. We have to stop them from opening that jar. If the Grizzly gets out again—"

"It'll be a fun time in Disneyland," Jess mumbled. "Y'all think we could arm Mickey? He might be badass with a gun."

Abigail slapped him lightly on the arm. "What do we have to do, Ren?"

"Get his jars before they do."

It amazed Jess that Ren could make the impossible sound easy. Too bad reality didn't go that way. "Does Coyote know where it is?"

"I don't think so. But then, neither do we. Choo Co La Tah should be able to track it . . . if we can get *him* to wake up. However, the one who spilled Guardian blood has to make an offering on the sacred ground to appease the ancient elements before sunrise. Otherwise all of the jars will open . . . at once . . . which would then also blow open the Gate and all that concentrated evil would pour out of it."

Oh yeah, that would seriously suck. "Did they launch that last space shuttle yet?"

"I don't follow," Ren said.

"I'm just thinking maybe we should evacuate the whole planet. I've heard the moon is kind of nice this time of year."

Both Abigail and Ren let out mutual sounds of aggravation.

"Focus your ADD, Jess."

He rolled his eyes at Ren's quip. "I gotcha, brother. What you're forecasting is six more plagues coming out of the northwest at maximum velocity with a mild chance of survival. Followed by the world getting swallowed whole into a vat of evil."

"Well, yeah. That's exactly what I'm saying."

"Nice to know I didn't misunderstand and all." He purposefully exaggerated his drawl on that. "Ah, hell, y'all lucky I can follow anything, especially given how many times I got kicked in the head when I's a kid." Sobering, Jess let out an irritated breath.

Instead of Renegade, his name should be Mary Sunshine. "I'll get Abigail to you as soon as I can."

"I'll keep working on Choo Co La Tah. You be careful."

"Same to you. Let me know if anything changes. I could really use some good news right about now." Jess hung up and turned to face Abigail. Unfortunately, she had her clothes buttoned up all the way to her neck.

Damn.

She let out an exaggerated breath. "I don't want to know about Choo Co La Tah, do I?"

"Not really. Kind of wish I didn't know." Jess toyed with the keys that dangled from the ignition while he watched the wasps continue to swarm outside. He didn't like the idea of being trapped, and he wasn't keen on the idea of being beholden to Sasha for anything.

"Ah, screw this. I'm not going to wait for rescue like a puppy on a float. Buckle up. We're going for it."

Abigail wasn't sure she liked the sound of that. But what choice did she have? Jess was in the driver's seat.

Besides, she was with him on this. No need in waiting around when they could at least be trying to get home.

She snapped the belt over her lap and braced herself. "All right, cowboy. Let's do it."

Jess put the car in gear, then opened the garage door with his powers. The wasps immediately swarmed inside. Something that didn't faze Jess at all. She admired that.

He gripped the wheel, then tore out of the garage as fast as he could. The lights were dimmed by the number of wasps gathering around them.

But that wasn't the worst part.

She cringed at what awaited them on the street. Everything had gotten worse. There was no movement from any-one, anywhere. Businesses and homes had their windows drawn shut, and most were dark—as if afraid that the light might attract more wasps.

It terrified her.

But at least there was no sign of the mountain lion. He appeared to have moved on.

Needing to understand what was going on in the world around them, she turned the car radio on and scanned the channels until she found the local news.

The reporter's voice was thick with concern, and it made her own throat tighten. "There's no explanation for this rash of insect uprisings or these unprecedented weather fronts that keep moving in. The authorities are advising everyone to stay calm and in their homes until the experts have figured out what's causing it. As of now, several roads and highways are being closed, and everyone is be-ing told to watch out for flash flooding. They also want us to remind everyone that wasps can and do sting even after death, so please don't pick up any of their remains without gloves or some other form of protection. Officials are ad-vising everyone to turn off any light that might attract more wasps. And if you have pets in your yard, please do not venture out to get them."

Flash flooding? The dark sky above them was com-pletely clear.

She turned the radio off. That hadn't been very helpful.

"Guess they can't report that it's the end of the world, huh?"

"It's not the end."

She stared at the wrecked cars and bodies they passed. The people who'd posted handmade signs in the windows of their homes asking for God's forgiveness and warning others to repent. "It sure looks like it from my seat."

"Ah, now," Jess said in that exaggerated drawl she was beginning to recognize as his way of keeping things either in perspective or light. "Buck up, little camper. It ain't over yet. We're far from out of this."

That was the problem. They had a long way to go, and she didn't see an escape for them.

Jess kept his attention on the road as he navigated hazards every inch of the way. He was trying to be positive for her, but inside, he was worried fierce. Why had Old Bear been holding the key to the West Gate? Why take the chance? It should have been cast out to sea or something.

For that matter, couldn't the First Guardian have locked up butterflies or something equally harmless in those jars?

No. People had to have their misery, and Old Bear would have to have the pimp daddy of plagues waiting for discovery.

Give me locusts and boils. Hell, he'd even prefer pimples on his private parts. Anything would be better than Coyote taking over the world.

At this point, they were mired so deep in the mud of Shit City, he might as well have his mail forwarded.

I swear, Coyote. If I live through this . . .

You won't.

13

Jess let out a relieved breath as he pulled into his driveway while rain pelted the car so hard, it sounded like a sledgehammer pounding on metal and glass. Man, what a night. He was exhausted already, and it wasn't even late yet.

Of course, another round with Abigail and he'd definitely perk up.

Don't go there.

Please, go there. . . .

'Cause honestly, he'd much rather think about her naked in his arms than think about doing what they were going to have to do and then walking away and never seeing her again.

I thought the good guy was supposed to get the girl. That was the theory, anyway. Too bad he had enough life experience to know that it definitely wasn't the case.

Nice guys got shot by their best friend.

He shook his head to clear it of *that* nightmare and turned his attention where it needed to go.

Their friendly neighborhood plague.

At least it was raining heavy enough to drive the wasps back into submission and disperse them. Especially since Talon had added a little god power to it to shock and numb them.

Things were almost back to normal.

Yeah, right. Things were about as normal as a Luddite working for Bill Gates. But then, wishful thinking was about all he had left right now. That and the fierce desire to find Coyote and beat the ever-loving shit out of him.

He parked in the garage and looked over at Abigail. Her features were pinched by dread and determination, and still she was the most beautiful woman he'd ever seen. What he wouldn't give to be able to crawl into bed with her for a week and not come up for air until they both were near dead from lack of food.

Yeah, she'd be worth starvation.

And as he met her gaze, regret slammed hard into his gut. How he wished they'd had more time tonight. More time to explore and taste her.

More time to just . . .

He forced his thoughts away from that train wreck. What good were druthers, anyway? They just made you ache for things you couldn't have. And the one thing his childhood had taught him was not to dwell on what-ifs.

What was it Nietzsche had said? Hope was the worst of all evils, for it prolonged the torment of man?

Props to the philosopher. The man was definitely right in this case. Hoping for something better wouldn't make it manifest. It would only remind him of decisions he'd made that he couldn't undo.

He had a job to do, and it wasn't just to protect her. He had to save the rest of the world, too.

Steeling his own determination, he inclined his head to Abigail. "You ready for the next part?"

Apprehension lined her brow as she stared at her hands held clenched in her lap. "Like an adrenaline shot straight into my heart via my eyes." Her voice was faint and pain filled. "Weirdly, I think I dread meeting Andy more than fighting off Coyote."

He would laugh if she wasn't right. He had the same

rock in his stomach at the thought of how the kid would react to seeing his car mangled in its current condition. Definitely not something he was looking forward to.

Time to face the music.

After turning the engine off, he opened the door and got out while Abigail followed suit. He'd barely shut the car door behind him before he heard the agonized scream coming from the house.

"What have you monsters done?"

Abigail's face blanched as she froze in place.

He quickly moved past her to intercept Andy on his way to the car. He tried to shield the car with his body, but Andy was having none of that. Andy dodged left. Jess went right. Andy pivoted right. . . .

Jess held his arms out to stop him before he saw all the damage. Dang, the kid should have played ball. He'd seen less slippery piglets.

He offered his Squire a sympathetic nod. "You might want to order a new one."

Andy groaned in pain, then raked his hands through his hair in a way that would make James Dean proud. "I can't believe you tore up my car! My car! My precious baby. Sheez, Jess. What did you do?"

Well, there was one thing he definitely wasn't going to mention. That would only wig the kid out even more, and he would definitely never hear the end of that.

Not to mention Abigail would probably gut him if he told anyone what they'd done.

Jess dropped his arms and shrugged. "All I can say is, it got hairy for us."

"Hairy?" Andy covered his eyes with his fists and made the sound of ultimate suffering. Damn, the boy knew how to overreact. It was actually impressive. If the Squire gig failed, he could always get a job playing Oedipus. All he needed was to plunge two brooches into his eyes and stumble offstage. "My car looks like the stunt double for the Charger in *Burn Notice*. How could you? Jeez, Jess. Really?" He gestured toward the car. *"Really?"*

Abigail took a brave step forward. "I'm so sorry, Andy. It's all my fault."

He glared at her as if he was imagining her in little bloody pieces spread out through the house. He raised one hand as if about to lecture her, but honestly, he was so upset that all he could do was sputter indignantly.

Jess clapped him on the back. "You'll live. It's just a car, kid."

"And hell is just a sauna." Each word dripped with indignation and outrage.

Wincing, Andy sucked in a deep breath and appeared to get a hold of himself. "Fine," he said in a falsetto. "You're right. I'll live, even though right now it feels as if my guts have been yanked out through my nostrils and laid on the floor for your bitter amusement. You insensitive bastard! Just wait till I pick up your bike from the Ishtar. Let's see who laughs then."

"You hurt that bike, and I'll rip out your spine."

Andy paused. "Point taken." He looked at his car and sighed. "It could be worse. No one threw up in it. . . ." He widened his eyes, as if even more disturbed. "Did they?"

"No," Jess reassured him. "No one tossed cookies."

"All right." He straightened up and seemed to be true to his promise to let it go. "I will be a man about this."

That lasted until he saw the scratches on the hood from the mountain lion and the front fender, where Abigail had dragged it off the driveway.

Wailing, he went to it and sank to his knees. He sprawled over the hood and laid his head on the damaged fender. "I'm so sorry, Bets. I should have hidden the keys. Booted your tires. Something. I had no idea anyone would abuse you so, baby. I swear I'll never let anyone hurt you again. Ayyy, how could they do this to you? How? Oh the humanity!"

Jess let out a deep *heh* as he locked gazes with Abigail. "I really need to get that boy a girlfriend—" He glanced over to where Andy was now stroking the hood. "—or at least laid."

Abigail laughed.

Pushing himself back, Andy hissed at them. "You mock my pain, sir."

"Nah," Jess drawled. "I mock your idiocy."

Andy curled his lip. "Go on. Get in the house. Leave me to my suffering, you insensitive monster. You've done enough damage."

Jess shook his head. "Too bad the Razzie committee can't see this performance. We might actually have a winner if they did."

Hoping the boy would get over it without needing a therapist, he headed toward the house.

Abigail went over to Andy. "I really am sorry about your car. I mean it."

He looked up with a sincere stare that gave Jess hope Andy wasn't completely shot in the head. "It's all right. It's just . . . a . . . car. I'll get over it eventually." He pushed his bottom lip out to pout like a two-year-old.

In a weird way, it was almost adorable.

Abigail wanted to reach out and soothe poor Andy, even though his reaction was way over the top. Maybe it was ridiculous, but she felt terrible about it.

Because of her past, she tended to bond to objects more than to people, too. Objects could be stolen, but they didn't leave voluntarily. They were always there when you needed them, and they didn't say or do anything to hurt your feelings.

It killed her that she'd damaged something that obviously meant so much to him.

I'm becoming a massive walking disaster area. She was the opposite of Midas. Instead of turning to gold, everything she touched turned to dust.

Even her best friend . . .

Her heart caught on that. She still couldn't believe

everything that had happened tonight. Her friends were her enemies, and she was depending on her enemy to help save her life. Nothing in the world made sense right now.

Honestly, she just needed a few minutes of peace before the next catastrophe. A moment to ground herself before another storm blew through and swept her over the edge of insanity. But that was a luxury none of them had.

Unwilling to think about what was coming for her next, she followed after Jess, who'd already vanished into the house.

By the time Abigail caught up to him in the kitchen, he was standing with Sasha and a blond man she'd never seen before. Not quite as well muscled as Jess, the newcomer was by no means small. He had short tousled blond hair and tiny braids that fell from one temple. Dressed in jeans and a gray T-shirt, he had arms covered with black Celtic tribal tattoos. There was something about him that screamed ultimate badass.

And he pierced her with a suspicious look the moment he sensed her presence. That look pinned her feet to the floor and kept her from taking another step.

At least until Jess turned around and offered her a kind smile. By the friendly expression on his face, she knew it was safe to approach the other man.

She hoped.

Jess motioned her forward. "Abigail meet Talon. Talon, Abigail."

Relaxing a bit from his tough man stance, Talon inclined his head to her. "Hi."

Well, at least he was friendlier toward her than Zarek had been. Not that that was saying much. *They'd probably be a lot friendlier if you hadn't killed their brethren.*

In all honesty, she was lucky he wasn't attacking her, and she wouldn't blame him if he did. There was no telling how long he'd known the ones she'd killed. How close they'd been.

I'm so sorry.

Life seriously needed an undo button. The coward in her wanted to turn around and run. But she'd never been craven a day in her life, and she wasn't about to start now when they needed her to stand strong.

Clearing her throat, she forced herself to join them at the stainless steel island. "Are you the one responsible for the rain?"

"Yeah." Talon glanced at Jess and cracked a devilish grin that said there was an inside joke between them.

Jess made a face of supreme pain. "You're not still busting on Storm, are you?"

"Ah, hell yeah, you know it." Talon let out an evil laugh. "There are truly few things that give me more pleasure."

"You are all kinds of wrong." Jess shook his head before he explained it to her and Sasha. "Talon's brother-in-law is a professional rainmaker. So every time poor Storm tries to make it rain, Talon stops it. At this point, he's beginning to get a complex over it."

Pride gleamed bright in Talon's eyes. "I know it's cruel, but I can't help myself. Little bastard deserves it after all the grief he gives me over his sister. Not to mention I really like the little girl sound he makes when he fails."

Sasha snorted. "And you people think I'm twisted. Damn, that's so cold."

"Speaking of, Weatherman," Jess said. "You can probably kill the rain now. I think the wasps are pretty much shocked and driven back."

A loud clap of thunder shook the house. "Yeah, but it's fun."

"Might be, but you're flooding out parts of the city."

Talon grimaced. "Make me feel bad, why don't you? Fine, it's canned."

Abigail was intrigued by his powers. It was one she hadn't known a Dark-Hunter could have. "So can you summon tornadoes or earthquakes?"

"Earthquakes aren't weather related." Talon winked at her, then sobered as if he caught himself being too friendly. "And no offense, I don't feel comfortable discussing my powers with someone who might try and use them against me one day. So I'll be keeping all details close."

Pain stabbed her hard in the chest. "You're right. I deserve that. I shouldn't have asked."

The expression on his face said that he felt as bad about his words as she did.

Jess put his arm around her shoulders. "Go easy on her, Celt. She was protecting her family. We've all done things we regret while trying to help the people we love. It doesn't make her an enemy."

"True. It just makes her human." Talon held his hand out to her. "Truce?"

Offering him a shy smile, she took his hand in hers and shook it. "Truce." The moment she touched his skin, she felt something strange on his palm. Scowling, she turned his hand over to see a nasty burn scar there. "That looks really painful."

Talon actually smiled as if the memory warmed him. He pulled his hand away. "A very small price to pay for all I gained. Trust me. Had it been necessary, I'd have given the whole arm." He passed a look from her to Jess that sent a shiver down her spine.

It was like he knew what they'd done.

A light smile played at the edges of his lips. "Speaking of, I need to be getting back home. Last thing I want to do is stress out Sunny. My luck, she'd show up here and in her condition I'd have to kill someone if they upset her. Since I don't want to kill myself . . ." He scanned the three of them. "Good luck. For the gods's sakes, don't fail."

"Don't intend to," Jess assured him.

Talon vanished.

Abigail shifted nervously as Sasha arched a brow over the fact that Jess still had his arm around her. She'd shrug it off, but didn't want to do anything to make it stand out more. Besides, she liked it.

Ignoring Sasha's curiosity, she spoke to Jess. "I take it Sunny is his wife and she's pregnant?"

"Very."

She nodded as she absorbed that. Along with a new fear for herself. "I didn't think Dark-Hunters could have families or make someone pregnant."

A light appeared in his eyes that said he might actually be reading her thoughts.

She gave him a stern glare.

Panic flared deep in his dark gaze before he stepped away from her as if wanting to put distance between her and his so-called tender parts. "Didn't do it. I swear, and no we can't. Talon's no longer one of us and hasn't been for some time. Sunshine freed him."

Really . . . there was another thing she'd never known was possible.

Before she could speak again, Ren's deep, stern voice rang out. "You need to take it slowly."

"I say, stop mothering me, Ren. I'm not an invalid, you know? Fall into one little trance while taking care of something, and now I have a hen on top of me. I swear if you don't stop, I shall rename you."

Abigail quickly hid her amusement as Choo Co La Tah came into the kitchen with Ren. The expression on Ren's face could freeze fire.

Unlike her, Jess had no problem laughing at them both. "Anything I should know about?"

Choo Co La Tah stiffened indignantly. "Yes. Your friend here is a bit of a faffer, and I've had enough of it for one day, thank you very much."

Ren sighed in irritation. When he spoke, it was to Jess, not Choo Co La Tah. "Talon brought him out of the trance. I'm thinking now, though, that we should have left him there."

Abigail hated to interrupt, but . . . "Off topic—what's a faffer?"

Ren's face turned bright red.

Luckily, Choo Co La Tah smiled at her. "Someone who fusses, my dear."

Ah. No wonder Ren was so furious. Not the manliest of descriptions, by any means.

"May I also ask why you speak with an English accent? It seems . . ." She couldn't say *odd* without offending him, and that was the last thing she wanted to do. She actually liked the old elder a lot, even if he wasn't always the most likable of people. "Different."

Ren put his hands on his hips. "He learned to speak English from the original British settlers and never quite adapted to the modern accent."

Choo Co La Tah gave him a withering stare, as if he didn't appreciate Ren's explanation. "I like the way it sounds better. Besides, it throws everyone off balance when they hear it, and I like that even more. Always keep them guess-ing about you, my dear. Nothing ever makes them so crazy."

She appreciated that thought.

"How are you feeling?" Jess asked Choo Co La Tah, changing the subject.

"Weary. And we've wasted enough time. We need to get going so that we can reach the high point before dawn, make our offering, and secure the jars."

A tendril of fear went through her as she realized that the offering most likely would be her life. *I'm not ready for this. . . .*

Jess saw the fear in Abigail's eyes. Wanting only to soothe her, he took her hand in his and squeezed her fin-gers in a silent promise that he wouldn't let anything hap-pen to her. He meant that, too. So long as he had breath inside him, nothing would get to her.

Choo Co La Tah dropped his gaze to their hands, and something akin to approval crossed his face.

Weird.

But Jess didn't have time to think about that. "Let's head to the Bronco and get started. It's a little over an hour to get there from here. We should have plenty of time before dawn, but with what all Coyote's been throw-ing at us, who knows."

Ren hesitated. "My powers are waning. I think I'll fly in and meet you."

He had a point, but . . . "You sure about that? Snake

could open a can of whoop-ass on us, too, and we don't know what his plagues are. Do we?"

"Flesh-eating virus," Choo Co La Tah said. "And bloodfire."

Sasha screwed his face up. "Bloodfire?"

"My personal fave." Ren's tone was thick with sarcasm. "It's blood drops that fall from the sky and explode like wet dynamite."

Jess nodded as Ren proved his point. "Not exactly something you want to have hit you when you're out in the open."

"True, but I'm stupid enough to chance it. I need to recharge if we have to fight, and I'm sure you do, too."

Jess cursed the man's stubbornness.

And his sacrifice.

"You be *really* careful," he warned.

Ren gave him a cocky grin. "Always. You have to be careful when you fly, or you end up smeared on the side of a building."

"You're not funny."

"I'm hilarious, crabass." Ren's gaze went to Abigail, and a shadow passed across his face. One that Jess sensed was extremely important. But as quickly as it came, Ren covered it. "Save our girl. Won't do us any good to get there without her."

"Don't worry." He wasn't about to let her go. Not yet, anyway. "Peaceful journey, *penyo*."

Ren saluted him, then went to the front door. He opened it before he turned into a crow and flew away.

Sasha let out a sound of disgust. "What? Was he raised in a barn? Didn't he ever learn how to close a door?" He flung his hand at the door and slammed it shut without touching it. "Amateur shape-shifters . . . No manners whatsoever."

Jess was puzzled by the lycanthrope's distemper. "Do we need to get you a Midol before we go?"

"I'm not that easy to soothe, cowboy. My peeves are on a cellular level."

Jess shook his head, then fell silent as he looked at Abigail and saw the tiniest spark of red in her eyes. The demon was trying to surface again. He wondered if she could feel it when it did that. "Are you all right?"

"Yeah, why?" Well, that answered his question. Obviously, she had no idea.

The red faded out.

His gut drew tight. That couldn't be good either. He'd be more concerned with it, but right now, they were on a tight schedule.

"Never mind." Taking her hand, he led them out of the kitchen and down the barrel-vaulted hallway to the other side of the house.

Abigail was floored as they kept walking and walking. In the back of her mind, she'd noted that his house was huge, but it wasn't until now that the full size of it hit her.

Dang . . .

He opened the door to another garage that housed a huge collection of cars and motorcycles. It had more in common with a warehouse than a garage, except for the fact that it was immaculate and ornate. The gold trim even appeared to be gilded. "Just how big is this house?"

Jess grinned sheepishly. "Andy's doing, not mine. Don't ask, 'cause it's just obscene. And no, with the exception of the black Bronco, nothing in here belongs to me. Since Andy lives in the apartment over the garage, this is his domain."

"And how big is Mr. Andy's apartment?"

He actually blushed. "Sixty-two hundred square feet, and I'm pretty sure it's why he picked out this house. Though he denies it."

Holy snikes . . . Well, that explained the huge feel of the place. Her house was one quarter of the size of Andy's apartment.

"And why's your Bronco in here?"

Jess continued on through the huge place toward his truck. "He was hauling tack earlier, and he didn't want to risk dinging or scraping one of his darlings. Since I don't drive it all that much, he left it over here."

She was strangely amused as she counted Andy's impressive super car collection. "If he has sixteen cars, why does he care about the Audi so?"

He opened the door for the Bronco and passed her a defiant grin that set fire to her blood. Oh, to have five minutes to nibble those lips. "That's his newest, and honestly,

I think the boy just wants something to moan about. Pay him no heed."

Abigail climbed into the backseat, leaving Choo Co La Tah to sit up front with Jess while Sasha climbed in beside her.

Jess adjusted the seat and mirrors to accommodate his size. Before he started it, he pinned a meaningful glare at Sasha through the rearview mirror. "Everyone buckled in?"

Sasha snorted, then gaped as he realized Jess wasn't joking about it. "Really? Is there anyone here one hundred percent human? No. I think dying from an unbuckled belt is the least of our concerns right now."

"And I don't put it in drive until everyone's secure. That means you, wolfboy."

Sasha's exasperated expression was priceless. "Unfrakkin'-believable. I'm in hell. With a lunatic. Might as well have stayed with Zarek. Next thing you know, you'll be drowning pancakes with syrup, too." He made a grand showing of buckling himself in. "Hope you get fleas," he mumbled under his breath.

"Thank you." Jess pulled out of the garage.

She pressed her lips together to keep from laughing at them. No doubt they'd take turns beating her if she did.

Curling his lip, Sasha sarcastically mocked his words in silence. "By the way, cowboy, you do know that if we were to wreck, I can teleport out of this thing. Right?"

"Is Scooby still bitching?" Jess asked Choo Co La Tah. "Remind me to check his vet record when we get back. I think he might have distemper or rabies or something."

Choo Co La Tah laughed.

Abigail shook her head at their antics. She wasn't used to people so at ease with danger. They were either the bravest creatures ever born . . .

Or the most reckless.

And as they headed back out into the darkness, she felt a chill run down her arm. *I'm being watched.*

It's Ren. Don't worry about it.

Maybe, but it didn't feel like Ren.

It felt like evil.

Coyote felt the fire in front of him flare as he walked with his mind through the realm of shadows to spy on his enemies. Even with his eyes closed, he could see himself in the cavern. The fire licked against the logs in front of him, casting eerie shadows from the stalagmites and stalactites onto the rock walls around him.

But that wasn't what held his focus. His enemies did.

They were together, and that made him seethe so deep inside, he was sure it burned a groove into his soul. "Why won't you die," he snarled. "All of you."

How many times did he have to kill Buffalo before he stayed dead?

As for Ren . . .

"What's happening?"

He opened his eyes to find Snake walking toward him from the dark opening that let out onto the hills he'd called home for centuries. "They're heading to the Valley."

Snake cursed. "We have to stop them."

Like he didn't know that? "Why are *you* panicking when I'm the one who has everything to lose?"

"You're not the only one, Coyote. I don't want to retire any more than you do."

But this wasn't about retirement. It was about payback. A betrayal so foul that no amount of time had lessened the burn of it.

How could I have been so stupid?

The First Guardian was still tormenting him. He could feel it. Why else would he have made the mistake he made all those years ago?

I killed the wrong one. Only the First Guardian could have pulled off that deception and protected the girl from him after he killed her mother.

And he needed that key. It was the only way to have his vengeance. The only way to survive this.

I will not fail. Not this time. He'd waited for centuries, and it was the season for his patience to be rewarded.

He rose to his feet and started for the entrance.

Snake caught him and held him by his side. "What are you doing?"

"I'm going after them."

"You can't. Outside of the Valley, we're like gods."

Inside, they weren't. It still mystified Coyote that the woman had been able to kill Old Bear. Something that should have been impossible even for her.

And if she could kill a Guardian outside of the Valley, then Buffalo most likely could do it, too. "I have to stop them."

"Then stop them, my brother . . . with others."

Coyote shook his head. "I've unleashed my plagues."

"Then I will unleash mine." Snake placed his hand on Coyote's shoulder in brotherly solidarity. "We are in this to the end."

Snake for the power.

Coyote for blood.

He nodded to the South Guardian. "At dawn we will feast on the hearts of our enemies."

"And bathe in their blood."

A warrior's bond.

Snake tightened the grip on his shoulder before he released him. "I will summon the bounty hunters." He started away.

"Wait." Coyote hesitated to say more. He didn't want to show his weakness to anyone. Ever. But he had no choice. "Tell them not to harm the woman. I want her brought back to me."

"Intact?"

"Preferably."

"May I ask why?"

The answer smoldered inside him like a pressure cooker that was about to explode. "It's personal."

Confusion marred his brow, but Snake didn't pursue it. "I'll make sure it's done."

Good. Coyote watched Snake make his exit while his emotions churned inside him. But it was his rage that flared brightest. "You owe me!" he shouted, his voice ringing through the cavern. And this time, he would collect on that balance.

Jess Brady would die, and he would finally have the reward he'd been promised.

14

Jess cursed as he swerved to miss a pedestrian while they drove down the Great Basin Highway toward the Valley of Fire. All over the interstate, people had abandoned their cars which had been wrecked during either the wasp attack or subsequent storm Talon had sent.

In spite of the media telling everyone to remain in their homes, thousands of people had tried to evacuate and were now walking on the side of the road. Many were screaming that it was the end of the world while others trudged on in grim determination to get wherever they were headed.

It was an ugly sight, and it made Abigail pray that whatever plague Coyote unleashed next didn't make it to them.

Cell phone lines were completely jammed, which only added to everyone's panic. There was no way to reach anyone inside or outside the city. Maybe that was what had caused them to try and leave. That need to find your family and hold on to them in a crisis.

Even though she'd lost her parents as a child, she still had that urge to crawl into her mother's arms whenever something awful happened. That burning need to talk to her and have her chase away all the monsters and fears.

It never went away.

Abigail wanted to weep over what she saw. She wanted to weep for the people who'd been hurt because of her stupidity. "I can't believe I did all this." Surely, she would burn in hell for it.

Choo Co La Tah turned in the seat to face her. "It's not entirely your fault, dear. Don't take that guilt into your heart. The Balance is fragile, and it controls everything in the cosmos. If the scales ever tip—"

"We get screwed," Sasha said in a chipper tone with a big grin.

"You're not funny, Sasha," Jess snapped.

"Sorry. Trying to lighten the mood." He met Abigail's gaze. "If it makes you feel any better, this isn't my first apocalypse. There is hope."

She wasn't sure what to make of that. "Obviously the world survived."

Even in the darkness, she could see the pain those words brought to him. "Yeah, not really. It kind of blew everything back to the Stone Age. The good news is, people are resilient, and that which doesn't kill you merely serves as a cautionary tale for others." He glanced out the window and sighed. "It also makes one hell of a bedtime story, especially if the Crypt-Keeper's your audience."

She sucked her breath in sharply at the unspoken agony that lay beneath those words. "What happened?"

"What always happens when preternatural powers are unleashed or go to war, and no one cares about the collateral damage during the battle." He gestured toward the people on the street. "I lost my entire family in the blink of an eye. But hey, I saved a lot of money on not having to buy Christmas cards."

How could he make light of something that was obviously so painful for him?

Without thinking, she reached out and touched his hand.

Sasha didn't look at her, but he closed his fingers around hers and gave a light squeeze that said he appreciated it.

Sasha cleared his throat. "So, Choo? How many apoc-alypses have *you* survived?"

"More than you, Wolf. More than you."

Abigail was humbled by their experience. The misery they'd seen. It was easy to lose sight of other people's pain when your own was so strong. What was it that Plato said? Be kind to all you meet, for everyone is fighting a hard battle?

It was so true.

"Are you all right?" Jess asked.

She caught his gaze in the rearview mirror. "Yeah."

No. Not really. Her guilt ate at her.

And one question hung heaviest in her mind. "How did you learn to live with being a hired killer?"

"It's just like any other act of cruelty. You lie to your-self. You say that they deserved it. You create stories to justify why they needed to die and tell yourself that if you hadn't struck first, they'd have done it to you. In the end, you do your damnedest not to think about it all."

Yeah, people did have a nasty tendency to excuse their bad behavior and then to hold it against others whenever they did the same thing.

Sasha let go of her hand. "Hey, Choo? Wanna take odds on our survival tonight? We are in Vegas, after all. I think we should up the ante and have a huge payout for whoever calls it." When Choo Co La Tah failed to re-spond, he turned his attention to Jess. "What about you, cowboy?"

Jess scoffed. "I only gamble with my life."

"Ah . . . explains so much about you. And off on a random topic in an attempt to divert our attention from the fact that we're all most likely speeding to our impending doom, how did you get the name Sundown, anyway?"

"You want to know that now?" His tone was incredulous.

"Why not?"

Jess shook his head. "Why?"

"It's just an odd moniker for an outlaw. Figured it had some deeper meaning."

"A newspaper reporter gave it to him," Abigail said quietly. She'd read the article in something Jonah found years ago. "The man wrote that everyone called him Sundown because he did his best and most gruesome work after dark."

"You believe everything you read in the papers?" The anger in Jess's tone cut through the truck as an angry tic beat a fierce rhythm in his sculpted jaw. "They get all the facts screwed up, and I think most of them are so crooked, they have to screw their pants on in the morning. Hell, most of them have to go diagonal just to walk in a straight line."

Obviously that had struck a nerve with him. "It was wrong?"

Sasha gave her a no-duh stare.

"Yeah." Venom saturated his voice. "It was wrong. Some . . ." He paused as if he was about to say something offensive and then caught himself. "Trying to take credit for something that has nothing to do with anything he did. My real name is Manee Ya Doy Ay . . . it means 'sundown' in my mother's language."

How beautiful. She doubted she could ever say it properly, but it sounded wonderful as it rolled off his tongue. "Really?"

He gave a subtle nod. "It was her favorite time of day. When the sun must make peace with the moon and for a few brief moments, the two touch in mutual friendship and respect. Perfect balance between the light and dark. A time for reflection and for preparation."

What a wonderful way of looking at things, and it made her ache for his loss. A woman so kind shouldn't be taken from her loved ones. No more than her own mother had. "She sounds incredible."

"She was."

"She was Cherokee, right?"

"Tsalagi," he corrected. "It's what they call themselves."

Abigail frowned as she saw a strange expression cross Choo Co La Tah's face. It was like he wanted to say something, but knew that he shouldn't.

Before she could ask him about it, something hit the car. Hard.

And set it on fire.

"What the—?" Jess swerved again as more fire rained down on them. It hit the hood like a gel egg and splattered, spraying flames that clung to the metal.

Abigail gasped as some hit the window, staining it red. Blood red. "Is that bloodfire?"

Choo Co La Tah nodded. "The worst part? It burns in water."

Lovely. Couldn't anyone ever invent a friendly plague? Something like raining daisies? Euphoria? Dancing flying pigs?

Nah. They always had to be nasty.

"Uh, guys?" Sasha said in a droll tone. "It's not just a plague."

Abigail understood what he meant a heartbeat later when the Bronco was literally swatted off the road so hard that it bounced over the concrete bridge wall on Interstate 15 to land them beneath it on Highway 93. Even after the jarring crash, the Bronco continued to roll fast and furiously toward the area where several tractor trailers were parked.

By the time they stopped moving, she was completely disoriented.

And upside down.

She lifted her hand to her brow and touched something wet along her eyebrow. Crap, she was bleeding. At least that explained her sudden headache. She glanced to Jess to make sure he was all right. Like her, he had a head injury on his temple, and his left hand was bleeding. Other than that, he appeared fine. Choo Co La Tah seemed to be the one with the least injuries. He held one arm over his head, bracing it against the ceiling to hold his weight so that his belt wasn't cutting in to him the way hers was.

Gravity was a definitely a bitch right now.

Sasha groaned from beside her as he struggled with his belt. "I think I'm going to barf a hairball."

Jess let out a frustrated breath as he tried to loosen himself. "You can't. You're canine."

"Tell that to the hairball in my stomach."

Jess cursed as his hand slipped while he was trying to get loose. "Bet you're glad I made you fasten that seat belt now, aren't you, Mr. I-can-flash-myself-out-if-we-get-hit?"

Sasha groaned. "Shut up, asshole." He glared at Jess. "And I would have flashed out of the car, but because we were rolling, I didn't want to get hit by it. Damn those Rytis laws."

Abigail wanted to ask what that was, but there was no time as they were hammered with more bloodfire. The smell of gas was thick. If the Bronco wasn't currently on fire, it wouldn't be long before it ignited from the rain.

"We have to get out of here." Jess kicked at the broken windshield with his booted feet.

Sasha flashed out.

Abigail tried to undo her seat belt, but she couldn't. The buckle had broken during the crash. "I hate to be all girly, but I'm trapped."

"Where's Sasha?" Jess asked.

The answer came from just outside her window. "Getting his ass kicked while deflecting this asshole from you. Any time you want to help me, Jess. Step right up."

Jess snorted at the acerbic shape-shifter as he cut his belt, then slammed down to the ceiling. "Whatever you do, keep him busy."

"No problemo. Using my face as his punching bag seems to be working. I'll just need you to help me find all my teeth later."

Abigail saw Sasha hit the ground near them. Oooh, that looked really painful. His face turned deadly before he pushed himself up and vanished out of her line of sight again.

Choo Co La Tah was strangely calm while the scent of gas grew stronger. And her breathing became more labored. It was hard to draw a breath while the nylon belt dug into her.

"Guys!" Sasha shouted. "You might want to think about getting out now. Flames are spreading all over the bottom of the truck."

She could hear the fire and feel the heat of it. *I'm going to die.*

And yet she had no fear. No idea why. It made no sense whatsoever. In fact, she was strangely calm, too. Like a part of her might even crave it.

Lying on his back, Jess kicked furiously at the windshield. "Damn. It. Break. Already. You. Sorry. Son. Of. A.

Biscuit. Eating. Cat." He had the most colorful way of speaking as he punctuated every word with a solid kick.

Something let out a high-pitched whine. A second later, the windshield flew out onto the ground. Jess moved toward her.

She shook her head. "Get Choo Co La Tah first."

He hesitated.

"No," Choo Co La Tah snapped. "Free her. I'll be out in a second."

She saw the indecision in those lush dark eyes. "He's more important than I am."

Not to me he isn't. Jess barely bit those words back before he said them out loud. Every part of him cringed at the thought of her being hurt any worse. He couldn't stand to see her trapped and bleeding. It brought back memories he didn't understand.

Not memories of Matilda. These were something else. Faded images of a time and place he didn't understand.

But he saw her face so clearly.

Her face. Same black hair and that sassy smile that dared him as she crooked her finger for him to follow after her.

I will always come for you, Kianini. Nothing will keep me from it.

She laughed as she pulled him into her arms and stared up at him coyly from beneath her lashes. *And I will never leave you, my heart. Forever yours.*

Those words whispered in his ears.

"Get her free."

It took him a moment to register Choo Co La Tah's words, which had been spoken in a language he'd never heard before. Yet he completely understood them.

Blinking, he moved to comply as Choo Co La Tah crawled out through the missing windshield.

Abigail met Jess's determined gaze, and the horror in his eyes told her that the clock was ticking down for them. The sound of fire was now deafening. More than that, the pungent gas odor clung to them so thickly that she tasted it and it made it even harder to breathe.

Undaunted by the danger, Jess struggled to cut through the belt. The car thudded and popped.

Her time could be counted in heartbeats now. But it touched her that Jess was still helping her.

Moronic, but touching.

She put her hand over his to stop him from cutting the belt. "Go. There's no need in both of us dying."

He lifted her hand to his lips and kissed her knuckles. "I'm not leaving you. If we go, we go together."

"Don't be stupid, Jess."

He scoffed as he returned to sawing on the belt. "Brains don't exactly run in my family. Suicidal lunacy, on the other hand . . ."

"Runs thick?"

He grinned at her. "Move back."

The metal whined a warning to them as the belt finally snapped.

Jess caught her against him and took a second to savor the feeling of her there before he kissed her temple, then pulled her from the wreckage.

They barely cleared the Bronco before it exploded into one impressive display of pyrotechnics. Fire shot up to the dark sky while pieces of the truck rained down all over them. Jess snatched Abigail under him to protect her from the shrapnel.

Abigail couldn't breathe with his heavy weight pressing down on her. But she was grateful to have him as her shield. Her only hope was that nothing hit him.

Jess froze the moment their eyes met, and he caught the full force of the adoration in her gaze. It stole his breath. She lifted her hand and laid it gently against his cheek. The warmth of her hand set him on fire.

Suddenly, the sound of a loud dragonesque call caught his attention and shattered the spell.

Abigail turned her head in synch with Jess. She gaped at the sight of Choo Co La Tah, Ren, and Sasha embroiled in a bitter fight with the most hideous thing she'd seen since Kurt's attempt to cut Hannah's hair when they were kids.

Solid black, it was extremely tall and thin with spidery limbs that twisted out like living tendrils. Whatever it was, it could sling its arm out like a whip and crack it against their friends. It moved so fast, it was hard to follow, and it said a lot about their fighting skills that they were able to stand toe to toe with these new creatures.

Jess pushed himself off her and ran to join the fight.

Rolling over, Abigail got up, intending to join them in battle. But before she could move or Jess reached the fight, Ren appeared in front of him.

"Get back."

Jess shook his head. "We can't let Choo Co La Tah get hurt."

"He's expendable, Jess. You and Abigail aren't."

That news floored her.

Jess scowled. "What?"

"Do what he says!" Choo Co La Tah shouted as he drove one of the creatures back while another one moved forward to fight him. "Both of you have to live."

Jess would argue, but honestly he wanted to protect her. Fine. He would trust them.

"What are these things?" she asked him as he returned to her side.

"A good fable gone bad."

"What?"

Ren kicked the one he was fighting away from him. "They're tsi-nooks."

He said that like she should understand it. "Gibberish is not my native tongue, Ren. What's a tsi-nook?"

No one answered, as they were a little occupied by fighting them, and while they were getting in some good blows, they didn't appear to be winning.

Abigail hated the feeling of being so vulnerable. She had no idea what she was up against or if she should poke out their eyes or kick them in the knees. Though to be honest, she wasn't sure they had either one. "Okay, I don't care what they are. How do we kill them?"

"With great skill, my girl. With great skill." Choo Co La Tah uncoiled his feathered bracelet from his arm. As he unwound it, it grew into a staff almost as tall as he was. One that expanded so that he could attack the tsi-nook nearest him.

But that didn't work. It seemed to only upset the beast. The tsi-nook fell on the ground. On its back. At least that's what she thought was its back. Their forms were so twisted, it was hard to tell for sure.

After it landed, she saw its face clearly for the first time. Strangely, it reminded her of a wooden mask. Weathered with deep lines all over its features, the eyes were nothing more than slits, and it didn't appear to have eyelids. For that matter, it didn't seem to blink.

In one word, they were ugly.

As if it sensed what she thought about it, it turned to face her and let out a piercing shriek. Apparently in freak-speak, that was some kind of rallying call because the moment it started, the others stopped to glare at her and Jess.

It was never a good thing to be the center of unwanted attention, and right now she felt like Carrie at the prom. Or more to the point, the only steak in a dog kennel.

Her heart pounded as fear tackled her to the ground and held her there.

Moving with an eerie fluid grace and a speed that shouldn't be possible, they ran in her direction. Jess went to fight them, but they actually ran past him and kept going full speed.

At *her*.

Abigail's eyes widened as she realized they didn't care about the men. She was the target.

The only target.

C-r-a-p.

She braced herself for the fight. *What am I doing?* There were more than a dozen of them, and there was only one her. One. While it was noble to be brave, it was stupid to be suicidal. Fighting a dozen . . . when she didn't have a weapon and didn't know how to kill them flew right past the realm of noble and landed solidly in the kingdom of stupid.

To quote her favorite play of all time . . . *Run away!* She turned and headed for the desert as fast as she could.

Jess went cold as the tsi-nooks ran for Abigail. His vision darkened at the same time fear for her rushed through him. For one second, he was mortal again, and then the sensation was gone.

"Oh no you don't." His powers surged in a way they hadn't in decades. Suddenly, he felt stronger than he ever had before. Something deep inside him snapped, and out came what he could only describe as an inner warrior. One who knew the taste and feel of the tsi-nooks' blood on its hands.

No one would harm Abigail.

He went after them. And as he neared her, he realized her eyes were turning red. The demon was taking possession of her again.

It could be a good thing.

Or a really bad one.

Since the tsi-nooks, much like a traditional Daimon, preyed primarily on human souls, they might not want any part of a gallu demon. Or if they were like the new generation of Daimons, eating her soul might charge their powers and make them stronger.

Either way, he wasn't going to chance it. Not tonight.

Jess reached deep inside and tapped the only other power he did his best not to use. One so strong and painful that later it would make him wish he were dead.

But first, it would save their lives.

Closing his eyes, he conjured a gun—and not just any gun. The one that had made him infamous. An 1887 lever-action Winchester with a five-round tubular magazine. Not that it would need that tonight. His powers would make sure he didn't run out of rounds.

The smell of blood permeated his nostrils. His nose always bled whenever he accessed this power, which was why he almost never used it. That and the vicious headache he'd have later from it. So much for Dark-Hunters not getting those.

But if it kept her safe, it was worth it.

Abigail froze as she caught sight of Jess approaching her with long, determined strides. The desert wind whipped at his long black duster, stirring it back from his muscled body. The grim lethal glare on his chiseled features promised the tsi-nooks hell wrath and then some. This wasn't the tender man who'd made love to her while cramped in a tiny car. Nor was it the goofball who joked with and teased her.

This was the fierce, cold-blooded killer who'd left legions of dead and a legend so terrifying that one marshal had surrendered his badge rather than take Jess's horse into custody.

True story.

And Jess had been only seventeen at the time.

No wonder his partner had shot him in the back. She doubted anyone with a brain would ever assault this version of Jess Brady while he was facing them. Even she had a chill running down her spine as the hairs along her arms and neck raised. While she was pretty sure he wouldn't hurt her, she really didn't want to find out for sure.

Without breaking stride, he cocked the lever of the shotgun across his chest, took aim, and blew the tsi-nook closest to her apart.

She flinched in reaction to the ringing sound of the gun

followed by the shrill scream of the tsi-nook. Blood from the creature sprayed all over her body. She tensed, unsure of what to expect from the blood touching her skin. Luckily, nothing happened.

Before she could think to breathe again, Jess kept firing, rapidly blowing apart every one of them in turn. Their screams echoed around her until the night swallowed the sound and silenced it forever.

Until he took aim at her head.

Eyes wide, she seized in terror. *What did I do? Why would he kill her now?* She stared straight into the barrel. Black and evil, it gave her a profound understanding of the people he'd killed.

Don't. The word caught in her throat.

His features stone cold, he fired.

Abigail sucked her breath in sharply at the sound, expecting pain and a recoil that would knock her off her feet. Instead, she remained intact.

No pain. No impact.

Jess continued toward her, taking aim again. It wasn't until he fired another round that she realized he was shooting past her and not *at* her.

Thank God, she hadn't moved. Then he might have really killed her.

In fact, he didn't stop shooting until he was standing right beside her. Only then did he put the gun down and scan the darkness to make sure there was nothing else out there.

The wind whistled around them, and out in the distance, she heard the cry of a single coyote. Though to be honest, she was amazed she could hear anything, given the last few minutes.

"Is that our friend?" she asked Jess.

"No." Jess tilted his head back and sniffed the air like a lycanthrope might if he was tracking someone. "They're bounty hunters."

"Pardon?"

Jess's memories burned as he was pulled back in time to age fifteen. Then, as now, there had been a chill in the warm air. But no one except him could feel it. Bart had left him holed up in a small dugout on the side of a mountain out in the middle of nowhere Arizona. A posse had been chasing after them, and he'd had nothing more than a handful of bullets.

He'd been dead asleep and then awakened to nothing other than his heart racing. As he tried to force himself back to sleep, he'd smelled that haunting stench that defied explanation.

It was the same odor he smelled on the wind now. He glanced over to Choo Co La Tah. "What's going on?"

"We must get to the Valley. Quickly. Coyote is growing desperate."

Putting his hands on his hips, Sasha stopped in front of them. "Coyote got boys." He jerked his chin toward the bodies. "And a lot of them. What the hell did we just fight?"

Abigail was even more grateful to the wolf. "Thank you for asking. That's what *I* wanted to know."

Jess didn't answer as he locked gazes with Choo Co La Tah. "What is out there?"

"You're asking me a question you already know the answer to. And yes, they have been after you before. . . . Many times."

Ren sighed. "They're skinwalkers who lost wagers to Coyote. Now they serve as his bounty hunters."

"They're the same as you?" Abigail asked.

Ren shook his head. "I'm a shape-shifter, not a skin-walker. They are the nastiest of creatures. Evil so foul that it rots them from the inside out." He turned to Jess. "That's the odor you smell. Nothing else like it."

Sasha growled. "What are their powers?"

"They can track as well as you do. Maybe better. They can shift forms, but only so long as they hold the pelt or feather of the animal they want to become next to their skin. Superhuman strength."

Choo Co La Tah agreed. "And halitosis so bad, it could knock down a building."

Great. Just great. Jess was really getting tired of being hunted. "I understand why they're after us tonight. But I remember them chasing me when I was human."

Sasha whistled. "Let's come back to the why in a few. First things first. What the hell is lying in pieces on the ground around us? I'm Greek, remember? So all this is . . .

non-Greek to me, which means I know nothing about it. And I need to know in the event I have to fight it again. Obviously shotguns are effective against them. What else?"

Jess rested his shotgun over his shoulder. "The term is tsi-noo. Tsi-nooks for the plural. Not to be confused with the Chinook Nation, because they have nothing to do with each other. . . . In short, they're our version of Daimons."

"Apollo curse them, too?"

Jess snorted at Sasha's irreverent question. "No. They were humans who committed crimes so unspeakable and horrific that the winter winds turned their hearts to ice. Now they can only live off the souls of humans."

"And they were one of Snake's plagues," Ren added. "Which means he and Coyote will be even more hell-bent on finding Old Bear's."

Sasha nodded as he listened. "Point taken there. Now, the important question, so pay attention, ye ADD degenerates. How the *F* do I kill them? 'Cause no offense, I was trying and they were kicking my ass all over the place. It really wasn't pretty and didn't do much for my ego either. My only reprieve is that no one I have to face on a regular basis witnessed my beating. Don't know why you wanted me here when I'm about as useful as a wart on Artemis's bum."

Smiling at his rant, Choo Co La Tah melted his staff back down to the bracelet, then coiled it around his wrist again. "Simple, Wolf. Like a Daimon, pierce the heart and the ice shatters inside. They die instantly. As you saw from Sundown, a shotgun will blow the heart apart and end them."

Sasha narrowed his gaze on Jess. "How you know that, cowboy?"

"Didn't. But a twelve-gauge round to the head or heart will take down just about anything. And if doesn't, kiss your ass good-bye and run like hell."

Abigail crossed her arms over her chest and drummed her fingernails on her biceps. "By the way, you and I need to talk about how you got that gun when I know it wasn't in the truck." She raked him with a glance from head to toe that succeeded in making him flinch. "You've been holding out on me."

Help . . .

How in the world could he be more afraid of her, a tiny little slip of a woman, than he'd been of the tsi-nooks?

"Um . . ."

"What was that?"

They all turned to look at Sasha who was staring into the darkness.

Jess frowned. "What?"

Ren stepped back as if he might have heard it, too. "We need to get going."

Sasha gestured toward the smoldering remains of the Bronco. "How? Are you an African swallow in another form or something?"

Choo Co La Tah scowled. "African swallow? What are you going on about now?"

"Oh c'mon, surely all of you get the Mon . . . ty . . . Python . . ." Sasha paused as if he remembered his audience. "Never mind."

Jess rubbed at his jaw. "He's right. It's too far to walk, and with the exception of Sasha and Ren, we don't have a ride."

Choo Co La Tah pointed to the parked tractor trailers. "What about one of those?"

Jess considered it. "Someone might have left keys in one. Let's go see."

Abigail walked in the center of the men while she listened for another attack. It was so dark, she could barely see. There was a low-lying cloud cover that held back the stars. It made the air feel heavy. Ominous. Or maybe that was from the fact that she knew what was out to get her.

Without thinking, she reached out and took Jess's rough hand. When he laced his fingers with hers, it warmed her in spite of the cold desert wind. She took strength from his nearness, and it made her wish that they didn't have to do this.

Made her wish that she could find some way to end the nightmare and return to a normal life.

Your life was never normal.

That was certainly true. But for the first time, she

wanted normality. She craved it now that it was too late to claim it. She'd already cast her die and come up bust.

One way or the other, her life was over. If by some miracle she did survive all of this and convince Choo Co La Tah not to sacrifice her to the spirits she'd offended, she had no doubt that one of the other Dark-Hunters would kill her for what she'd done.

There was no hope. Not now.

How could I have screwed up my life so badly?

The same way everyone did. She'd listened to and trusted the wrong people. Had put her faith and energy into the wrong things, only to learn too late that she shouldn't have harbored hatred.

I'm so stupid.

Jess paused as they reached the trucks. He and Abigail searched the first one for keys while the others spread out to check the rest.

One by one, they reported failure.

"Hey!" Sasha shouted after a minute. "I don't have keys, but this one's open. Anyone know how to hot-wire?"

Ren gave him an arch stare. "Can't you use your powers to start it?"

Sasha raked him with an equally offended sweep. "Can't you?"

Abigail held her hands up. "Step aside, boys. I have the evil powers for this."

Jess smiled as she climbed inside the cab and vanished

under the dash. "My lady got mad skills," he said, imitating the slang Sasha used.

Then he sobered as he realized what he'd done.

He'd claimed her. Publicly. But that wasn't what shocked him. The fact that he truly thought of her like that did. She was a part of him now. Even though they hadn't known each other long, she had breached his defenses and wormed her way into his heart.

Oh my God. The very idea terrified him.

He wouldn't call it love.

Would he?

It wasn't what he felt for Matilda by a long shot, and yet there were enough similarities that it left him wondering. When had he known he loved Matilda?

The day he'd realized he couldn't live without her.

Bart had told him that he wanted to move on. That it was time for them to find a new base of operations. Normally, Jess would have been packed up in a few hours and been ready to ride. Instead, an excruciating pain had ripped him apart when he thought about not seeing Matilda again. It'd been so debilitating that it brought him to his knees.

Nothing had struck him like that since.

Not until he'd seen the tsi-nooks going after Abigail.

I would die for her. That fact hit him like a punch in the jaw. He really would. She had a power over him that not even Matilda had possessed. *I'm so screwed.*

The semi started up, startling him away from his train of thought.

Blinking, he realized the other men were staring at him like he'd grown a third head. "What?" he asked defensively.

Sasha snorted. "I have never in my extremely long life seen anyone take so long to answer a question. It's like you went into your mind and got lost. You need a bread crumb, buddy?" He made a noise like he was calling his pet. "Here, Lassie, here. Come back, girl."

Jess shoved at him. "Shut up. What did you ask me, anyway?"

Sasha slapped himself on the forehead and groaned. "Really? Good thing I didn't tell you to duck a bomb."

He started to respond, but Abigail's frantic voice stopped him.

"Gentlemen. We have company."

15

The men climbed up the sides of the truck to
see why Abigail had called them. Ren and
Sasha on the passenger side. Choo Co La Tah
and Jess on hers.

Jess stood in the open door with one hand
braced against the top, looking down at her.
"What is it, babe?"

Stunned, all she could do was point at the herd of . . . whatever it was, speeding toward them. The group was stirring up a huge cloud of dust in their wake. Not even the darkness could conceal their presence. Mostly because their number was just that impressive.

Some she knew to be tsi-nooks. Others were definitely coyotes and the last group she assumed were the bounty hunters they'd been talking about.

Ren's jaw went slack.

Jess's tensed.

Sasha outdid them all. He laughed. "Now there's something you don't see everyday. Gah, I hope there's no human roaming around with a video recorder or cell phone. Be a bitch to explain that. Easier just to kill them."

Ren ignored him. "Did they open the Gate already?"

That would explain it.

But Choo Co La Tah shook his head. "They're trying to scare us."

"Working. 'Cause the wolf here is definitely feeling an 'oh shit' moment." He glanced over to Abigail. "You wouldn't want to change my diaper, would you?"

Jess shook his head at the wolf. He started to take the wheel from Abigail, then paused. "You know this is one of those moments when you think about the fact that you didn't quite complete the plan."

She frowned. "How so?"

He glanced around their small group. "Anyone know how to drive a semi?"

Ugh! She could kick herself for not thinking of that. Since they'd trained her to go after Dark-Hunters, Jonah had taught her the skill of hot-wiring—just in case she needed a quick getaway. She even knew how to start electronic and digital ignitions.

Why hadn't she ever taken the time to learn a standard transmission?

Sasha and Ren exchanged a bemused stare. "I don't drive," they said simultaneously.

Her heart sank. Of course they didn't. Ren flew as a bird and Sasha did that flashing thing. When would *they* have ever needed a driver's license?

"Can't you flash us out?" she asked Sasha.

He let out a fake, hysterical laugh. "My powers were strangled by a bitch-goddess as punishment for my gross stupidity. I'm lucky I can still flash myself, never mind other people. All I have is raw power and sexy, fighting prowess. Well, okay, if I had to, I might teleport one, maybe two others. But I wouldn't bet my better body parts on it."

Ren frowned. "I didn't think you could lose psychic powers."

"*You* can't, Dark-Hunter boy. But mine weren't a gift. I was born with them. Total different standard. Lucky me."

Jess arched a brow at her. "Can you drive it?"

"No. I can't drive a stick at all. It's why I took Andy's car and not one of yours."

"Oh people, for goodness' sake . . . Move over." Choo Co La Tah pushed past Jess to take the driver's seat.

Curious about that, she slid over to make room for the ancient.

Jess hesitated. "Do you know what you're doing?"

Choo Co La Tah gave him a withering glare. "Not at all. But I figured someone needed to learn and no one else was volunteering. Step in and get situated. Time is of the essence."

Abigail's heart pounded. "I hope he's joking about that." If not, it would be a very short trip.

Ren changed into his crow form before he took flight.

Jess and Sasha climbed in, then moved to the compartment behind the seat. A pall hung over all of them while Choo Co La Tah adjusted the seat and mirrors.

By all means, please take your time. Not like they were all about to die or anything . . .

She couldn't speak as she watched their enemies rapidly closing the distance between them. This was by far the scariest thing she'd seen. Unlike the wasps and scorpions, this horde could think and adapt.

They even had opposable thumbs.

Whole different ball game.

Choo Co La Tah shifted into gear. Or at least he tried. The truck made a fierce grinding sound that caused Jess to screw his face up as it lurched violently and shook like a dog coming in from the rain.

"You sure you don't want me to try?" Jess offered.

Choo Co La Tah waved him away. "I'm a little rusty. Just give me a second to get used to it again."

Abigail swallowed hard. "How long has it been?"

Choo Co La Tah eased off the clutch and they shuddered forward at the most impressive speed of two whole miles an hour. About the same speed as a limping turtle. "Hmm, probably sometime around nineteen hundred and . . ."

They all waited with bated breath while he ground his way through more gears. With every shift, the engine audibly protested his skills.

Silently, so did she.

The truck was really moving along now. They reached a staggering fifteen miles an hour. At this rate, they might be able to overtake a loaded school bus . . .

By tomorrow.

Or at the very least, the day after that.

". . . must have been the summer of . . . hmm . . . let me think a moment. Fifty-three. Yes, that was it. 1953. The year they came out with color teles. It was a good year as I recall. Same year Bill Gates was born."

The look on Jess's and Sasha's faces would have made her laugh if she wasn't every bit as horrified. *Oh my God, who put him behind the wheel?*

Sasha visibly cringed as he saw how close their pursuers were to their bumper. "Should I get out and push?"

Jess cursed under his breath as he saw them, too. "I'd get out and run at this point. I think you'd go faster."

Choo Co La Tah took their comments in stride. "Now, now, gentlemen. All is well. See, I'm getting better." He finally made a gear without the truck spazzing or the gears grinding.

Abigail cringed as she saw the whites of the eyes of their pursuers. "They're almost at our tailgate."

"Excuse me, darling." Jess slid over her lap to roll down the window.

She started to ask him what he was doing, but before she could, he held his hand out toward Sasha.

"Gun."

Sasha handed it over like a surgical assistant.

Jess leaned against the door with one leg braced over her lap. He pressed his thigh lightly against her stomach as he started shooting at the ones chasing them. The rapid fire rang in her ears as she felt his muscles contracting with each movement. He leaned out further.

Choo Co La Tah snatched the wheel to avoid an abandoned car in the road.

The motion tipped Jess so fast that he lost his balance and fell forward, through the window. Terrified he was about to fall to the street, Abigail wrapped herself around him to hold him in place.

Jess couldn't breathe for a second. He'd bruised the shit out of his ribs when he'd slipped and slammed his side into the door. Not to mention, Abigail had him pinned in a bear hug so tight he was amazed he wasn't turning blue.

But he didn't mind the pain. She felt so good, he was willing to suffer.

Unfortunately, he couldn't shoot this way.

"Sweetie?"

She looked up at him.

"I need my arm back."

Her face turned bright red. "Sorry." She quickly released it, but she kept her arms around his waist, anchoring him to her.

His heart pounded at the sight she made holding on to him to keep him safe. He wanted to kiss her so badly, he could taste her lips.

First, he had to protect her. Returning to his post, he started picking off their pursuers while Choo Co La Tah floored it. They were finally going fast and putting some distance between the truck and their pursuers.

Jess kept firing as the wind rushed around him. A tsi-noo screamed in frustration. *Yeah, that's right. Cry, baby, cry. Go home to your daddy and tell him you failed. Let him kick your ass.*

"Jess?"

He felt Abigail tugging hard at his shirt. Ducking back into the cab, he arched a brow. "Yeah?"

Choo Co La Tah cleared his throat then asked in the

calmest of tones. "You wouldn't happen to know how to stop one of these devices, would you?"

Oh please no . . .

Surely he'd misheard that. "Come again?"

Choo Co La Tah pressed the brake pedal all the way to the floor. A loud sound echoed

Nothing happened. The truck didn't slow in the least. Jess's stomach sank to his feet.

His arms spread wide over the giant steering wheel, Choo Co La Tah held on with a grip so tight his knuckles blanched. "I'm sorry to say, there seems to be a little bit of a problem. As you can see, it doesn't respond when I apply the brake."

And they were approaching an almost ninety degree turn they'd have to make onto the Valley of Fire Highway.

Jess considered their options. "Keep going straight. Don't try to make the off ramp."

"And again I say we have a bit of a problem."

Jess dreaded the next word. "Yeah?"

Abigail swallowed hard before she pointed down the road. "There are two jack-knifed trucks blocking it."

Shit.

And they were going way too fast. He'd say to ram the trucks, but one was hauling gas. They'd go up like a Roman candle.

Why, Lord, why?

Sasha leaned forward. "Hit the brake again."

Choo Co La Tah complied. Air blew back on him as a loud *sssshhhh* sound filled the cab. "I fear they're in ill repair, my boy."

"Yeah, but I think I know what it is." Sasha dove at the floorboard and started pounding against it with his fist. "C'mon, you little bastard. Work." He hit the brake with his hand.

As before, nothing happened.

Sasha growled low in his throat. "Send the wolf to watch them," he mocked in a falsetto. His nostrils flared. "I swear Z, if I live, I'm going to rip that damned goatee off your face and stick your shaving cream in the fridge." He locked gazes with Jess. "I'll be right back."

Abigail bit her lip as fear darkened her eyes. "Where's he going?"

Jess shrugged. "No idea."

"Oh dear . . ."

Since his back was to the windshield, Jess really didn't want to look at what had alarmed the ancient spirit. He'd much rather stare at Abigail.

But the compulsion was too great.

He turned, then wished he'd listened to himself. *Ay carumba!* They were way too close to the wrecked trucks. One lay on its side like it'd fainted while the other was sideways on the highway. No way to avoid them.

We're going to burn . . .

Suddenly, something was slamming hard at the floorboard underneath Choo Co La Tah's feet.

"Hit the brakes!" Sasha's muffled shout was barely audible even with Jess's super hearing.

Choo Co La Tah stomped the brakes and everyone held their collective breath and prayed.

Nothing happened. Jess felt his heart stop as he realized they were going to crash. He wasn't worried about himself. He would survive.

Abigail might not.

"Again!" Sasha shouted.

Choo Co La Tah obeyed. Jess tensed in expectation of their oncoming crash.

Then, to his utmost shock, the truck finally began to slow. He couldn't believe it. Sasha flashed back into the cab with a proud grin on his face.

Abigail leaned her head back on the seat and returned his smile. She high-fived Sasha.

Until Choo Co La Tah cursed—something he never did. "Hold on everyone."

Jess was tossed forward as they left the interstate and flew down the exit ramp at a speed that would have probably gotten them arrested had a cop seen it. Luckily there were no concrete barriers or anything significant around. Only small road markers that warned of the drop off the shoulder that they plowed over.

Please don't tip, please don't tip.

And don't plow into the Casino Smoke Shop Truck

Stop. The owner definitely wouldn't appreciate it. That had now become his biggest concern. Killing someone other than them.

The truck shimmied and shook as if it wanted to flip. But through some miracle, it didn't and in a few seconds, they were slowed to a safe speed while Choo Co La Tah headed toward the Valley.

Sasha fell back and laughed. "All right, everyone. Fess up. Who just shat in their pants? C'mon. Admit it." He raised his hand. "I know I did and I'm wolf enough to own it."

Jess ignored him. "Are you all right?" he asked Abigail. She was still a little too pale for his tastes.

"I think I'm going to own Sasha's question. Definitely put me on your list."

Jess laughed, then looked over at Sasha. "So Wolf, what did you do?"

"You mean before or after I soiled my jeans? Which, by the way, I want kudos for coming back in the cab when I could have gone home." Sasha sobered. "The foot valve was stuck. It doesn't happen often. But it can happen as you just saw. If you're lucky you can pop it back out from the cab. Obviously, given the horrors of this night, I wasn't lucky so I had to crawl under the damn thing at ninety miles an hour and pound it out from underneath. I don't *ever* want to hang like that under a speeding vehicle again. I swear I lost eight of my nine lives."

"What is it with you and the cat analogies?"

"Long, really not boring story. Anyway, I'm just glad I knew what it was."

Impressive, but . . .

"How did you know?"

"Video games," Sasha said proudly. "Never let it be said they're a waste of time. But for them, we'd be toasting some better parts or flipped and bleeding. And speaking of, we probably want to leave a note for whoever owns this thing so they can get it fixed. We don't want a human getting hurt over bad maintenance."

Choo Co La Tah checked the side view mirror. "I hate to be the one to cut in on the reverie and congratulatory sentiments, but we still have our friends following behind us."

Jess let out a long breath at their persistence. "What I wouldn't give for a case of C-4." And then the worst thing happened.

The pain from conjuring his gun hit.

Abigail gasped as Jess pressed his hand to his forehead and doubled over in the seat. "Jess?"

"It's okay," he said between clenched teeth. "I'll be all right."

In spite of those words, fear gripped her. "You don't look all right."

His nose started pouring blood.

She widened her eyes. "Honey?"

Sasha manifested a small hand towel and threw it over him.

Jess held it to his nose and tilted his head back. Terrified, Abigail ran her hand through his hair. "Is there anything I can do?"

He shook his head.

"All right, my boy. Now that we're on the back road . . ." Choo Co La Tah begin chanting something under his breath. Light in tone at first and then in crescendo. Louder and louder it went like a frenetic dance. Acapulco and harmonious, she couldn't understand a word of it. Only the beauty of the sound.

And as he spoke, the dirt outside began to swirl and spin, rising higher like small tornados.

Abigail was floored by what she saw. In a matter of seconds, they had a dust cloud surrounding them. The only problem was, their sight was limited by it.

"Why didn't you do this before?" Sasha asked. "When it could have really helped us?"

Jess shifted the towel that was fast becoming drenched in blood. "He needed to be close to the Valley to draw the sand."

And it wasn't just any sand. It rose up into the shape of an angry fist and rushed back toward their enemies like a landlocked tsunami. She could hear their screams as the sand blasted and pelted them.

Yeah, that had to sting.

In a matter of minutes, the swirling sands had settled and there was no one on the road but them.

Abigail took that moment to relax, hoping that this time it would last a little bit longer than a few ragged heart-beats. She needed a small break. They all did. This had been an incredible nonstop journey.

Jess watched the relief play across Abigail's delicate features as she lay back with her eyes half closed. The light of the cab cast shadows over her face. Her soft hands stroked his hair while he tried to breathe through the pain pounding in his skull. He had no idea why this power took its toll on him. For that he'd like to beat Artemis.

But if it meant being held so tenderly by Abigail, he was willing to suffer.

No one spoke as they traveled down the lonely desert road. They were all too relieved to be alive and not have to fight for it. The silence seduced them with her well needed tranquility. Only the sound of the engine and the tires rolling on asphalt reached them.

But all too soon they reached the Valley—something he'd been dreading for hours. Choo Co La Tah slowed down even more so that he could scan the surrounding landscape.

"What are you looking for?" Jess asked.

"The mound that marks our trail."

Abigail looked around at the dips and crevices of land and rock that now lined both sides of the highway. She'd never been to the Valley before. It was spooky at night.

Skeletal bushes and shrubs rose out of the ground to tower like evil spirits. A part of her even felt like they were watching her.

"Do you feel it?"

She glanced over at Choo Co La Tah. "Feel what?"

"The manitou? The energy of the earth that flows through everyone and everything. It's a living creature that can feel our pain and our joy. Everything we are, feeds into it and it leaves a lasting impression on the earth after we're gone."

Sasha sat up. "So it's like a ghost?"

Smiling, he shook his head. "It's hard to explain. You must feel it."

Abigail tried, but the only thing she felt was the weight of Jess's head in her lap and the heaviness of her conscience that still flogged her over all of this.

Choo Co La Tah's words didn't help her any, either. If anything, they made her feel worse. Her lasting impression was four plagues and untold horrors played out on innocent people.

Part of her wished she was twisted enough to not care. But sadly, she did.

Choo Co La Tah pulled over to the side of the road and parked the truck.

Jess sat up slowly.

"Are you any better?"

He pulled the towel down and she cringed. He was

still bleeding pretty badly. "Sasha? I need some tissue to pack my nose with."

The wolf gave him a suspicious stare. "Is that hygienically sound?"

"Sasha . . ."

"Fine, but if you get toxic shock up your nose, buddy, remember I warned you." He held his hand palm up and a box of Kleenex appeared.

Jess pulled a couple out and wedged them into his nostrils. He gave Abigail a sheepish smile. "Sexy, right?"

"Oh yeah, baby. You're so hot right now, if I was chicken I'd lay hard-boiled eggs."

Sasha fell back laughing.

Jess chucked the box of tissues at him. "At least I don't lick my own crotch."

"Hey!" Sasha snapped. "That's just rude. And for the record, I don't. We do have full cognitive functioning in our animal forms and that's all I'm going to say on the matter. I refute your mean lies." He sat up again and laughed at Jess. "By the way, you really need to check yourself out in the mirror."

"I'm really not going to." There were some things a man didn't need to know about himself. How much a goober he appeared to a woman he had the hots for was one of them. His imagination was bad enough. God forbid the reality be worse than the image he had in his head.

He wouldn't be able to recover from that blow.

Sasha flashed out of the cab while the rest of them climbed down.

Jess made sure to take his gun.

They met up at the back of the trailer while Ren swooped down from the sky and returned to his human form.

Abigail was impressed at how he did that. One second he was a bird and then after a small flash of light that could be easily missed if you weren't paying attention, he was human again.

Ren shook his head at Choo Co La Tah. "Nice driving. I honestly thought you guys were dead, especially when you hit that off-ramp at warp speed."

Sasha snorted. "So did we. Be glad you weren't there for the screaming."

Abigail rubbed her hands down her arms, trying to banish a sudden chill. "So what do we do now?"

Choo Co La Tah pinned her with sinister stare. "We find the sacred rock and you make your sacrifice."

16

Abigail took a deep breath to quell her rising fears. This was what she'd come here to do. Trade her life for the world.

You can do this.

No, I can't. I can't. I don't want to die. Not now that she had a real reason to live. She wanted to hang on to every heartbeat.

Every breath. Because every one of them meant something now in a way they never had before. After a lifetime of waiting for something, anything special, each second with Jess was an extraordinary adventure in discovery . . .

Of him.

Most of all, herself. She'd learned about a whole new side of her that she never knew existed. He brought out a sense of wonder and showed her miracles in the smallest things, and she didn't want to leave that. Not so soon.

One more day, please . . .

Panic set its steely talons against her courage, and it wouldn't let go of her.

Until she met Jess's dark gaze. That centered and calmed her nerves. Yeah, he looked like a silly kid with his nose packed full of Kleenex. Still, it didn't detract from how gorgeous he was with his dark windswept hair falling gently into his eyes. Those sharp cheekbones and soft lips that she could nibble on until her mouth was numb. From that tough aura of I-am-here-to-kick-your-ass-and-make-it-count.

Only Jess could make Kleenex sexy.

And that brought home one simple truth. *I won't die to save the world.*

But she would die for him.

He didn't deserve to pay for her stupidity. He'd suffered enough in his life. It was her turn to make a sacrifice. To grow up and face the consequences of her actions. Yes, she'd been lied to, but she'd let them deceive her. There was no one else to blame.

She'd dragged an innocent man into all of this . . . True, she'd seen his face that night in her room, but the woman in her now knew the man, and while she had no doubt he could have murdered her father without a second thought, Sundown would never have been able to hurt her mother.

Not like that. And there was absolutely no way he would *ever* search for a child to kill it. He was lethal, but never intentionally cruel.

Jess was innocent and she most definitely wasn't. She deserved to be punished for what she'd done.

Her entire body quaked from fear, yet she refused to let anyone know that. She wouldn't be a hypocrite. Lifting her chin, she nodded at Choo Co La Tah. "Where do you need me?"

"Follow me, my dear."

She took a step forward.

Jess cut her off. "We don't need to do this. I can fight Coyote. We have the ability to defeat him."

Sasha laughed hysterically. "Are you out of your effing mind? Hello? Where have you been for the last two days? I want whatever screwed-up glasses you're looking through. 'Cause from where I've been standing, we've been getting our asses seriously kicked around the block. Up a few stairs and down again."

Jess let out a sound of supreme exasperation as he cut a killing glare toward the wolf. "We're not dead yet."

"*Yet* is the operative word. If that's all that's in the way, I'll kill you and end it. Ren? Give me your knife."

Ren shook his head. "It's their decision."

Sasha curled his lip in repugnance. "Oh, that's it. You're fired, buddy. Get off my island until you learn to be a team player."

Abigail ignored his tirade. The only one who had her attention right now was Sundown. "It's okay, Jess. I'm ready."

"I'm not." Those dark eyes scorched her with emotions she couldn't even begin to understand. Was it possible she might mean something to him after all?

Dare she even hope for it?

She walked into his arms and held him close against her, wishing they had one more night together. *I would give anything for it.*

But it wasn't meant to be. And for that alone, she wanted to weep.

Jess couldn't breathe as he held on to her and pain ripped him apart. Every inch of her body was pressed against his, making him hunger for her in a way he'd never hungered for anything.

How could he lose her now when he'd only just found her? The depth of his feelings for her didn't make any sense. She had knocked him senseless, literally, from the first time he'd laid eyes on her and she kept him off-kilter.

There was no denying the agony that blistered him from the inside out at the thought of not seeing her again. The very concept of losing her staggered him.

He couldn't let go. Not of this.

Not of her.

I'm not strong enough to lose another woman I love. Yeah, he could take a savage beating and not blink. He could walk through hell itself and taunt the devil while Lucifer's demons flogged him every step of the way.

But living without her would break him. As bad as losing Matilda had hurt, this was so much worse. He wouldn't just lose the woman he loved.

He'd lose the only woman who'd ever seen the real him. The only person who knew his true feelings. He'd never been so honest with anyone.

Not even himself.

I can't let you go. . . .

Abigail ran her hands over his muscled back and savored this last connection to the one person she'd waited her entire life to meet.

The man she loved with every part of her.

Squeezing him tight, she forced herself to let go and step back. He stared down at her while she reached into his front pocket and pulled out his watch. Opening it, she stared at the face that had changed him forever. The face that had saved him from himself and given him back his soul.

The woman he'd sold his soul to avenge.

His was the face she would carry in her watch if she had one.

Heartsick and weary, she shut the watch and placed it in his palm, then folded his fingers around it. Lifting his hand to her lips, she inhaled the deep masculine scent of his skin, then kissed his scarred knuckles. A permanent reminder of how difficult his life had been and how hard he'd fought for it. "You will always belong to Matilda, Jess. I understand that now." Just as she understood what Jess had told her about his relationship with her mother.

Being in love was vastly different from loving someone. When you were *in* love, it consumed you. Devoured you.

And made you deliriously happy.

That was what he did for her.

Take care of our boy, Matilda. I won't fight you for his affections.

She'd been lucky enough just to know him for a short time.

Holding back her tears, she stepped around him and climbed up the dark ground to where Choo Co La Tah waited for her.

Don't look back. Don't torture yourself. But she couldn't help it. She had to see him one last time.

Her throat tight, she turned to find those dark eyes

never wavering. The look of tormented pain on his face seared her, and it made her wish she could steal every bad memory from him and replace it with only happiness.

Time seemed suspended as they stared at each other. Even her heart seemed to stop.

"Abigail . . ." Jess started forward, but Ren stopped him.

"She has to do this alone, *penyo*."

That familiar tic thumped against his lean jaw. She watched the battle he waged with himself. The indecision he had. Finally, he shoved Ren aside and sprinted up the hill to where she stood.

He took her hand into his and placed his watch in her palm. It was still warm from his touch.

She frowned at him. "What are you doing?"

"I don't want you to be alone anymore." He closed her fingers around the watch and kissed her hand just like she'd kissed his.

Those words and that single action brought her to her knees. They shattered her facade and succeeded in wrenching a sob from her. She understood exactly what he was saying. He was giving her his most prized possession.

He loved her.

And that made her cry all the harder. "Damn you, Jess," she breathed, despising her weakness in front of the others. "I hate you."

He flashed that charming grin that was as much a part

of him as his slow Southern drawl. "I know . . . Me, too."
He clutched her hand in his.

Don't let go of me.

"Abigail? We must go."

She wiped the tears away with the back of her hand.
There was so much she wanted to say to him. So much to
tell.

I love you. How could three small words like that become lodged in her throat?

Jess had been right. The hardest words to live with
were the ones you didn't say that you should have.

Summoning her courage, she pulled away and went to
Choo Co La Tah.

Jess couldn't breathe as he watched her vanish into the
landscape. *How could you let her go?*

Duty. Honor. He could come up with "noble" reasons
all night long. But none of them made this tolerable.

One life to save the world. It was a fair exchange. The
only problem was that one life had become the entire world
to him.

And he'd just sent her off to her death.

Alone.

A*bigail clutched Jess's* watch to her heart and held it there
as she followed Choo Co La Tah into a cave that looked
like something other than nature had hand-carved it out of

the hills. Once the darkness had swallowed them whole, he clapped his hands together three times, and on the last one, a fire ignited between his palms. He spread his arms wide, allowing the light to arc between his hands. It grew taller, stretching for the earthen ceiling far above them. Blues, greens, reds, and oranges burned in the fire, entrancing her like a melody for the eyes.

Then it shot around the room, lighting sconces she hadn't even known were there. A living entity, the candlelight danced against the walls in a way that made it appear the myriad of petroglyphs were moving.

The one on the far west side drew her attention. It showed a man with a buffalo skin holding the hand of a woman with butterfly wings. But what kept her spellbound was the design of the wings.

She'd seen that before.

Where?

Choo Co La Tah moved to stand behind her. "Open your mind, Abigail. Don't be afraid."

Something about his voice lulled her senses. Suddenly her eyelids were heavy. So heavy, it was hard to keep them open.

Stay awake.

She couldn't. Against her will, they closed and the images continued to play behind her eyelids.

Cool wind blew on her face as she ran by a small pond, searching for something.

No, she was searching for some*one*.

"Where are you?" she called in a loud whisper.

When no one appeared, she became frantic with worry. Where was he? Had something happened? He was never late. Terror flooded every part of her body. What would she do if he was gone?

"I would never leave you, precious."

She laughed at the deep, resonant voice that breathed in her ear. "You know not to do that to me."

He laid his lightly whiskered cheek against her smooth one, then enveloped her in his arms. Ahh . . . This was what she'd been craving all day. Smiling, she allowed him to rock her while they listened to the waves lap against the edges of the pool and the birds serenade one another.

He kissed her neck. "Have you told him yet?"

That question pierced her happiness with an arrow of sorrow. "No. I dare not."

"Then you will marry him?"

"No," she said, dipping her chin coyly. "That I cannot."

He tightened his arms around her. "Those are your only two choices."

But she knew better. There was a third option as well. "We could run away together." She pressed his hands closer to her skin. "Just the two of us. We'd be free, and no one—"

"I have responsibilities." His tone sharpened to a dagger's edge. "Would you have me turn my back on them?"

"Yes," she answered honestly.

He clenched his teeth. "No."

That word wounded her deep in the heart that beat only for him. "Don't you love me?"

"Of course I do."

She turned in his arms so that he could see her desperation for himself. "Then come away with me. Now. Today."

His eyes glowed with warmth as he watched her giddy playfulness, and that succeeded in taking the anger from his tone. "I can't." He gave her chin a gentle caress. "You have to tell him about us."

Guilt stabbed her breast as she thought about the man who loved her as much as she loved the one before her. A man who had proven exactly how much she meant to him in a way no one ever had.

Why can't I love him? It would be so much easier if she did, and she'd tried. She really had.

Unfortunately, the heart played its own tune, and it was deaf to what the head tried to tell it.

"It will crush him, and that's the last thing I want to do. He's given me so much and been so kind . . ."

Anger slapped at her from his dark eyes. "Then marry *him.*"

Those words stung her like a slap. And she didn't deserve them. "You shouldn't say that if you don't mean it. What if I did what you said?"

His nostrils flared. "I would cut his heart out and feed it to him."

Now he scared her. Was this the real him that he was showing to her because her love had made him comfortable? "What's happening to you?"

"The woman I love won't come to her senses. That's all."

She shook her head as every instinct she possessed denied his words. "There's something else. You're . . . different."

"I'm the same as ever."

But she knew better. This wasn't the man who'd conquered her defenses and laid siege to what no other man had ever claimed. "Is your post corrupting you?"

He scoffed. "I'm stronger than that."

Everyone had a weakness. Everyone. "Where is your arrogance coming from?" She didn't understand it.

"The truth isn't arrogance."

She gaped at him. "Who are you?"

"I'm the man you love."

And those words hurt her most of all. "Are you not the man who loves me?"

"Of course."

She shook her head in denial. "No, that's not what you said. You put the order there that matters most to you. All you care about it is you."

"I did not say that."

"You don't have to." Tears began to flood her eyes

until her vision drowned in misery. "Your words betray your thoughts." She tried to leave him, but he stopped her. She tried to gain her release. "Let me go!"

"Not until you learn to be reasonable."

Learn? She was not some infant who needed lessons. She was a woman full grown. How dare he not see that. "I'm not the one who's changing. There's something dark inside you that wasn't there before."

He scoffed. "You don't know what you're talking about."

But she did, and that knowledge beat painfully inside her.

He leaned down, his eyes glacial and foreign. "If you love me, you will tell him."

Why did she have to prove her love? Was it not enough that he saw it with his own vision?

She wrested her arm from his grasp. "I must go."

He didn't speak as he watched her walk away.

A shadow unwrapped itself from his and peeled itself from the wall. As full figured as a man, it walked toward him to stand behind his shoulder and whisper in his ear. "I told you so, didn't I? Women are ever fickle. There's no man who can keep one forever satisfied."

"Butterfly is different. She is all things good."

"And you are not."

No, he wasn't. He was a warrior, and his skin had been bathed in blood more times than he could count. It didn't pay for him to show mercy or patience. He wasn't supposed to.

At the right hand of his chief, he had slain innocents aplenty. It was his job. But now that they were at peace, he was lost.

Until he'd seen the Butterfly. She had tamed the savage inside him. Made it content to sit before hearth and watch her gentle ways. He didn't understand it. But so long as she was with him, he had no desire to pick up knife or spear.

He wanted only to please her.

Abigail blinked as the vision faded. When it was gone completely, she realized she was still standing in front of the wall with Choo Co La Tah behind her.

"Now you know," he said quietly.

Baffled, she turned to meet his kind gaze. "Know what?"

"Who you really are. Who Jess is."

More images flashed in her mind like a short-circuiting strobe trying to drive her mad. They came so fast that she could barely see them, and yet somehow her mind registered it all. "I don't understand."

He placed his hands on each of her arms. "You are the Butterfly, and Jess is the Buffalo. Peace and war. Two halves who were supposed to make one."

She shook her head in denial. "What have you been smoking or snorting or inhaling?"

"Do you not feel the connection here?"

Weirdly enough, she did. But that only freaked her out more.

Choo Co La Tah sighed as he realized she still wasn't ready for the truth. For all these centuries, he'd hidden her and waited for her to find a way to free herself from the curse. And still she was bound.

What a pity.

Maybe in her next life . . .

"Come." He gestured toward the rock in the center of the room that lay like a bed beneath a cluster of shimmering stalactites. She was strong in this lifetime. Stronger than she'd ever been before. He saw the rebellion in her eyes that he'd waited a millennium for.

She squelched it and then went to obey. Even so, it was obvious that her submission grated against every part of her being. Her teeth thoroughly clenched, she climbed up and lay back against the cold stone slab.

Choo Co La Tah began chanting as he summoned the sacred breath to cleanse them both.

Abigail listened to his song, but she zoned out as she conjured an image of Jess in her mind. A smile spread across her face as she saw him in the car again. As she felt the memory of his touch on her body. She cupped his pocket watch in her hands and held it on her stomach.

"Choo Co La Tah?" She hated to interrupt his ceremony, but this needed to be done.

"Yes?"

"Once I'm dead, would you please return Jess's watch to him?"

"Why?"

She ran the pad of her thumb over the engraved scrollwork. "He loves it."

"Is his happiness all that matters to you?"

"No. But I don't want him to have any regrets. Not about me."

He inclined his head to her, then went back to his chanting.

Abigail was patient at first, but as it dragged on and on, it began to wear on her nerves. Why couldn't he kill her already? Was the torture part of it?

Perv.

When he started on another chant with no letup in sight, she lost all semblance of manners.

"Choo? Really? Is all this necessary?"

He paused midsyllable. "You're ready to die, then?"

Oh . . . there was that.

She turned her head to look at him. "May I have what's behind door number two?"

He actually laughed. "You already chose."

"I know." She swallowed hard and closed her eyes. "I'm ready."

She felt Choo Co La Tah move to stand by her shoulder. The faintest whisper of metal scraping leather let her know he was drawing a knife. Bracing herself, she conjured Jess's face and imagined herself in his arms.

No, on a beach. A little difficult, granted, since he couldn't be in daylight without bursting into flames, but she'd loved the beach when she was a kid. And since the Apollites had the same spontaneous combustion issue with the silken sands, she hadn't been on one since her mother took her there for her fourth birthday.

But she was there now. Jess in a Speedo.

Just kidding. That was too bold a look even for him. Maybe a . . .

Naked. Yeah, naked. She liked that best of all. The two of them lying in the surf like the old movie her mother had loved, *From Here to Eternity*.

Something cold and sharp touched her throat. Tensing, she braced herself for the cut that would end her life.

"Do you not want to fight me to live?"

Hold on to Jess. Naked. Beach. Naked.

"Answer me, Abigail. Do you want to live?"

"Of course I do." What kind of question was that?

"Then why don't you fight me?"

Abigail didn't answer. She had to hold on to Jess's face or she would be fighting him with everything she had.

"Why don't you fight?"

She opened her eyes to glare at him. "Don't you understand? I *am* saving my life."

"I don't follow. You're doing this to save the world?"

She shook her head. "I'm doing this to save Jess."

"For him I can cut your throat?" He laid the knife across her neck. So close, she couldn't swallow without cutting herself. She kept her eyes open this time.

Screw it. If he was going to kill her, he could do it looking at her.

"Yes."

His gaze softened immediately as a slow smile spread across his face. "That's the right answer." He pulled the knife away.

Completely confused, she scowled at him. "What are you doing?"

"You made your sacrifice. You can get up now."

She still didn't understand. "I have to die. Don't I?"

"Not all sacrifices involve death, child. As the Enapay used to say, the noblest sacrifice of all is to open your heart up completely to another person and give them the dagger with which to slay you. . . . You were willing to die for Jess. Bravely. You proved it. That's enough for the Spirit to see and be appeased."

Incredulous, she gaped at him. "Get out." Could it really be that easy?

"No getting out, I'm afraid, my dear. All we need to do now is make your offering and then locate those jars to protect them."

She bolted upright. "I really don't have to die?"

"Are we going to be doing this all night? Should I book us a reservation at Redundancy?"

She laughed. Until her gaze went past his shoulder to . . .

It took a moment for her eyes to see it again and then to realize what it was. . . .

That familiar shadow she'd seen on her wall as a child. The one that had whispered to Buffalo.

And before she could make a single sound of warning, it attacked.

17

Jess paced back and forth like a caged cougar on steroids. Every time he started to go after Abigail, Ren grabbed his arm and stopped him.

The bastard was about to get a boot kicked so far up his ass, he'd be burping shoe leather for the rest of his immortal life.

Jess started for the cave again.

Ren cut him off. "You can't."

"Bull. Shit. What I can't do is leave her. Don't you understand?"

Ren laughed bitterly. "Yeah, I understand better than
you can ever imagine. I know exactly what it's like to want
something so bad, you can taste it and to have to watch as
it voluntarily goes to someone else and then wish them
both the best and try to mean it. I know the bitter taste of
gall as they sit down at your table and you have to smile
while inside you die every time they touch or exchange
love-saturated glances. Don't talk to me about torment,
Jess. I wrote the fucking book on it."

Now, that was something Ren had never shared with
him before. He had no idea his friend had been through
an experience like that. Ren never talked about his past.
Hell, Jess didn't even know why Ren was a Dark-Hunter.

Because of his own past, he'd never wanted to pry into
someone else's. He figured they'd tell him what they wanted
him to know, and if they didn't volunteer it, then there
was probably a real good reason why.

Far be it from him to stick his nose in it.

Jess inclined his head respectfully. "I'm sorry, Ren."

Ren wore an expression that said, *You have no idea.*

From up the hill where the cavern was, a fierce battle
cry rang out. One that sounded like Choo Co La Tah's.
Jess's heart seized as a bad feeling tore through him.

Please let me be wrong.

As fast as he could, he ran up the red-soiled hill while Ren turned into a bird to fly and Sasha took his wolf form.

By the time Jess reached Choo Co La Tah's private cave, Sasha, still in wolf form, was fighting a coyote and Ren was nowhere to be seen.

Neither was Abigail.

That didn't make him happy at all. Was she dead?

He ground his teeth as agony poured through him. It was the same aching, desolate feeling he'd had the night he sold his soul to Artemis.

Abigail was gone.

Please don't be dead.

"Jess?" Choo Co La Tah's voice pulled him back to their present situation. They were in the middle of an attack, and he had to focus if they were to survive. Six bodies of coyotes lay nearby as a gruesome reminder of everything at stake. Blood was splattered on the walls and pooled on the floor, under the bodies.

Choo Co La Tah took a step toward him, then slipped and fell on the blood-drenched ground.

He didn't get back up.

Jess sprinted toward the elder, who lay in a small crevice on his side. A quick visual skim of his injuries said that it was a miracle he was still alive.

Coyote had been playing for keeps. But by the looks of it, so had Choo Co La Tah.

Jess reached down to gently roll him over so that he could see the extent of his injuries. And they were extensive. The coyotes had torn him up badly. "What happened?"

He swallowed hard. "They jumped us."

"Us?"

Choo Co La Tah cleared his throat. "They took Abigail before I could complete the ritual. We have to make the offering by dawn . . . or else."

Hell would rain down on them in biblical proportions. Boy, would his snooty neighbors be pissed. They didn't like him on his best day anyway. Not that he cared.

"Do you know where they took her?"

Choo Co La Tah rubbed at his bleeding forehead while Jess tried to tend the wound. "Most likely, Coyote's den . . . and you can't kill him there, Jess. We have to get him here in the Valley."

Jess glanced around to see Sasha defeating his playmate. "Where's Ren?"

"He went after Coyote and Abigail. You have to find them, Jess. Bring them back."

"Don't worry. I won't fail."

He hoped.

Abigail *fought hard* against the ropes that bound her hands and feet together, but there was no give with them. As Jess would say, she was bound up and dressed like a Christmas goose.

And in total darkness. If only she knew where she was.

Then she heard a deep voice from the other side of whatever she was in.

"I'll deal with him later," a man growled in a voice that was familiar, yet she couldn't identify it.

A second later, the door opened and relief poured through her at the sight of a friendly face. And here she'd thought she was in danger.

Thank God.

She smiled at him. "Ren. It's so good to see you. You won't believe what happened."

He curled his lip at her, silencing her happy greeting. "Do I look like that piece of shit?"

Okay . . . Obviously he equated Ren with something bad. Which was strange, since they were virtually identical. Same black hair, dark eyes. Refined features. But now that he mentioned it, there was a difference.

Ren wasn't crazy. This man was.

Did he have multiple personality disorder?

"Are you a shape-shifter?" she tried again.

"Are you stupid? Of course I am."

He acted like she should know him and yet claimed he wasn't Ren. What was she dealing with? "Are we playing a game?"

He snatched her closer to him. "I don't play games. Ever."

Psycho it was. She would take that category and run with it.

And he got even weirder a few heartbeats later when he leaned over her and brushed his hand through her hair. He picked a handful of it up and held it to his nose so that he could sniff it. "So beautiful."

Ew . . . where's my Perv Be Gone? Had she known she'd be facing him, she'd have brought extra.

He brushed his lips against her forehead. The moment he touched her, a bright image appeared in her mind.

She saw the Butterfly again, and this time she was talking to . . .

Ren?

"I can't marry you, Coyote."

That name slammed into her like a truck. For a full minute, she couldn't breathe.

Coyote was an identical match for Ren? WTF? Why hadn't Ren mentioned that fact? Wouldn't something like that be a *little* important?

Especially since they were at war.

That thought made her blood run cold as another one followed right behind it. Was Ren a spy for Coyote?

It made total sense. No wonder Coyote kept finding them and Ren kept vanishing. He was probably heading straight to his brother every time he took flight.

She was the only one who knew. *I can't die until I let the others know, too.*

And still the images of the past played in her mind. . . .

Coyote's handsome face was a mixture of equal parts

horror and hurt over Butterfly breaking up with him. His breathing ragged, he shook his head in denial. "I don't understand. More than anything, I love you. Why would you want to leave me?"

Guilt hung heavy in her heart. The last thing she'd wanted to do was make him hurt. "I love someone else."

Coyote shot to his feet to confront her. "No. It's not possible."

Of course it was possible. It'd already happened. She started crying. "I'm so sorry, Cy. I never meant for this to happen. I did want to marry you, but then we met and . . . and . . . I haven't been the same. Please be happy for us." Her smile turned dreamy through her tears. "He understands me in a way no one ever has. I feel so alive, and all I have to do is think of him."

Coyote's face turned beet red from his fury, and for a second, she thought he might actually strike her.

Girl, get out of there. This was the part where Freddy Krueger or some other ghoul jumped out and killed the hapless victim.

Why wasn't Butterfly standing up for herself?

Coyote sneered in her face. "Never meant for this to happen?" He mocked her tone of voice. "Is that the lie you tell, you whore? Where did you meet him? Was it before or after I was tortured for over a year for protecting you?"

Guilt gnawed her into pieces. He was right. He had suffered so much for her.

But it was wrong to throw that in her face, and she knew it. "I'm sorry. I am. I didn't mean to hurt you. Please understand. I know in time you will."

She turned and walked across the floor, toward the door.

"I'll win you back, Butterfly!" he shouted after her. "Watch me. You'll see. You're mine. Now and always."

What a jerk . . .

"Shhh," Coyote whispered to her as he rubbed her forehead and her dreams of the past dissipated. He traced the line of her brow. Something that made her skin crawl.

"What do you want with me?" she asked him.

"For you to fulfill your promise."

Abigail widened her eyes. "I didn't promise anything."

He gave her an evil smirk. "You always had trouble remembering your promises. Keeping your word. But not this time. You *owe* me. And I intend to collect it."

Yeah, she had something she was going to pay him with. But she could pretty much bet he wouldn't like it.

He definitely wouldn't enjoy it.

Pulling away from her, he cocked his head as if he heard something. He shoved her back into the darkness and withdrew, then shut the door.

That's right. Run, Coyote, run. No matter what Choo Co La Tah or Coyote thought, she wasn't Butterfly. She was Abigail Yager. And she didn't give up or give in.

Yes, she'd spent her childhood in fearful submission to

her Apollite parents. But that had ended when they died. From that day forward, she'd been reborn as an assertive woman who refused to cower to anyone.

"Abby?"

She stopped her tirade as she heard the most wonderful voice in the world in her head.

"Sundown?"

"Yeah. Are you okay, baby?"

She definitely was now. *"Didn't I tell you to stay out of my thoughts?"*

"You can beat me later. Just do it naked."

In spite of the danger and her being tied up, she laughed at his humor.

Until she remembered Ren might be with him. *"Jess, listen. We have a spy in our midst."*

"What?"

"It's true. Did you know Coyote is Ren's brother?"

"No. No way. It's not possible."

"It's definitely possible and extremely creepy. Keep your eye on Ren. Whatever you do, don't turn your back on him."

"Okay. Are you somewhere safe?"

She glanced around her jet black prison. *"I really can't answer that. I'm tied up in some kind of little room without any light whatsoever."*

"All right. I have Sasha tracking you. I'm going to stay here in your head with you until we get there . . . if that's all right with you, that is. I don't want to intrude."

Those words made her smile in spite of her danger. *"Thank you, Jess."*

"There's no reason to thank me, Abby. You say the word, and I will always come for you. No matter what."

That promise choked her and brought tears to her eyes. Never in her life had she had that kind of security.

Not even with Kurt or Hannah. As the oldest of the three of them, she'd allowed them to rely on her. Not the other way around.

The closest thing she'd had, had been Jonah. But even he hadn't been reliable.

I love you, Jess.

How she wished she could say that to him. But she knew she couldn't. He would always be a Dark-Hunter, and they couldn't marry.

"You still with me, Abby?"

"I'm here. How many more hours till dawn?"

"Less than two."

Ouch. They were running out of time. Choo Co La Tah needed to finish his ceremony and make an offering of her blood to Mother Earth.

"Where are you guys right now?" she asked.

"Not close enough to you for my money."

"How close would that be?"

"By your side."

"You keep talking to me like that, cowboy, and you might get lucky tonight."

"I already got lucky tonight."

"Mmm, so you're a one-shot-a-night guy, huh?"

He laughed in her head. *"Ah, now, sugar, I didn't say that. The stallion never minds an all-night ride, especially when it's a wild one."*

"Stallion? That's some ego you have there."

"It's not ego when it's true."

A chill went down her spine at that phrase. It was the same one Buffalo had used with Butterfly.

Could it be true?

Before she could pursue that thought, she heard a strange noise outside her door. Was Coyote coming back?

Something large struck the door hard a split second before it was wrenched open. Reacting purely on instinct, she charged the newcomer and kicked out with everything she had, hoping it would be enough to overpower him.

He fell straight to the ground, where he rolled back and forth on his shoulders in utter agony. A loud groan filled her ears. She moved to kick his groin again.

"Abigail!" he snapped, lifting his arm to prevent her infamous nut-cracker stomp. "Stop!"

Unsure whom she was dealing with, she narrowed her gaze on the man. "Are you Ren or Coyote?"

He flashed into the body of the crow. But it didn't last long. A heartbeat later, he returned to his male form.

Granted, he was still a little green around the gills . . . and cupping himself. But he was Ren again. And he was whimpering.

"Oh, come on, you big baby. I didn't hit you that hard."

"I completely disagree. You kick like a damn mule, and I swear both my testicles are now lodged in my throat." He let out a long breath as he pressed his hand to his groin. Then slowly, he rose to his feet. Biting his lip, he let out several sounds of severe pain before he stood and glared angrily at her.

She backed up, unsure of his intent. Would he kill her for his brother?

"What's wrong with you?"

Abigail hesitated. "I'm fine. What's wrong with *you*?"

"You kicked me in the balls."

There was that. And then there was the other matter. "What are you doing here?"

"I was trying to rescue you, but I'm thinking it was bad idea. And damn, you're still bundled up. I'd hate to see what you could do with unrestricted access."

Likely story. Who would have ever questioned him coming in to save her? But she wasn't that stupid. "How did you know where I was?"

"I tracked one of the coyotes back here." He pulled a knife out of his pocket and took a step toward her.

Abigail backed up in trepidation. "I'd rather wait till Jess gets here."

He didn't listen. Instead, he sliced through her bindings and let them fall to the floor. "We don't have time to wait. . . . Are you sure you're okay? You're as skittish as a cat in a Doberman factory."

She hesitated. Was he leading her home?

Or somewhere far more sinister?

"Abigail?"

"I don't want to go with you."

He recoiled as if she'd slapped him. "You don't have to worry about your privacy. I won't betray you."

"That's not what I'm worried about."

"What, then?"

"*Your* loyalty. You want to talk to me about Coyote and explain why he looks just like you?"

Busted. It was written all over his face. She could almost see the gears grinding in his head.

"Yeah," she accused. "That's what I thought."

He shook his head. "No. It's not what you think."

"I think you've teamed up with your brother and sold all of us down Shit Creek. Paddles are extra."

"I didn't. You remember the story I told you about the warrior and the Gate?"

"Yeah?"

"*I* was the warrior."

Her mind reeled with that knowledge. "No."

He nodded. "My brother hates me to this day, and I don't blame him. I was out of control."

"But why?"

"I told you why. Jealousy. I'd spent my entire life living in Coyote's shadow. Others flocked to him. And for the most part, I was good with that."

Ren clenched his teeth. "Until the day he brought you

home." He winced as if the pain was still too much to bear. "I'd never seen a more beautiful woman. For our people, butterflies are a symbol of hope. It's said that if you capture one in your hands and whisper your dreams to it, it will carry them up to the heavens so that the wish can be granted."

Sarcastic applause rang out from behind him.

Ren turned to find Coyote there.

"Nice, brother. You're still trying to get into her bed, eh?"

Abigail noted the pain in Ren's expression.

"I put it aside, Coyote. It's time for you to do the same."

Coyote shook his head. "No. The Butterfly belongs to me. I captured her. I tamed her. Most of all, I protected her."

"She's not a possession."

He smiled evilly. "Yes, she is. She's the most precious possession."

Abigail's head spun as the words they were saying now caused her mind to flash back to a time and place she still couldn't identify.

She saw Ren and Coyote in a meadow, where they were fighting just like now. Even the subject was the same.

Coyote sneered at Ren. "This is all your fault. You and your petty jealousy. Why couldn't you have been happy for me? Just once. Why? Had you left us alone, none of this would have ever happened. There would have been no Grizzly Spirit. No need for Guardians and he—" Coyote gestured to the floor with a knife. "—would never have come here."

Ren didn't respond. His gaze was fastened to the red on Coyote's hands. It went from there to the ground, where . . .

Buffalo lay dead in a pool of blood.

Ren winced. "How could you do this? He was a Guardian." *And my best friend in the world.* The one and only person who'd stood by him without question.

Even when evil had claimed possession of his body and he'd served it willingly, Buffalo had stayed with him. Protecting him.

Now he lay slain by Ren's own brother.

My cruelty drove him mad. . . .

Coyote spit on Buffalo's back. "He was a bastard, and he stole her heart from me."

Ren shook his head slowly as guilt and sorrow ripped him apart. "Hearts can never be stolen, Cy. They can only be given."

Coyote sneered at him. "You're wrong! That's your jealousy speaking."

But it wasn't. Ren had learned to banish that.

Now it was too late. He'd destroyed everything that was good in his life.

Everything.

Sick to his stomach, he went to Buffalo and knelt beside him to whisper a small prayer over his body.

A shrill scream echoed. Looking up, Ren saw Butterfly

as she ran to her Buffalo. She sobbed hysterically, throwing herself down on top of him.

"Why? Why? Why would you hurt me so?"

Coyote curled his lip. "You tore my heart out."

"And you killed mine." She laid herself over the Buffalo and wept.

Ren rose to his feet and left her there to grieve while he confronted his brother.

That was his mistake. He didn't think about what would happen if Butterfly was allowed to cry her misery out to the gods and spirits. To wail and shriek for her lost Buffalo.

But it was too late now. A howling wind came screaming through the woods, dancing around their whitebuckskin–covered bodies. Those winds joined together to form two trumpeters who blew their horns to announce the most feared creature of all.

The Avenging Spirit. Something that could be summoned only by the cries of a wronged woman who wanted vengeance against the ones who'd hurt her.

Nebulous in form, he was bathed all in white. His hair, the translucent skin that covered his skeletal features. His feathers and buckskin. The only break from the color was the dark blue beadwork along his neck.

"Why was I called forth?" he demanded.

Butterfly looked up. Her beautiful face contorted by grief, she looked old and haggard now. Her hair blew around her body as her gaze pierced them with her fury.

"The Coyote killed my heart. So I want his as payment for what he took."

The Avenging Spirit bowed to her. Then he turned toward the men. His face changed from an old gaunt man with stringy hair to the face of ultimate evil. He opened his mouth and it dropped to the floor, contorting and elongating his features. Abigail shivered in terror.

Out of his mouth flew a giant eagle with a lone ghostly warrior on its back. The warrior lifted his spear.

Ren stepped back to give the warrior room.

With a discordant cry of vengeance that shook the very fabric of Mother Earth's gown, he let fly his spear at Coyote's heart.

One moment Ren was standing out of the way. In the next, he was across the room, where Coyote had been a heartbeat earlier. Before he could gather his wits and move, the spear flew through the center of his chest, piercing his heart. The force of it lifted him off his feet and pinned him to a tree.

Pain exploded through his body as he gasped for breath. The taste of blood filled his mouth. His eyesight dimmed.

He was dying.

The warrior turned his eagle around and flew back into the Avenging Spirit's mouth. As quickly as they'd come, they were gone.

His breathing labored, Ren stared at his brother. "I would have given you my life had you asked for it."

"You taught me to take what I wanted." Coyote closed the distance between them and snatched the bone necklace from Ren's throat that held his Guardian seal. He untied the pouch from Ren's belt where he kept his strongest magic. "And I want your Guardianship."

"You weren't chosen."

"And neither were you." Coyote seized the spear and drove it in even deeper. He laughed in triumph as Ren choked on his own blood.

With one last gasp, he fell silent.

The pride on Coyote's face was sickening as he turned his attention to Butterfly. "I'm a Guardian now. You can love me again."

She curled her lip in repugnance. "I could never love you after what you've done. You're a monster."

He snatched her up by her arm. "You are mine, and I will never share you. Make yourself ready for our wedding."

"No."

He slapped her across the face. "You do not argue with me, woman. You obey." He let go of her so fast that she fell back across Buffalo's body, where she wept until she had no more tears.

She was still there when the maids came and dressed her for Coyote.

At sundown, he returned for her. But before they could begin the ceremony that would join them together, the

Keeper appeared in the middle of the meadow. His dark eyes radiated fury.

"I am here to claim the life of the one responsible for killing two Guardians."

Coyote gasped in terror. His mind whirled as he tried to think of some trick that could save his life. And while his brother's magic was powerful, it wasn't enough.

The Keeper crossed the room in a determined stride that promised retribution. From his belt, he drew the Dagger of Justice and without hesitating, plunged it straight into the heart of the one who'd caused such turmoil and misery.

Butterfly staggered back as blood saturated her dress and ran across her braids. Instead of showing pain, she sighed in relief. Blood ran from her lips as she turned to Coyote. "I will be with my love now. Forever in his arms." She sank to the ground, where she died with the most blissful of looks on her face.

Coyote sputtered. "I don't understand."

The Keeper shrugged. "You were the tool. Butterfly was the cause. Had she not been born, you wouldn't have acted."

"No, no, no, no. This isn't right. This wasn't how it was supposed to end." Raking his hands through his hair, he went to his one true love and cradled her in his arms one last time. She was so tiny and light. Her blood stained his wedding clothes, and he wept at the loss of her.

And it was his loss.

She wouldn't be waiting for him on the other side. Not now. The pain of that knowledge tore him apart. She would greet Buffalo.

Throwing his head back, he screamed in outrage. No, it wouldn't end like this. He'd been a good man. Decent. And one by one, all of them had killed that. His brother, Buffalo and Butterfly.

They'd ruined his life. There was no way he would let them live a happy eternity. Not after the way they'd tortured him. He reached into his pouch and summoned the strongest elements there.

"I curse you, Buffalo. You will live a thousand lives and never be happy in any of them. You will walk this earth, betrayed by all who look upon you. There will be no one place you call home. Not in any human lifetime. And you will never have my Butterfly." He blew his magic from his palm into the air so that it could be carried to the spirits who would make it so.

Then he looked down at the serene beauty of the Butterfly. So gentle. So sweet. The thought of cursing her stung him deep.

But she had scorned him.

"Because of what you did to me, you will never marry the one you love. He will always die on his way to unite with you, and you will spend your life mourning him over and over again. No peace. Not until you accept me. And if you do marry another, he will never trust you. You will never be happy in any marriage. Not so long as you have human blood within you." He reached into his pouch and drew the last of his magic, then sent it into the wind.

"Do you know what you've done?"

Coyote looked up at Choo Co La Tah's approach. "I settled the score."

Choo Co La Tah laughed. "Such magic always comes back on the one who wields it."

"How so?"

He gestured toward the sky and the trees. "You know the law. Do no harm, and yet you have done much harm here today."

"They hurt me first."

Choo Co La Tah sighed. "And you have sown the seeds of your ultimate demise. When you curse two people together, you bind them. With that combined strength, they will have the ability to break their curse and kill *you*."

"You don't know what you're talking about."

"Arrogance. The number one cause of death among both peasant and king. Beware its sharp blade. More times than not, it injures the one who wields it most of all."

Coyote dismissed the Guardian's words. He had no interest in them. He would never suffer.

But he would ensure that they did.

A*bigail came out* of her trance with a full understanding of everything around them.

Ren and Coyote were now in full combat mode, and they were going at it like nobody's business. They took turns pummeling each other through the tunnels of Coyote's den. She'd never seen a bloodier fight, which given the number of fights she'd been to over the years said a lot.

Glancing around, she looked for a weapon she might use that could help them.

Unfortunately, there wasn't one. But if arrogant belligerence could take down an opponent . . .

There was no telling who would win. It would definitely be close. But she knew which side she was pulling for.

Go Red Sox.

"Abigail?"

"I'm here, Jess."

"So are we."

Now, that was the best news she'd heard in days. Leaving Ren and Coyote to their bashing, she ran for the opening. At least she hoped that was where she was headed.

She knew she was going in the right direction when an explosion echoed and blew pieces of rock everywhere.

Yeah, her boys had arrived. Leave it to them to make a grand entrance.

She ran to launch herself at Jess.

Jess smiled as he felt her soft curves pressed up against his hard body. And when she kissed him, he held on to her tight. Until he sensed something that shouldn't be here.

Pulling back, he cocked his head to listen.

"What's wrong?" she asked.

"There are Daimons here."

She scowled. "No. Why would there be?"

"I don't know. But I can feel it. It's like a nest of them are nearby."

But that didn't make any sense. Why would Daimons be here with Coyote?

Unless . . .

"Coyote's a trickster."

Jess cursed as he came to the same realization she did. How could they have been so ever-loving stupid?

This was a trap, and they'd just barreled right into it.

18

Jess would laugh if it weren't so damn ironic.
One of his powers was the ability to know
when he was about to be ambushed. And the
den they were in had a damper on psychic
powers. Not that he and Ren needed that
right now, since they'd been draining each
other for the last few days.

At best, his powers were working only at

half-mast. And it wouldn't have mattered if they hadn't been. He still would have walked right into this.

For one simple reason.

He'd been so fixated on getting to Abigail and making sure she was safe, that he'd have been blind to everything else.

Oh, well . . .

Die and learn.

Cupping her face and soaking in that gleam in her eyes, he leaned his forehead against hers and took a moment to inhale the sweet scent of her skin. Yeah, this gave him strength.

"Um, guys?" Sasha said from beside them. "I hate to toss ice water on your mood, but we have a situation here, and you might want to look up and prepare or sneeze or something. Just saying."

Jess didn't have to look up. He could feel every pair of eyes on him. The three of them were standing in the center of a large round room deep inside a cavern. Pristine white and trimmed in black, the walls around them reminded him of a palace. Kind of place he'd never thought to see in real life back in the day when he'd been human.

Things changed. Not always for the good and not always for the bad.

Sasha stood on his left and Abigail in front. Because of his injuries, Choo Co La Tah wasn't with them, and Ren seemed to have disappeared entirely.

Again.

There were six Daimons coming at them. Three to his right, four to his left. And a herd of them in the back tunnel.

Ah hell, he'd had worst odds.

And that was just yesterday.

Abigail took a second longer to stare into those dark eyes that haunted her. Rising on her tiptoes, she kissed the tip of his delectable nose. "Thank you for coming for me."

"My pleasure."

She hugged him close. "And in case we don't make it out alive . . . I love you, Jess Brady. I just wanted you to know it."

Jess felt his heart swell over words he'd never thought to hear from another pair of lips that set his world on fire. "I love you, too."

She smiled.

Until Sasha barked. "They're attacking."

Jess savored the sensation of her skin against his for one second longer. "Aim for the heart."

Inclining her head to let him know she understood, she reached around his waist to pull the two weapons he had on the back part of his holster. He drew the ones in front.

They turned in synch and opened fire on their enemies. The first one he struck, flipped and landed at his feet. It didn't explode, so he took that to mean it wasn't dead or it was one of the new breed of killing machines.

Daimons were coming at them from every direction. It reminded him of the *Alien* video game. The more he shot, the more they grew. Only difference? Daimons didn't drop from the ceiling.

Yet.

Who knew what power they might develop at a later date. Every time he got it halfway figured out, they discovered something new—like eating a gallu to augment their powers. Who the hell thought of that?

Probably the same sick SOB who saw a chicken shoot an egg out its nether region and said, "Hey, y'all, I think I'm gonna fry that up and eat it. Wish me luck. If I get sick from it, someone fetch a doctor."

Abigail fired her last round and blew one of the Daimons into dust. She was having a serious crisis of conscience about killing people she'd have died to defend a week ago. But the fact that they were so determined to kill her if she didn't kill them made it a little easier to do.

She pivoted to her right and froze as she caught sight of Jess fighting. He fired a round from his shotgun, then used the stock to swat another. Turning in a graceful arc, he fired again at a new target, then ducked, slid along the ground on his knees to reach another bad guy that he slugged with the gunstock, then stabbed. He moved so fast that he was already two steps ahead of her before she'd done anything at all.

Incredible.

Another Daimon wielding an axe attacked. Completely calm . . . *freakishly* calm, Jess leaned his head back from the swing, letting the axe fly clear of his throat. Still, it'd been so close that she didn't know how he could trust himself not to have misjudged the swing.

Thank God he didn't. Otherwise, she'd be picking his head up right now.

As their ammunition ran low and the Daimons kept coming, Jess put himself between Sasha, who was in wolf form, and her. She loved the fierce protector in him.

Still he fought like a ninja. She was extremely impressed. And if the truth were told, she was amazed she'd been able to hold her own against him when they'd fought. Until now, she hadn't realized just how accomplished he was.

That boy had mad skills.

In no time, their rounds were spent, and they were retreating to the back part of the cavern while beating Daimons down as hard as they could.

Jess was really starting to miss his ability to reload his weapons. And create them. Damn his drained powers. It would make things easier, especially since Coyote had nothing here that could be used as a weapon.

Bastard.

"Can you hear the human souls releasing when you kill them?" Abigail asked.

"No."

But by the look on her face, he could tell that she did. "Are you all right about it?"

She nodded. "No," she said, contradicting the nod. "I keep thinking about the fact that my mother's soul was taken and consumed by a Daimon. No one freed hers."

"I'm sorry."

"Not your fault."

Maybe, but he felt bad for her anyway.

Sasha's powers were as limited by the damper as his were. They were fighting with their hands behind their backs, and the Daimons were all at their full psychic capacity.

Abigail began to panic as more Daimons showed up. They were breeding like cockroaches. "We're going to die, aren't we?"

"Hope not. I still have another episode of *No Ordinary Family* downloaded on my computer that I haven't had a chance to watch yet. Be a damn shame to miss it. Might have to hurt them if that happens."

She shook her head at him. "You're so not right." But that was what she loved about him.

They were backing up through the cavern and quickly running out of places to go.

When they got to the last of it, they formed a small circle.

Sasha sighed. "So this is it, huh? Not how I thought I'd go out." He glanced around at the extremely green cavern walls. "Well, at least we'll be all minty fresh when we go."

"Psst!"

Sasha turned around in a circle, looking for the source of the sound.

Jess arched a brow at Abigail.

"I didn't do it."

They looked at Sasha. "What? Some freak noise gets made, and you blame the dog? That ain't right. Next thing you know, I'll get blamed for gas attacks, too. I didn't do it."

"Psst! Abby!"

Abigail froze as she recognized Hannah's voice. She turned around to find her sister in a small hole in the wall. Dressed all in black, she looked like Spy Doll Barbie. If the point was to make her fierce, it was failing miserably. Hannah was too tiny, too blond, and too sweet looking to make anyone afraid of her.

"What are you doing here, H?"

"Saving your asses. Come on."

Abigail followed her without reservation.

"Keep your voices real low," Hannah warned in a whisper. "Some of the Daimons have really good ears, and the walls are thin."

"Do you know where Ren is?" Jess asked.

She nodded. "They're planning to sacrifice him at midnight. Right now, Coyote is torturing him."

Abigail frowned. Hannah acted like she was at home here and knew the schedule for everything. Best of all, she knew about this hidden passage. "I don't understand. How did you guys get hooked up with Coyote?"

"Jonah."

That unexpected response startled her so badly that she actually stumbled. "What?"

"You remember how Jonah did all that research into trying to find a cure for us?"

Abigail nodded. Everyone who'd ever met Jonah knew this story. He'd found some obscure text that said one of the local Nevada tribes had hidden a serum in the mountains that could cure any illness and transform someone's DNA into perfect structure.

Jonah had taken that to mean that it would repair whatever physiological damage Apollo had done to them when he cursed them.

Both she and Hannah had thought it was a load, but Jonah had insisted, and for years, he'd take night trips out to the desert to look for it.

"Jonah didn't find the serum. He found Coyote, who told him that the legend was real and that if he'd help Coyote find the two jars that contained it, Coyote would share. They were still looking for it when . . ." She passed a harsh stare to Abigail. "Jonah died. Anyway, they've been working together for decades now. So when Coyote called Kurt and asked him to round up Daimons to kill a Dark-Hunter, we came."

Abigail's heart stopped beating. "We?"

"I took gallu blood with Kurt. I don't want to kill humans, Abby, but I don't want to die either. I figure no one will miss a demon."

Grateful for her compassion and humanity, Abigail hugged her. "I love you, little sister."

"I love you, too. It's why I couldn't let them kill you. Even if you are with the enemy." Hannah pulled a small box out of her jacket and pressed a button on it.

Jess breathed a sigh of relief. She'd turned off the damper.

Hannah hung her head down. "I feel like I've just betrayed one family member for another."

Abigail shook her head. "You haven't betrayed Kurt. He doesn't want me dead, does he?"

"I don't know. He's so angry and hard to read. Especially when it comes to Jonah. You know how close the two of them were. But I don't want to live like that. It takes too much energy to hate. I'd rather get on with my life than worry about someone else's."

Jess cleared his throat. "Sorry to interrupt, but we need to find Ren."

"He's probably in the lower chamber."

Abigail arched her brow at that. Hannah had responded without any thought whatsoever. "How much time have you spent here?"

"Too much. Coyote . . ." Hannah paused as if seeking the right adjective for him.

"What?" Abigail prompted.

She squirmed like she used to do as a kid whenever she'd done something she thought their parents might punish her for. "Promise you won't hate me if I tell you something."

Abigail went cold with dread. What was wrong now? "Tell me what?"

"Promise me first."

Oh, she could wring her little sister's neck whenever she played these stupid games. "All right. I promise."

Hannah licked her lips and glanced about nervously. "Coyote was the one who killed your parents."

That news slammed into her with the force of gale winds and left her reeling. "What?"

She nodded. "He wanted your mom, but she wouldn't have anything to do with him. He'd gone to see her in various disguises and tried to seduce her. No matter what he did, she wouldn't look at him. Apparently the last time, she said something she shouldn't have and he killed them for it."

Abigail was flabbergasted. And she would have denied it, but it all made sense now. It hadn't been Jess in her room. It'd been Coyote wearing his skin. "How do you know this?"

"Jonah. He got drunk one night back when we were dating and told me all about it. He was there with Coyote when he did it."

It was just as she'd seen in her house. That was why the voice had seemed so familiar to her.

"I should have told you when I found out, but Kurt and the others were in love with the idea of turning you into their own personal Terminator to slay the evil Dark-Hunters. It's all they talked about. They saw you as the perfect weapon against our enemies."

The sad thing was, she had been.

And Abigail didn't know what to say to that. Raw emotions warred inside her. Anger, hatred, betrayal. And even relief. At least she finally knew the truth about the night her parents died.

"Thank you, Hannah."

"You're not mad?"

"Not at you." Kurt and the others, she could kill over it.

Most of all, it was Coyote blood she wanted. That need was so strong that it bubbled up inside her like a volcano.

"Hey, Jess?"

Jess turned his attention to Sasha. "Yeah?"

He pointed to Abigail.

Jess looked over at her, then actually jumped when he saw what she looked like.

Holy shit. She barely looked human right now.

In fact, all three of them took a step back as they saw her eyes. They weren't just red. They had stripes of orange laced through them.

Her teeth grew longer, and there was an evil aura around her that said she was open for business.

Jess approached her slowly. Any sudden movement might make her gut him. "Baby?"

Abigail put her hand on his chest to stop him from coming any closer. "Not this time, Jess." Her voice sounded like it had reverb on it. "I want the blood of Coyote, and I won't be stopped."

Normally, he'd have stopped her anyway. *But you know what?*

Payback's a bitch, and this one was way overdue. If she wanted to rip Coyote's head off and play basketball with it, he'd bring the net.

"I've got your back, Abs."

Sasha screwed his face up. "You're going to make me get her back, too, aren't you?"

He gave the wolf a droll stare. "You wanna live?"

"Some days." Sasha let out a long, tired groan. "Fine. I'll follow even if it kills me, and it better not."

When Abigail started toward the lower chamber, Hannah fell in line to go with them.

As soon as Abigail noticed her slinking behind Sasha, she stopped her. "I want you to sit this one out."

Hannah scowled. "I don't understand."

"If anyone sees you aiding a Dark-Hunter . . ."

"I'm aiding my sister."

Abigail was touched by the offer. But she knew exactly

what kind of repercussions Hannah would have. From everyone. "They won't see it that way, and you know it." They would make her life a living hell, and they might even drive her out of their community.

Hannah sighed. "Fine. Take care of you." It was a line from their favorite girl movie, *Pretty Woman*.

Abigail hugged her again. "Take care of you." Then she set her sister aside and accessed the part of her that was still foreign and terrifying.

The demon.

Jess exchanged a wary grimace with Sasha. The old school cowboy in him didn't like giving such a tiny woman the lead in anything so dangerous. His job was to protect the woman he loved. Not put her in the line of fire.

But he knew if he said that out loud, she'd have his boys for jewelry and make him pay for eternity for his chauvinistic ways. So he rode herd on his tongue, but stayed extra vigilant where she was concerned.

If anyone came for her, they'd answer to him.

And he'd gut them for it.

He didn't know how she did it, but she went straight to where Coyote held Ren like she'd lived here for years.

Jess winced as he saw the holding cell where Ren was strapped to a metal rod. Coyote had put him in with Tesla coils that were sending shock after shock to Renegade, who screamed when they hit him.

Yeah, that was the drawback to being immortal. If

someone wanted to torture you, you couldn't die to escape it.

Jess opened his mouth to ask Abigail what her plan was, but he never got the chance. His hotheaded woman stormed into Coyote's workspace without preamble and seized the ancient being by the throat. When Coyote moved to fight, she backhanded him so hard, he dented the wall.

Remind me not to make her mad.

Jess rushed to turn the electricity off in Ren's cell and stop the pain of his being electrocuted.

Sasha fell back away from the switchboard and room. "Don't shock me, man." It had really nasty consequences for Were-Hunters.

"Check on Ren."

Sasha snorted. "In the electricity cube? What kind of psycho are you?"

"Sasha . . ."

He bared his teeth in a purely canine gesture of defiance. "Fine. I get shocked, you better start checking shoes before you put them on." He went to comply.

Jess rushed to watch Abigail mop the floor with Coyote.

"How could you kill my mother? You bastard!" She slammed his head down on the ground repeatedly.

Coyote twisted and sent her flying. "I only wanted her to love *me*."

"So you killed her when she didn't? That's not love. That's sick."

Coyote kicked her across the chamber. "Don't you dare lecture me. I thought her soul was yours. You. You're the one who betrayed me."

"I have no memory of you, and I'm grateful for that."

The fury in his eyes was scorching. "You can't kill me."

Abigail glanced over to where Sasha was helping Ren. "Torture works for me. Besides, I've already killed one Guardian. What's another?"

He shoved the lab table at her.

Abigail caught it and sent flying back at his head.

Jess widened his eyes at her strength, but wisely stayed out of it.

"You're an animal," she snarled. "You've done nothing but destroy everyone around you."

"Me?" Coyote asked indignantly. "I'm not the animal." He glared at Ren. "He is."

Abigail pulled a knife from her boot. "Yeah, well, from where I call home, we put down rabid animals."

Snake entered the room at the same time Coyote ran.

All Abigail could see was her mother's killer getting away. Without a second thought, she threw her knife at his fleeing back.

One second he was there.

The next, he'd changed places with Snake, just like he'd done with Ren. Her knife buried itself straight into Snake's heart.

No!

Snake blanched as he looked down and saw the knife

sticking out of his chest. His breathing labored, he gave her such a sad, pathetic look that it wrung her heart.

"I'm so sorry."

He said something in a language she didn't know, then sank to the floor.

Abigail ran to him with Jess one step behind her. "Don't die, Snake. We can help you." She looked at Jess. "Can't we?"

But it was too late. His eyes turned cloudy and his last breath left him.

Abigail covered her eyes as the horror of it ripped through her. "I thought the Guardians were immortal. How could I have killed another?"

"They don't die of natural causes." Only unnatural ones.

She ground her teeth in frustration.

Sasha brought Ren over to them. Ren collapsed on the floor and leaned against the wall. "It wasn't your fault, Abigail. Trust me. He killed me the same way. Coyote's a trickster. It's what he does."

Jess growled as his own need for vengeance overwhelmed him. "We'll find him."

Ren shook his head "No. You won't. Not for a while. Not until the Reset of the Time Untime. He'll be in hiding now. Plotting for a way to get his Butterfly back."

"I won't let him."

"I know, but it won't stop him from trying." Ren sank

his hand in his pocket and pulled out a necklace. He handed it Abigail.

Her heart pounded as she saw the necklace Jess had given her mother on the day she died. "Where did you get this?"

"I ripped it off Coyote's neck while we were fighting. I thought you'd want it back."

She nodded as she clutched it to her chest. "Thank you."

"I would say no problem, but it really was." Ren let out a long breath and closed his eyes.

Jess cursed.

Abigail was almost too afraid to ask. "What?"

"It's dawn," he said in synch with Ren.

Jess sighed. "We missed the deadline for the offering."

Abigail groaned as she heard those dreaded words. "What do we do now?"

To her chagrin, both Jess and Ren started laughing.

Jess pulled her against him. "We do what we've always done. We protect . . ."

"And we fight," Ren finished. "But only after I have a nap, preferably away from electricity and daylight."

Sasha helped him to his feet. "Come on, Dark-Hunter badass." He looked at Abigail. "I'll take this one if you take yours."

"It's a deal."

She watched as Sasha and Ren limped away from them. Then she turned back to Jess. "Is it over?"

"For now. You've stopped your first apocalypse. You should be proud."

"I'm too tired to be proud."

He laughed. "I know that feeling." He fished his phone out of his pocket and called his Squire.

Abigail stood in silence as she listened to Jess negotiate a ride home for them in something that wouldn't cause him to burst into flames. From what she overheard, Andy wasn't willing to haul them anywhere since he was still mourning the mangling of his Audi.

After a few minutes of asking politely, then threatening his Squire with bodily harm, Jess hung up the phone. "Andy will be here shortly."

Yeah, right . . . She could see Andy taking his sweet time getting here and grumbling every inch of the way. They'd be lucky if he didn't let them starve to death before he made it out here.

Jess's gaze went past her to see something behind her that made his jaw go slack.

Her stomach shrank with dread. *How bad is it this time?* More to the point, how many whatevers were about to attack them?

Not quite ready for another round, she turned to find . . .

Her own jaw hit the floor.

Was that Choo Co La Tah? Gone was the old man and in his place was the younger version of him that she'd seen in her visions of the past. Strange that she hadn't noticed before how handsome a man he'd been. He wore his long black hair loose around his shoulders and walked with the swagger of a predator.

This was a warrior in the prime of his youth and that fact was evident in every bulging muscle and most of all in a stance that said he could kill you in a heartbeat.

Jess put himself between them as if to protect her.

Choo Co La Tah smiled. "Stand down, Jess. I'm not here to harm either of you." He held his hands out to his sides to prove his intent. "I do have to say 'thank you' to our Butterfly though."

Abigail frowned. "How so?"

"It appears we didn't miss the deadline as we feared. When they attacked us earlier and you protected me, you shed some of your blood on the cavern floor. Because of that the seals are still intact."

She wasn't sure if she should be grateful or ticked off at him. One day, they'd have to do something about Choo Co La Tah's penchant for withholding important details. "That was the offering I had to make?"

He nodded. "It also restored my youth and health. For that, my dear, I offer a resounding debt of gratitude. I haven't felt this strong in centuries."

Jess stepped aside as she moved forward to eye the ancient Guardian with respect.

"I don't understand," Jess drawled. "Why did you and Old Bear age while neither Snake nor Coyote did?"

Choo Co La Tah lowered his arms. "It takes more energy to not give in to the Dark One they chose to serve. Fighting them and staying true to our duties takes its toll. It's another reason why our posts are finite. There's only so long you can hold them back before the body wears out and leaves you defenseless." He swept his gaze to where Snake lay dead on the ground. Pain flickered deep in his dark eyes. "You were ever a fool, my friend. Ever led astray and for that I am truly sorry. May your soul find the peace your body never could." He looked back at Abigail. "You may lay your fear aside, child. I can hear it even from here. The ancients never held you responsible for the death of Old Bear nor will they for Snake."

His words confused her. "I don't understand. You said—"

"I implied and you inferred. You were only a tool Coyote used for his own purposes. The ancients are able to look past the event to see the true causation and who set it in motion. All of which go back to Coyote and his actions and greed. Just as I was trying to use you and Sundown to lure him to the Valley so that we could trap him. I knew he would follow you. But unfortunately, he's escaped again."

"We can follow once the sun sets," Jess offered.

Choo Co La Tah sighed. "We won't find him. He's clever that way and he will go to ground to lick his wounds and plot his next move."

Abigail felt a tingle of hope inside her at his words as another idea occurred to her. "Isn't the balance restored now that Snake is dead?"

"In theory."

She didn't care for his tone that told her it would never be so easy. "Theory?"

Choo Co La Tah fell silent for a bit as if thinking on how best to answer. "The balance is a very delicate thing. While Coyote and I may contain each other, we are still missing two Guardians. The jars aren't open, but their seals are weakened by the death of their Guardians. The Wind Seer could free herself now and then go after the Grizzly Spirit on her own. If she were to unite with him, they will rain down an apocalyptic hell that would impress even Sasha."

Great. But she wasn't ready to give up. "What of Jess and Ren? They were the original Guardians, right? Can't they step in and replace Old Bear and Snake?"

He shook his head. "Until the Reset, no new Guardians are allowed to be appointed."

Jess scowled. "Ren told me earlier that Coyote's actions had caused that to speed up."

"They have indeed. And we will have to stand strong against him to keep the Dark One from reigning during the next cycle."

"I'm ready," Jess said with conviction.

Choo Co La Tah smiled. "While I appreciate that, the last chapter isn't yours to write."

"What do you mean?"

"This is now between Ren and his brother. Your job was to stop him before he claimed the Butterfly and tainted her bloodline. You've done that and you kept him from claiming Old Bear's magic."

Abigail was even more confused by his words. "Tainted me how?"

"The Butterfly people were the guardians of the soul. They were born of the Light while the Coyote and Crow are the Dark that would cover the soul and turn it evil. While they, like all of us, were drawn to the Butterfly because of her magic and beauty, she was never theirs to have. The Butterfly can be captured, but never claimed. Her love is a gift that only she can bestow on her chosen one." He gestured to the petroglyphs on the wall where a butterfly flew around a white buffalo. "The Buffalo were the strongest warriors ever known. Intuitive. Brazen. They were fearless. Their job was to protect all of the people, especially those charged with our souls. It's why the two of you were forever drawn together—you were destined to join the two bloodlines. But in the first lifetime, Butterfly was too weak to stand with the Buffalo. She had to learn to fight for herself. To stand up and let the world know she was unafraid." He turned to Jess. "Buffalo was arrogant and egocentric. He had to learn to put the Butterfly before himself and to realize that she was the most vital part of him." He paused. "You both have done that. You understand that while you're strong alone, you're so much stronger to-gether. So long as you stand together, no one can tear you down."

Abigail swallowed. "We're still cursed."

"Yes and no. You two have confronted the Coyote over his evil and you no longer have human blood in you. Coy-ote's curse only applied so long as you were human."

She seriously regretted that decision. If only she could go back . . . "What about the demon inside me?"

"You're controlling it and you have Jess to help."

He made it sound so much easier than it was. Even now she could feel it inside her, salivating. It wanted to feed and it was hard to deny that craving. "But when it wants to feed . . . What do I do then?"

"You do what all of us should do when evil beckons. You beat it back into submission and rise above it. You are more than strong enough to succeed. I know it."

She wasn't sure she liked that answer.

Choo Co La Tah closed the distance between them and took her hands into his. "The Buffalo people had a saying. There is purpose in all things no matter how random they seem. Mother Fate is ever watching and ever working to aid us." He looked at Jess. "Your mother was the last of her people. She knew the Coyote wanted you and it's why she never told you who you really were. Who her people really were. She hid your true tribe from you and married your father, hoping his lineage would disguise you and give you a fighting chance to fulfill your destiny." He tightened his grip on their hands. "It did and because of your mother's sacrifice, you evolved into what you needed to be. It's why you came so close to marrying your true Butterfly then. Unfortunately, she hadn't metamorphosed enough. Matilda was still too weak to stand by your side." He reached for Abigail's. "Now you are ready."

He put their hands together between his. "In spite of all the enemies who would seek to destroy you, you two have found each other again. As the Tsalagi would say, the future path is the one you choose to follow. The journey what you make of it. You both have come so far in this lifetime and those before. I know that this time you will have the life you've dreamed of." He squeezed their hands, then released them. "Now I must go and rest. The fight between the Dark and Pale One is upon us. We will need all of our strength for the battle to come." With those words spoken, he vanished.

Abigail stood there for several heartbeats, absorbing everything that had happened. She didn't know what the future held and that terrified her. For a woman who'd had her entire life mapped out, it was scary to stand here with no clear cut path to follow. She'd chosen the wrong way so many times that she wasn't sure she trusted her instincts anymore.

But she trusted Jess.

She looked down at their combined hands. Who would

have thought? While looking for her enemy, she'd found her best friend. "So where does this leave us?"

Jess froze at a word he hadn't thought about in a long time.

Us. Two united beings.

For the first time in over a century, he wasn't alone.

He stared at how delicate the bones in her fingers were. At how warm her touch made him. It was a sensation, he never wanted to lose again. "I hope it leaves us together."

"Is that what you want?"

"Absolutely." How could she ever doubt it? "Marry me, Abigail, and I swear this time, curse or no curse, I will make it to that damned altar. Even if I drag the devil with me to be there on time."

She offered him a smile. "I will definitely marry you, Sundown Brady. And this time, I will kill anyone who tries to stop you from making it to that altar."

He leaned in and gave her the sweetest kiss of her life. And when he pulled back, her lips were still burning.

"So tell me . . ." she whispered. "How do we get you free from Artemis's service?"

19

A *week later*

*The hardest part of living is making peace
with your past. Most of all, it's making peace
with yourself.* Ash's words hung in Jess's mind
as a sober reminder of how hard the journey
had been to get to this one perfect moment.

He'd never thought to have that peace, but as he watched Abigail napping on his couch after an entire day of exploring each other, he knew the past no longer mattered to him at all.

Only tomorrow did.

Smiling, he got up to find a blanket for her.

Abigail knew the moment Jess had left the room even though she was sound asleep. She wasn't sure where that power came from. But it was there.

And it let her know that something else was here with her.

Her eyes flew open as she jumped to her feet to find an unknown man in front of her. She started to attack until she saw the double bow and arrow mark of a Dark-Hunter on his cheek. He was one of them and yet . . .

The demon in her recognized the demon in him. He was much more than what he appeared and what he appeared to be was a vicious predator. He wore his dark hair swept back from a handsome face that could only be described as pitiless. There was no compassion or even kindness evident in any part of him.

"Nick? What are you doing here?"

She turned to see Jess rejoining them.

That dark, scary gaze left hers to meet Jess's. "I was told you wanted your soul back."

"I thought Ash would be the one to bring it."

Nick curled his lip at the mention of Ash's name, but

he didn't say anything about him. He merely reached into his long black coat to pull out a small wooden box. Delicate scroll work decorated the top of it.

Without preamble, he handed it to Abigail. "Make sure you truly love him before you even attempt to restore it. If you fail, you will kill him and there are no second chances."

Before either of them could speak, Nick vanished.

Abigail shivered at the sudden coldness Nick had left in the air. "Is it just me or was that creepy and weird?"

"Yeah, Nick isn't exactly . . . right. He's the youngest of our kind and I guess he hasn't settled in yet."

She started to mention the demon inside Nick that she'd sensed, but then thought better of it. If Nick didn't want anyone else knowing about it, he might go to war with her over it. The last thing they needed was another enemy coming for them.

Curious about the contents, she opened the box. There on a nest of black velvet was the glowing red medallion that housed Jess's soul. It was so beautiful that she instinctively wanted to touch it. But Jess had already warned her that it would sear her skin and leave a scar on her hand like the one Talon had.

Jess moved to stand in front of her. "What are you thinking?"

She smiled at the fact that he didn't pry into her thoughts. "How much I love you."

"I love you, too." He peered over the lid to see the medallion. "You'll have to kill me to restore my soul into my body."

"I know, but . . ."

He arched a brow at her hesitation. "But what?"

"I'm not so sure about this. We still have Coyote out there, gunning for both of us. If I put this in you, you'll be mortal again and you'll be able to die."

"I can die now."

She shook her head. "Not as easily and you know that."

"I'll still have my powers though."

True, but she wasn't sure it would be enough. There was no telling what tricks Coyote might come up with next. "It's not the same. Do we have to do this?"

"No. I have my soul back. Technically, I'm out of Artemis's service. As far as I know, there's nothing that says I have to restore my soul once I have it again. But we won't be able to start a family without it."

"We already have a family. You, me . . . and one irritated Squire."

He laughed at that. "Yeah, I guess Andy is our illmannered adopted son."

Abigail closed the box. She had a bad feeling deep inside that wouldn't ease. Something more was out there and it would be coming for them. "I don't want to take a chance on losing you, Jess. Not again. Let's wait on this."

He took the box from her hand. "All right. We'll wait."

That was one of the things she loved most about him. He never pushed his will onto hers. The decisions they made, they made as a team. Together.

She looked down at the simple wedding band that rested on her left hand. Even though Dark-Hunters couldn't marry, they'd eloped six nights ago. It was Vegas, after all. And Sin had a small chapel inside his casino that had provided a perfect setting. Zarek had been the best man and Hannah her maid of honor. Kat, Sin, Sasha, Choo Co La Tah, Ren and Andy had also been there as witnesses.

Yes, they'd jumped the gun, but given everything that had happened to them, it'd seemed most appropriate. And neither of them had wanted to take a chance on anything else going wrong.

Carpe Noctem. Seize the night. That was exactly what they'd done.

"You sure you don't want a diamond to go with that?" Jess had been nagging her about that since she'd declined an engagement ring. But that wasn't her style.

"I have everything I need and he's standing right in front of me."

Jess savored those words that had been her wedding vow. Even with her in front of him, he couldn't believe she was here and that they were finally together. That it was her face he now carried in the watch she'd returned to him. "I will spend the rest of my life, however long it is, making damn sure you always feel that way."

In the deepest part of himself, he sensed that Coyote would be coming for them again. He didn't know what tomorrow would hold, but today he knew what he would be holding.

Her.

And that was all he needed.

Bonus Scene

Holding on to her husband's huge, strong hand for dear life while they were surrounded by their closest friends and family in the bedroom of their home, Soteria Parthenopaeus leaned her head against the stacked pillows behind her and pushed with everything she had.

Ah, gah, it hurt.

It really, *really* hurt!

And it hadn't stopped for hours or was it days or weeks? Funny thing about labor, it made time slow down so that one minute in human time equaled three hours to a laboring mom. Maybe longer.

Yeah, definitely longer.

She reverted to her breathing techniques that all three (because her husband's paranoia feared one might not be good enough) of her midwives had taught her, but that was about as useful as all the pushing she'd been doing.

And the breathing was making her feel like a hyper-ventilating dog after a long race. Not to mention dizzy. She glanced at her husband who was coated in as much sweat as she was. He hadn't left her side for a single second since it started. His long black hair was pulled back into a sleek ponytail and his swirling silver eyes stared at her with pride and love.

She adored, loved, and worshiped him so incredibly much, would crawl naked over broken glass just to see him smile, but right now in the throes of ten hours of hard labor pains, she really wanted to grab the most tender part of his body in a set of pliers and squeeze his junk until he could fully understand how much childbirth sucked. "I swear if that's a pair of demon horns digging into my belly and stabbing me right now, Ash, I'm going to beat you after it's born."

'Cause face it, horns on the head didn't come from my side of the family or genetic code.

He actually had the nerve to laugh at her threat. Was he out of his mind? Just because he was an eleven-thousand-year-old Atlantean god with omnipotent powers didn't mean she couldn't make him suffer. Not that she ever would, but still. The least he could do was pretend to be afraid of her.

He kissed her cheek and brushed her hair back from her face. "It's all right, Sota. I have you."

"Apostolos, adjust her pillows higher," her mother-in-law snapped at her husband. "She doesn't look comfortable. I don't want my daughter in any more pain than necessary. You men have no idea what you put us through." While Apollymi couldn't physically leave her prison realm, her astral projection could travel without her. And it'd been pacing near Ash's oldest daughter Simi since the labor had started.

Simi rolled back and forth and spun around on Ash's wheeled desk chair. Dressed in a neon pink lab coat and black and white striped leggings with thigh high laced platform boots that went all the way up to her black lace mini-skirt, she was adorable. Her face was mostly covered by a black surgical mask with a matching pink skull and crossbones on the right side of it. Her glowing red eyes were empathized by her solid jet-black pigtails and dark purple eyeliner. She'd been so excited about the impending birth of the baby, that she'd been dressing that way for a month and shadowing Tory's every step. If Tory so much as hiccuped, Simi had whipped out a black baseball glove and asked, "is it time yet? The Simi's gots her glove all ready to catch it if it is,'cause sometimes they come out flying."

Simi couldn't wait to be a big sister again.

Kat, Ash's other daughter who was married to Sin Nana, sat in the window seat, holding her sleeping daughter on her lap. Her long flowing blue jersey dress was as serene as she was. "Grandma, please. It's okay. Dad's doing a great job. I give him kudos for at least being calm and rational, and not losing his temper with everyone around him who isn't in childbirth. And he has yet to start shooting lightning bolts at people. Poor Damien still has a burn scar."

That thought actually made Soteria laugh as she pictured it. Sin did have a temper where his wife was concerned.

Breathtaking, blond, and statuesque as the daughter of two gods should be, Kat smiled at Tory. "If it makes you feel any better Tory, they were just as bad when Mia was born. At least you don't have Sin, Kish *and* Damien running around, trying to boil water for no other reason than that's what someone had told Sin husbands are supposed to do and since Sin doesn't know how to boil water, he had to micromanage the other two incompetents who'd never done it either. I'm amazed they didn't band together to kill him during it or burn down the casino. And don't get me started on my mother trying to murder my husband in the middle of it or her fighting with grandma over whose labors were more painful. Or," she cast a meaningful glance to Simi, "someone setting my mother's hair on fire and trying to barbecue her to celebrate the birth."

Simi stopped rolling and pulled her black surgical mask down to show them her proud fanged grin. "That an old Charonte custom that go back forever 'cause we a really old race of demons who go back even before forever." She looked over to where Danger's shade glittered in the opposite corner while the former Dark-Huntress was assisting Pam and Kim with the birth, and explained the custom to her. "When a new baby is born you kill off an old annoying family member who gets on everyone's nerves which for all of us would be the heifer-goddess 'cause the only person who like her be you, Akra-Kat. I know she you mother and all, but sometimes you just gotta say no thank you. You a mean old heifer-goddess who need to go play in traffic and get run over by something big like a steamroller or bus or something else really painful that would hurt her a lot and make the rest of us laugh." She put her mask back on. "Not to mention the Simi barbecue would have been fun too if someone, Akra-Kat, hadn't stopped the Simi from it. I personally think it would have been a most magnificent gift for the baby. Barbecued heifer-goddess Artemis. Yum! No better meal. Oh then again baby got a delicate constitution and that might give the poor thing indigestion. Artemis definitely give the Simi indigestion and I ain't even ate her yet."

Kat let out an exaggerated sigh as she passed a bemused stare to Tory. "There's a reason Mia is currently an only child. Family drama takes on a whole new meaning when they're feuding gods who can't stand the sight of each other and always try to kill one another whenever they're in the same room."

Tory laughed, knowing just how right Kat was. It was why Xirena was downstairs with Alexian and Urian, eating her out of house and home. Simi's older sister couldn't stand Apollymi and the two of them had been fighting so badly that Alexian had volunteered to babysit the demon downstairs until the birth.

Tory loved her huge family, quirks, thorns, fangs, horns and all. She only wished her cousin, Geary, who was like a sister to her could have been here too. But Geary was about to give birth herself and was on bed rest for it.

She couldn't wait. Their babies would be like twins.

Acheron brushed her damp hair back from her face and started massaging her temples. "Is there anything I can do for you?"

She grimaced as more agony lacerated her abdomen. "Stop the pain."

He pressed his cheek against hers and gave her a gentle squeeze. "You know I can't."

Because they weren't sure what it might do to the baby or how it might unknowingly affect it and they'd decided together, as a family, that no one was going to lay a preternatural hand on the infant no matter what.

Not after what had been done to Acheron when he'd been born.

"Fine," she breathed. "But next time you're the one who's doing labor duty. I get to sit there and hold *your* hand."

And again he laughed.

She glared at him. "You have no sense of self preservation, do you?"

"Not really."

"Akra-Tory want some of my barbecue sauce to use on akri if he don't behave?"

Tory laughed again. "It's all right, Simi. I'll . . ." she screamed as something twisted inside her that felt like a broken bottle scraping her stomach lining.

Ash went pale. "Tory? Is something wrong?"

She couldn't answer. All she could do was try to breathe.

Ash looked at Tory's best friend Kim who was their lead midwife. Her features were drawn tight as she and Tory's other best friend, Pam talked in a low whisper.

"What's going on?" Ash demanded.

Kim turned to Danger. "Hon, can you go get Essie

from downstairs?" Esmerelda Deveraux was another friend who was practically family. While Kim was a medical practitioner and experienced midwife, Essie was a medical doctor with an additional twelve years of experience with delivering babies at home.

Danger left immediately.

Tory screamed as the pain worsened.

Acheron's skin turned from olive to mottled blue as his panic rose. "Answer me, Kim. What's happening?" Oh yeah, the god tone came out. It was so deep a growl that it vibrated the room.

Luckily, Kim knew he was a god and she never panicked over anything. "I don't know, sweetie. I've never delivered a nonhuman infant before. I don't know if this is normal or not. That's why I want a second opinion."

"How about a third?" Menyara asked as she, Essie, and Danger spilled into the room.

Ash stood up. "Don't touch the baby, Mennie."

Menyara cocked her hip and head at his concern. Dressed in a flowing orange skirt and cream peasant blouse, she had her sisterlocks held back from her face by a striped red scarf. "Now I know you didn't just come at me with your attitude, Mr. High And Mighty Atlantean God. Believe you me, if there's one thing I know how to do it's birth nonhuman infants. Been doing it since before even your old ass was born."

"Men—"

She held up her hand, cutting him off. "You know me better than that. I would never do *anything* to harm your baby and I'm not about to curse or mark it. Now let me take a look and see what's going on."

Ash stood down. "I'm sorry, Mennie."

"It's all right. I know where you're coming from and I know you're stressed. But don't worry. We'll take care of it."

Ash returned to Tory's side.

Tory took his hand again and did her best not to scream out anymore. Her poor baby. From the moment she'd told him she was pregnant, he'd been terrified. He didn't say it, but she knew. His childhood had been made so violent and traumatic by those who sought to destroy him that it'd left scars inside him that not even eleven thousand years could ease.

And all because his goddess aunt had touched his skin when she delivered him.

"It's okay, baby," she said to him.

But still she saw the fear in his eyes. *I can't lose you, Sota. I can't.* He sent those words to her and her alone.

She smiled at him through her pain as she used the powers he'd given her to respond. *I have no intention of leaving you. Ever.*

"Is it supposed to do that?" Kim asked Menyara.

Menyara swallowed. "I've never seen anything like this."

"What's wrong?" Tory's heart pounded as her panic rose. For Menyara to say something like that . . .

It was bad.

"We need to do a c-section." Menyara directed the others as they scrambled to make preparations.

Ash went to look, then stepped back.

Tory panicked even more. "What is it?"

"Stay calm," Apollymi said. "It's fine."

But it wasn't fine and she knew it. That fact was etched in the horror on all their faces. More pain stabbed at her.

Within minutes, they had her prepped. But when Essie went to make the cut, the blade snapped in two.

The room began to shake.

Tory screamed as the baby rolled inside her. It was as if he was angry at all of them and taking it out on her.

The midwives looked hopelessly at each other. "What do we do?"

Tory's vision dimmed. She was shaking uncontrollably.

"Do something!" Acheron shouted.

Essie swallowed. "We don't know what to do."

They couldn't take her to a hospital because of the fact that the baby wasn't human. If he were like his father and had mottled blue skin and horns, it was going to be a little difficult to explain.

Apollymi gestured to Menyara and Acheron. "Use your powers to pull it out."

Ash paled even more. "What if it damages the baby?"

"Oh for goodness sakes, child. The baby will never be left alone and unprotected." She gestured to the crowded room. "There's not a being here who wouldn't lay their life down for him. He is not you, Apostolos. We don't have to hide him."

Pam looked up from the monitors. "Tory's blood pressure's too high. We have to calm her down or she's going to have a stroke."

"Calm her down? How?"

Tory screamed as the baby moved again. It felt like he was trying to rip her in half.

Kim blanched. "We're going to lose them both."

Ash couldn't breathe as he heard those words.

In all of his extremely long life, he'd never been more terrified. He couldn't lose his wife. He couldn't.

Hoping he didn't do it wrong, he reached with his powers to pull the baby out.

Lightning burst in the room, ricocheting all over it. He had to duck to keep from getting blasted.

Tory screamed even louder.

And the baby stayed inside her.

"Oh that's not good," Menyara whispered. She moved him aside. "Let me try."

This time, the lightning slammed her into the wall.

Ash looked at his mother who shook her head. "I've never seen anything like this."

Pam turned the monitors toward them. "She can't take much more."

Ash met Tory's gaze. The utter agony and terror there stabbed him. What were they going to do?

"Her heart's failing."

Tears welled in his eyes. If she died because of this, because of him, he'd never forgive himself.

"Call Mom."

Ash frowned at Kat. "What?"

"She's a goddess of childbirth. She was only a few hours old when she delivered Apollo from her own mother. If anyone knows what to do . . ."

Yes, but she was also his worst enemy. They hated each other. Why would she help?

And then another fear stabbed him. What if Artemis was doing this? She'd been known to kill women in the throes of labor. Could she hate him so much that she would kill Tory just to get back at him?

Of course she would

Tory screamed again.

Wincing, Ash teleported himself from his home to Artemis's temple on Mount Olympus. He would rather be flayed, which he'd been many times, than come here. Only fear for Tory's life would have him in this hated place.

Her receiving hall was completely empty. "Artemis!" he called, heading toward her bedroom. If she did have something to do with this, he would turn Simi loose on her. Fate and order be damned.

Artemis appeared in front of the doors.

Ash hesitated. There was something different about her. She still had the flawless beauty that had always been hers. The long curly red hair and eyes so green they betrayed her divine status, but there was a serenity to her that had never been there before.

"Are you all right?" She actually managed to look concerned.

"Tory . . ." he choked at saying her name as unimaginable fear and pain ripped him apart. "She's in trouble. The baby won't come and she can't survive it. I need your help."

Her eyes darkened. "You would dare come here about that after all you've put me through?"

Oh yeah, there was the old Artemis he knew and hated. No mention of the fact that she'd stood and watched while her brother disemboweled him at her feet. Or of all the times he'd been beaten and humiliated while she watched on.

But none of that mattered to him.

Only Tory did.

Swallowing his pride, he kept the hatred from his gaze. "Please. Whatever price you demand of me, I will pay it. Anything, Artie. Just don't let her die."

"She, a pathetic human, really means that much to you?"

"I would die for her."

Artemis pressed her lips together as tears glistened in her eyes. "You loved me like that once."

And he'd paid for that love in the most violent ways

imaginable. "Please, Artemis. If you ever loved me, don't make Tory pay. I'm the one who wronged you. Not her."

A single tear slid down her cheek. "Would you have ever begged for my life?"

"When I was human. Yes."

She reached out and laid her hand on his cheek. "I did love you, Acheron. As I have never loved anything else, other than the child you gave me. And you're right to hate me. Because I'd never loved anything, I didn't know how to take care of it. I didn't know how to take care of you." She pulled his head down to hers and whispered softly in his ear. "I'm sorry." She placed her lips to his cheek and kissed it.

Then she vanished.

Ash scanned the room, trying to locate her. "Artemis?" Where had she gone? He shoved open the doors to her bedroom. "Artie?"

Still no answer.

Had her apology meant that she was sorry she wouldn't help? Terror tore through him.

What have I done?

Ash raked his hands through his hair as he fought down his panic and rage. Fine, if Artemis wanted to be a bitch, he'd find some way to save his wife.

Closing his eyes, he went home.

And froze in the corner as he saw the most shocking thing of all time.

Artemis with Tory.

"That's it, Soteria. Breathe easy." Artemis had one hand on Tory's forehead while she gently rubbed the other over Tory's stomach. "See how calm he is now?"

Tory nodded.

"He feels what you feel. He's trying to protect you both." Artemis looked at the others. "All of you need to leave."

Kat stood up slowly. "Mom . . ."

"Leave, Katra. The baby wants peace."

"We'll be downstairs," Menyara said.

Ash hesitated. "Am I to leave too?"

Artemis shook her head. "If you go, you'll always think I've done something to the child to get back at you. Stay and know that I'm not hurting him."

One by one, she pulled all the monitoring devices from Tory. Then she cupped Tory's face in her hand.

"Breathe slow and easy, then push. Not hard, but gently. Let him know that it's safe and that you want him here to be loved."

Licking her lips, Tory nodded and did what she ordered.

"Again."

After the fourth time, Artemis went to her feet. Then turned toward Ash. "Come, Acheron. Be the first to welcome your son into his new life."

She was right, he was still suspicious of her. All their

centuries together, the only thing he'd ever been able to count on was her willingness to hurt him anyway she could.

But he did as she said. He went to Tory and with one more push, his son slid into his hands.

For a full minute, he couldn't breathe as he stared at the tiniest, most perfect creature he'd ever seen in his life.

"Is it a smurf?" Tory asked.

Ash laughed. Since he was blue in his natural god skin, Tory had been joking with him that she wasn't having a baby, but rather a smurf. Artemis cut and sealed the cord, then took the baby and woke him.

He let loose a wail that would have shamed Simi.

Artemis wrapped him in a blanket, then took him to Tory. "Meet your son, Soteria."

Tory stared in wonder at the tiny baby who, even now, looked just like her husband. He was perfect in every way. From the top of his head that was covered with blond fuzz to the bottom of his itsy bitsy toes.

Artemis started to move away.

Tory took her hand to stop her. Her emotions swelled inside, choking her. "Thank you, Artemis. Thank you."

Artemis smiled at her. "I hope he brings you as much happiness and pride as Katra has always brought me."

Ash came closer. "Thank you, Artie."

She inclined her head to him, then moved to leave.

"Aren't you forgetting something?"

She paused at Ash's question. "What?"

"Your payment."

Artemis shook her head. "The happiness on your face when first you touched him was enough. I only wish you'd been there when your daughter was born, but that was my fault. I've had a lifetime of joy, hugs and love from her and you missed all of that because of my stupidity and fear. His life is my gift to both of you. Let's hope the future is much kinder to all of us than the past has been." And then she was gone.

Tory stared in confounded disbelief. "What did you do to her?"

Ash shook his head. "I don't think it was my influence."

"Then who? 'Cause that's not the Artemis who came at me over you."

Ash shrugged. "I don't know. She's been hanging out with Nick."

"Nick? As in I-hate-your-guts-Ash-go-die Nick?"

He nodded.

"Whoa." Tory looked down at her son while he kicked and squirmed. There was no way to describe what she felt in that moment. This was her baby. A part of her and Ash. The best part of them.

Ash held his hand so that the baby could wrap his tiny hand around his pinky. "So what are we going call him?"

"Bob."

Ash laughed at the name Zarek used for his son because he detested the name Astrid had picked out. "Really?"

Her smile set his entire world on fire. "No. I think I'd like to name him Sebastos Eudorus."

Ash arched a brow at her choice. "Why that?"

"Sebastos was the name my parents picked out for me, had I been a boy and I always thought it would make a great name for my son. And Eudorus because he was the son of Hermes and Polymele. As a boy he danced in Artemis's chair to celebrate her. When he grew up, he was one of the fiercest, most venerated of Achilles' Myrmidons and Homer wrote more lines about him than anyone else. Plus it means gift of joy, which he is. And while we've had our issues with Artemis, but for her I wouldn't have you and neither of us would have had the baby today. "

Only his wife would know all of that off the top of her head. Ash laughed. "Sebastos Eudorus Parthenopaeus. He is really going to hate us when he has to learn to spell all that."

"Probably, but I think I'll call him Sebastian. That way he can grow up and confuse people with his name just like his father does."

"Yeah well, I still haven't figured out how you got Tory out of Soteria." He leaned down and kissed her gently. "Thank you for my son."

Her eyes glistened and the love he saw there never ceased to amaze him. "Thank you for my life."

He could stare into her beautiful face all day.

She patted him lightly on the cheek. "You should probably let the thundering horde in from downstairs. Let them know Artemis didn't kill us."

"All right. You sure you're ready?"

"Absolutely. And before you start posting photos on Facebook for the rest of the Dark-Hunters to see, make sure I have on makeup."

He scoffed. "You don't need makeup to be beautiful."

"And that's part of why I love you so much. But the rest of the world doesn't look at me through silver swirling eyes."

"I love you, Tory. I know I say it a lot, but . . ."

"I know, baby. I feel the same way about you. Those words never convey what goes through my mind and heart every time I look up and see you sitting in my house. Funny thing is, I always thought my house was full and that there was nothing missing in my life. I had a job I loved. Family who loved me. Good friends to keep me sane. Everything a human could want. And then I met an infuriating, impossible man who added the one thing I didn't know wasn't there."

"Dirty socks on the floor?"

She laughed. "No, the other part of my heart. The last face I see before I go to sleep and the first one I see when I get up. I'm so glad it was you."

Those words both thrilled and scared him. Mostly

because he knew firsthand that if love went untended it turned into profound hatred. "And I hope you never change your mind about that."

"Never."

Foolish or not, he believed her. But the one thing he knew for certain. He would never be able to live without her.

Author's Note

As a woman of mixed Tsalagi (Cherokee) heritage, I've always been fascinated by the beliefs and legends of all the Native American Nations. I spent untold hours as a child, combing through the library, reading any and everything I could find that would give me insight into that part of my family history as well as listening to countless stories told to me by my family, all of whom wove great magic with their words.

When I first started writing the Dark-Hunter series back in college, I decided to base it around Greek mythology with one notable exception. The Daimons. A cursed vampire-like demon that wasn't immortal and rather than feed from blood, they fed from something a little more . . . robust.

The human soul.

While I created the curse and the mythos around the Atlanteans, Apollites and Daimons from my own mind, there was one thing I did borrow from my ancestors. Part of the tsi-noo (chenoo) legend.

When I was a child, the tsi-noo was the bogeyman my mother would threaten me with if I didn't behave (she also used the Manitou, but that's another story).

A Wabanaki legend, the tsi-noo began life as a human who was either possessed by an evil demon or one who committed some atrocious crime (usually cannibalism) that caused his heart to turn to ice. Also known as an Ice Cannibal, the tsi-noo stayed alive and grew stronger by consuming humans, especially their souls. This was why my mother told me it was imperative to say my prayers at night and to ask God to keep my soul safe while I slept. If I failed to do so, one could slip into my bed (or my dreams) and steal it away from me . . . because everyone knew that a child's soul was the most coveted by the tsi-noo and if you weren't careful, you could easily give your soul to one. I'm pretty sure all of that last bit was made up by my mother for the sheer fear factor of it as I haven't been able to find any corroborating story about it.

But as a little girl, the idea of having my soul stolen or being able to lock one up fascinated me and as an adult, I decided to borrow it for my Daimons.

I also incorporated the tsi-noo, as well as several other monsters, into this book. It's something I've been wanting to do for a very long time. I introduced Sunshine Running-wolf into the series at the beginning (she was the heroine of the second published Dark-Hunter novel, *Night Embrace*). A woman of mixed Native American heritage, she, like me, treasures both sides of her ancestry. And from the moment, I completed that novel, I've been aching to return to my roots and explore them more.

Finally, in this book, I was able to pay homage to many different Native American legends and beliefs, including those of my family, and to explore them more fully.

That being said, I've also created my own Native American history for the purpose of the book. The original tribes/clans, creators and Guardians I've used, as well as some of the monsters, are not taken from any Native American belief system or religion. This was done out of respect and on purpose.

As a very spiritual person who comes from a mixed

religious background, I have a deep and abiding love and respect for all religions and points of view. I would never intentionally insult or otherwise offend anyone.

The Time Untime is a real Cherokee belief that I couldn't resist borrowing a bit from and it was another story I grew up with. However, I have tweaked it a bit and will continue it on in the 2012 Dark-Hunter novel that will follow this one.

I can't tell you how much I've enjoyed my foray into another pantheon. I knew when I sat down to start Jess's story that it would grab my heart and make me laugh and cry. It did both many times.

As with all of my books, I'm very proud of this one and I hope you enjoy taking this journey with me. Now I must get back to the voices in my head who, I pray, will never leave me alone and who will sing their songs to me for many years to come.

But before I go, I'd like to leave you with the first words my uncle taught me to say in Tsalagi. *Wa-do* (wah doe). Thank you.

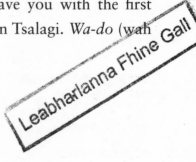